DECEPTION

DECEPTION

KATELYN ALEXANDRIA

Deception
Shattered Ties

This book is dedicated to those who struggle to love and be loved.
Your forever is just around the corner.

Trigger Warning

I would not categorize this book as a dark romance; however, it does display heavy themes and depictions throughout the story. Therefore, if you wish to go in blind this is my warning before you do so. However, for those of you who wish to have a heads up of some of the heavier and darker topics mentioned in this book I have included a list of trigger warnings to look out for.

Trigger Warnings include but are not limited to:

Rape, Domestic Violence, Mention of Suicide, Drug Use, Alcohol Use, Smoking, Blood and Gore Depiction, Blood Play, Violence, Mention of Miscarriage, and Murder

Soul Bound

My mind is asleep until you come into view
Since it is because of you that my whole body awakens too
My dreams have been haunted but then I think of you
You encompass all the good I need to see past the darkness that looms
You and I put on a mask when it comes to those around
But it comes off when it's just us two, for our souls are bound

Prologue

CAIN

I look out into the city I have been blessed to call my home. My very own sanctuary and paradise. The one place where I can revel in all of their desires and not feel the judgment that is only felt by the righteous. For the past thousand years, I have been condemned to a life of isolation and rejection. Forced to wander and relive my most *horrific* sin - over and over again. However, when I finally thought my life had no purpose, no meaning, my savior found me. The morning star himself.

Left to rule over his army in his absence, I return back to my throne settled in the middle of the room in my own section of our kingdom. I glance over to the smaller throne to the side of it- encased in gold and blood red velvet. A seat meant only for a queen.

Rose, how I have waited centuries for her return. Her time has officially run out and what was once promised to me, will now be mine. Now, all I have to do is drag her soul down to hell, where her and I will be together forever.

As I allow the memories of my promised lover to play in my mind, I can envision her luscious caramel hair flowing down her back. I relish in her beauty and the peacefulness of her being. How I long to see her.

I still blame myself for what happened. I shudder, every time I think about the pain she suffered at the hands of that human waste. His hands rummaging her body, not once showing any remorse for his actions, I fought with everything in me to save her. The agonizing wait, the despair. She needed me and I couldn't help her. My only satisfaction was the look of terror on his face when I arrived. Too late to save my beloved but in time to see her save herself. The wrenching pain coursing through his body as he watched his own blood pool itself around him was enough to console my regret. I underestimated her. She truly had the purest of all talents when it came to torture. So many wounds yet, he was still alive, doomed to a slow and painful death. In hindsight, I should have plunged my hand through his chest and grabbed his soul at that very moment. Instead, I convinced myself to allow patience to dominate. Surely, his descent to hell would be more enjoyable.

But alas his soul never arrived. Michael once again denied me the pleasure of my own enjoyment. Instead, he opted to make that piece of human waste a soldier of Lucifer, as if he deserved such a privilege.

I needed to rid my mind of these thoughts. I will never claim such a monster as one of my warriors. He had harmed *her*, and for that he will pay.

I walk into my bedroom and lock the door craving the silence. The commotion in the adjoining rooms felt too intrusive when it came to my thoughts. Right as I am about to sit on my bed, a knock is heard at my door. I let an annoyed huff escape my lips as I make my way back to the door and unlock it. To my surprise, Marie, dressed in her best black silks, stands in front of me. Difficult to resist, I gaze up and down at her. She is gorgeous, there is no doubt about it. I sometimes wonder if she realizes that we could have been the strongest and most powerful of all the soul ties in our world, but her selfishness ruined everything.

"What?" I grumble, not in the mood for anything more. She only takes my annoyance as an invitation to follow me in. I go back to my bed as she closes the door behind us. I sit looking forward as she stands allowing her silk robe to drop below her left shoulder displaying her lingerie. Her legs were completely accentuated by her extremely high heels.

"I want some fun, I'm bored." She whines, giving me a pout. Her actions are fruitless against me. She begins to take off her robe as she walks closer to me. My eyes linger on her exposed breasts as they practically spill from her corset.

"Come on, you like having fun." She argues walking even closer until she is finally in front of me. I look at her with a quizzical stare, acknowledging that allowing her to have her way would be a bad idea, but my animalistic desires overrule. I allow her to come closer, desiring her body to press against mine.

"Fuck." I groan, feeling defeated as I push her down and pin her to my mattress.

"Imagine, what we could've been if you would've chosen me." I remind her, as I stare into her big brown eyes filled with anticipation of what I would have in store for her this time around. Sex was never an issue with her- it was always sinister. She showed no regret. My cruel words, a reminder of her greatest sin, had no effect on her. She didn't even flinch.

"I will never regret my decision Cain. Women like me are not meant to be tied to anyone. That's what makes me so fun." She says as she pulls from my grasp and wraps her arms around me pulling me closer, licking the side of my face then pulling back to meet my lips. I allowed her as I picked her up from where we laid, wrapped her around me and pinned her to the wall.

"If you're all about fun, let's see how much fun you can take." I smirked as I released my grip around her body and instead ripped open her corset. Throwing it to the floor as I crouched down and delighted myself in kissing her bare skin. I ripped the little pieces of fabric still covering her skin, causing her to shriek in surprise. The smirk on my face only grows wider.

"I can take a lot." She states as she runs her hands through my hair. I look up at her with a challenging grin and let my true face show, the one picked by Lucifer himself and bite into her thigh. She moans in ecstasy. After drinking just enough to entice myself, I release my fangs from her delectable flesh and kiss my way back up to her lips. Blood now smeared all over her. Her true face is now displayed as well, and without any warning she bites into my shoulder. I grab hold of her, squeezing her ass as she wraps herself around me.

I throw her back onto the bed and position myself on top of her. She might have not been the most docile of humans, however, she was submissive when it came to her pleasure. And in that, I knew I had full control over her. I could bend her to my will, and she would allow me to. Her screams of absolute pleasure could be heard throughout the whole realm. I was in the middle of using one of her favorite sex toys, when the door flew open. I looked up, not feeling the slightest bit shy about her or even myself being naked, when we both paused, realizing that the prince himself had just walked into my room.

"Cain, you are needed amongst the others. There is a quarrel amongst the demons in the chamber of torture." Luke- the prince of hell- exclaims, displaying his authority. I looked over at Marie, letting her know play time was over. She sighed in frustration as she angrily grabbed her robe and placed it on her heavenly body.

"I am on my way." I reply, obligingly.

"Cain," Marie, states, "I will be back to finish our little game later." She smirks as she walks by Luke gently allowing her body to linger closer than needed as if inviting him to join in as well.

"Remember gentleman, this is the realm of lust and desire. There are no rules. I will see you both later." She continues as she walks out of the room. Luke follows, as I stand naked and alone, craving more. She always leaves me wanting more.

Chapter 1

ROSE

"Please stop!" I cry as I look into Pierce's blue sadistic eyes, begging him to get off of me. My panicked pleas only encourage him to be more forceful as I fight to get out of his grip. His face remains determined as he looks at me with excitement in his eyes while he holds my hands above my head. He was enjoying this. He loved knowing that he was stronger than me and therefore held all the power. The longer I fought the more anxious I became, and I couldn't help but give in to what he wanted most and screamed. I gave him the reaction that I know got him off and I screamed and thrashed around, praying to anyone who would listen to help me stop him this time. However, no one answered, and I had no more strength left in me. My body and mind are too worn out and defeated. He had won- like always. He'd managed to shatter me both physically and emotionally.

"Pierce please." I beg once more, my throat sore from my cries. I forced my eyes to look at him, so that he could see just how terrified I was, but instead of sympathizing he leaned toward me and connected his lips to mine. I wanted to vomit. I knew what was coming, but before he could deepen his one-sided obsession he was pulled back. I opened my eyes to see his disturbing grin gone and replaced with a look of shock. It took me a moment to realize what had caused him to stop. The warm feeling of his blood dotting my bare skin as a hand protrudes out of his chest, and in that hand is his heart. I scream in absolute horror.

Before I can plead with the mystery person for my life, Pierce is ripped off of me in one swift motion, everything fades to black and the only thing I can see of my mystery savior is their eyes: violet and intense. They stare right into me as if they were watching, to see what I would do next.

"Who are you?" I ask as I sit up and try to make out their nonexistent figure. The darkness was concealing them from me. However, I could still feel them, and they were moving closer and closer towards where I sat on the bed. When they were right in front of me, I managed to make out a body that was broad and definitely tall, but besides that, I had no idea who or even what was staring back at me. My body is paralyzed as I stay perfectly still waiting to see what would happen next. I can feel my breathing deepening as I try to calm myself. I feel the slight brush of a cold hand on my cheek, and the stickiness of the blood that belonged to Pierce.

"Beautiful." The phantom whispered, although after hearing the rough deepness of his voice, I knew that the being standing in front of me was a man. His voice both calming and cool, rubs me the wrong way. There was something about his presence that felt unsettling, besides the fact that he had just murdered Pierce.

"Please don't hurt me." I beg, not knowing what else to do. My high-pitched squeal causes him to let a low chuckle emanate from his lips before he shows me his shadow covered face. The only thing that I can see are those vibrant violet eyes.

All my warning bells and sirens are going off, but as scared as I should be at this moment, I'm not. I only feel a sense of curiosity and a sense of longing. It's as if his energy is pulling me towards him.

"I've waited centuries for you, Rose. You need to come find me. For I will unleash the darkness that resides within you, and we will become one when you die, you and I are soul tied." He chants repeatedly. As his words become clearer, the birthmark on the back of my right shoulder begins to burn. I scream out in pain.

"Who are you!" I cry out, desperately needing to know. The man doesn't answer, he only continues to chant, as if his voice was on a continuous loop.

"Come find me, for I will unleash the darkness that resides within you, and we will become one when you die, you and I are soul tied."

"Please stop!" I beg as the burning on my skin worsens.

"Stop!" I scream, shutting my eyes, fighting through the agonizing pain radiating from my shoulder. After a few moments the pain stops. I open my eyes realizing that I am now, back in my room and fully awake. It had been a dream- a really scary, freaky dream.

My body is sweaty and shaking from my vivid nightmare and I can't help but sit up in my bed and move my arm back to touch where my birthmark is. Just as my fingers touch the skin, I quickly pull them back as I hiss from the stinging.

"What the hell?" I mumble looking at my hand as I try to wrap my mind around everything that had just happened. The biggest question my mind seems to keep asking is who that man in my dream could be.

Still feeling his eyes watching me, I look around my room, trying to gain a firm grip of my reality, when the last few weeks came crashing back to me. I was safe and back at my childhood home in New York City. Pierce could no longer touch me, especially since

I left him for dead in Italy. Everyone around here thought he was missing, but I had killed him. And even though my mind had chosen today to play tricks on me and place my never-ending guilt on some imaginary man, I knew who the slayer of my true monster was...and that slayer was me.

I need to relax, before I officially get up to face the day, I pull a cigarette from my secret stash in my nightstand and light it. I then reach for my laptop and open up the book I have been working on for the past two years. Although, some would argue it's more of a diary, full of feelings and experiences.

To fall from heaven and to fall in love are both things you should always try to avoid doing. I know I've always tried to. However, as hard as I have always tried, I have also always managed to fail...miserably. To fall from heaven, you must commit a sin. To fall in love, you must rip a part of yourself out and give it to another. Both of these actions carry a certain guarantee of self-destruction. If I had to pick which one would hurt less, I would have to choose falling from heaven, by my own will or simply because I was casted out. I guess to a certain degree, I was casted out of my own paradise, even though it wasn't me who committed the sin, but instead it was him. I, however, had to pay the price. I was now an outcast amongst the others who roamed this wild dimension, I call New York City.

So, I ran from the city of dreams - my own personal heaven and fled to the city of angels, where maybe I hoped to find redemption with my fellow fallen celestials. After all, Los Angeles isn't too far from the city of Sin. I didn't mind being close to it as long as I wasn't in it. The drugs, sex, and alcohol reminded me way too much of my time spent with my own personal devil- Pierce.

LA was different. It was the perfect in-between. A temporary sanctuary where anything seemed possible. A new life, a new start- change. My biggest want from the moment I arrived, was to be someone else other than me, I wanted a new beginning and to forget the past- the past that still haunts me today.

I look up from the words typed on my computer screen- telling a small part of my story. My very own source of therapy. These words that will never leave the digital pages that fill the files in my computer, help me to cope. It reminds me that what I went through was real, that it wasn't something I had just imagined, it wasn't fiction. I owned it and in all honesty was profoundly grateful to be alive to write about it, even if I never publish it. I had my brush with death and survived. The fact that I had managed to run and be free for two years before having to come back to my home- New York City- seemed surreal.

I take one last drag of my much-needed cigarette when my mother barges through my door. The look of disappointment and annoyance never surprises me.

"Rose! Put that poison out before you burn down the building and get up, we have to be at church in the next thirty minutes." She practically barks, causing me to fight the urge to roll my eyes at her. I've officially been home less than two weeks from UCLA. I had just graduated with a degree in writing a couple months ago and call it the writer in me, but I had really hoped that with time she would have changed. However, from the moment I landed, I knew she was still the frigid, detached mother I had always known and rarely loved.

I look over at my phone and notice that it's almost ten in the morning. I put out my cigarette and slap a fake smile on my face, as I begin to get out of bed.

"I'll be ready in twenty minutes."

With one last look of disapproval, she turns and closes the door behind her. Violet Autry was the perfect picture of New York's Upper East Side. She was elegant and calculating. She knew how to kill with just the right smile, and she knew how to charm just about anyone through the sparkle in her eyes. Growing up in poverty had taught her that there were no lines that she wouldn't cross to remain at the top.

I was probably one of her biggest regrets. I guess you could say I was the stain she couldn't get rid of on her perfectly white Chanel suit. She just couldn't understand me. I missed my father, when he died, a part of me had died as well.

I finally head over to the bathroom and shower. Afterwards, I managed to tame my curly caramel hair and apply light makeup around my big brown eyes and long natural lashes. I cover my lips with a light pink lip gloss to help accentuate their natural plumpness. I put on my Cartier bracelets, placing one bangle on each wrist to hide my scars. I looked good, good enough to make my debut back into society. Since returning I hadn't really seen any of my family's inner circle of friends or acquaintances, just a few of my childhood friends.

I had no interest in playing the perfect daughter and putting the mask I once wore back on display. However, I had no option with Violet around. So, the mask of the New York City "It" girl was once again put into place.

I head over to my bureau where my purse sits and pull out my large black YSL sunglasses out of my bag, along with my wallet. I then proceed to rummage through my closet and pick out a beautiful white eyelet knee length dress and pair it with my favorite white Christian Louboutin kitten heels. I figured since this would be my first time back with these sharks, I might as well wear the bloody shoes. Feeling a bit more confident, I looked in the mirror and smirked.

I was ready.

Chapter 2

LEO

Human life can be best described as fragile and delicate, sort of like a piece of beautifully thin stained glass. Enchanting to look at yet so easily broken when touched. There was a time in my life when I would've cared if the broken pieces of glass that laid beneath my feet were there because of me, but now I relish in it. I enjoy hearing the shattering and the thuds from the glass hitting the floor from impact. Humans are nothing more than sustenance and entertainment. A delicious dinner and show, if you will. Today's pick is a beautiful, tasty blonde that was more than eager to take me back to her place and give me quite the performance. If only she knew what the price would be.

"Oh my God!" She moans loudly as I thrust into her. She arches her back as I go in deeper. I have no idea what her name is, nor do I care. I have never bothered to get to know any of their names, hers, or any other I have bedded. Their only purpose is to serve. However, what I do know is that she tastes delicious. Her warm blood still drips from my mouth as I bury myself deeper within her.

"Sorry to disappoint you kitten, but I am as far from God as one can be." I growl, before I lean down and whisper in her ear, "but you like that, don't you?"

I bite back down on her shoulder before she can reply and drink the delicious red liquid that flows through her as I thrust myself in and out of her. Her screams only make it more exhilarating and enjoyable. The screaming is what gets me most excited when I am with a human. I find it thrilling to feed in that way; it feeds my animalistic needs. I revel in the fact that she is smeared with her own blood as her body jerks underneath mine with each thrust. I move my mouth where I had been previously feasting and lick a strip of her bare skin where the blood from the previous bite was dripping.

"More!" She screams. I quicken my movements and manage to hit that one spot that all women come undone for. As I hear her screams of pleasure, I know I have done my job.

She climaxed four times during our time together this morning alone. As her orgasm takes a hold of her, I take the opportunity to once again bite down on her neck. Once satisfied, I withdraw my fangs and slide myself out of her warm wet cunt. I roll over and lay next to her for a moment. She is still shaking riding out her high. Once she manages to calm her body down, she moves over and touches me, but I immediately pull away and get off the bed. My flesh is sacred to me, it holds deep dark secrets that I live with every day. I never allow or display any affection after the fact. Besides, to be honest, not many of them mind. They already got what they wanted- me.

She doesn't question my movements since my compulsion is still glossing over her mind. She had been a willing participant in our overnight activities. However, I can't have her freaking out when my fangs come out - they always do. Besides, it's not as if they don't enjoy it.

"Mr. Lloyd, that was amazing." She praises. I give her a stiff smile and immediately go to look for my pants. I got what I wanted and now it is time to go. I was running late to meet with my best friend Elliot. I grab my clothes that are scattered all across the room, before noticing that this delicate creature is still dripping blood and cum while she watches me get dressed. I take a look at my surroundings; I truly do need to stop picking up girls from the strip club.

She looks saddened by my eagerness to leave, that's the one thing I hated most about these arrangements, they are always so emotional afterwards. It's so *human*.

"Can't you stay longer?" She pleads, her perfect golden hair now stained with blood, sticking to her sweaty face.

"I have to go." I replied coldly. She frowns at my shortness.

I have to admit there is temptation in the way that she looks, laying there teasing me to pounce on her and release everything within me. It has me second guessing my need to go to church this morning.

"Aren't you still hungry?" She asks so innocently, before moving a strand of her hair away from her slender neck. The once perfect skin was now covered in bite marks from our late night and early morning activities. However, my age makes me more than capable of having self-control, although I feel it slipping when I notice the blood from her neck was now seeping down and running onto her breasts. I lick my lips knowing I won't be able to resist her for much longer. She then sits up and moves closer to me, grabbing my hand and placing it onto one of her breasts, she shutters from my cold touch.

"Didn't you have fun?" She asks as she looks up at me through her large fake lashes, mascara stains her youthful face. She looks absolutely ruined from our night spent together- I had done that. She continues to look up at me the same way she had done when she had taken me in her mouth.

I massage her flesh with my hand watching as she closes her eyes and lets a loose moan slip from her lips.

I look down at her contemplating, feeding once again. My fangs descend right when my phone rings. She gives me a small frown and I find myself mimicking her same expression.

"I guess play time is really over, kitten."

I look into her eyes and compel her to forget everything that had happened between us. I puncture my finger and rub a few drops of my blood onto her open wounds. I can't have people knowing that vampires are running around the city, as it is this is the city that doesn't sleep.

I walk over to the front door and answer my phone.

"Elliot, I'm on my way." I state knowing he is already annoyed with me.

"Having fun with your meal again? How many times have I told you not to play with your food!" He scolds, his witchy judgment seeping through each word. I know he doesn't approve when I allow myself to embrace my true nature, but it has been a hard week for me. I promised myself that I would go back to strictly enjoying blood bags after today.

I walk out of the girl's apartment and walk over to my black Ferrari Spider and speed off to St. Patrick's Cathedral for Sunday Mass. It was a tradition Elliot made me uphold after a century long fight with my nonexistent humanity. He feels that by forcing me to go to a house of worship it will keep me somewhat grounded to what had been my human self's unshakable belief. I never fought against his pushing, because I did find some comfort in going, not that I would ever tell him that.

I have been back in New York City for about two years and have gone to the mass at St. Patrick's Cathedral almost every Sunday. Elliot is already there waiting for me by the entrance when I get there. I make sure to double check that I'm clean and that I don't have any evidence of my night and morning escapade.

Without a word, he walks inside, leaving me to follow behind as we both avoid the holy water bowl but still make the sign of the cross as we walk further inside. I'm fairly positive Elliot was never a devout Catholic in his lifetime, but it seems he finds a small amount of comfort in coming here as well.

We find our way to our usual seats in the back of the church. I stay silent listening to the light chatter happening around us as we wait for the sermon to begin. I look at my watch and notice that it's almost ten, when my body feels a surge of what I can only describe as sparks, flow through it. For a man who doesn't have a heartbeat, I swear on everything in this church, that I felt my heart begin to boom in my bloody fucking chest. I quickly snap my head up and I'm immediately met with an angel in white. She was the most exquisite beauty I had ever laid my eyes on- at least in the last three centuries of my existence. She quite literally made me feel human again for a split of a second, which was unsettling but somehow welcoming. I unapologetically looked her over. She must have felt my stare, because she gave me a quick glance and for a moment, I could have sworn I saw her falter. I wonder if she had been hit with the same feeling I had. I needed to know who she was, and I needed to know now. However, before I could say anything to her, she along with what I could only assume to be her mother and siblings and an older gentleman who I'd say is her father, except they shared zero resemblance, walked to the front and took a seat. Immediately after, the priest, Father John, came out and began his sermon.

"Who are those people?" I whispered to Elliot, hoping he had noticed them too. Elliot Lancer was kind of a gossip hotline. He knew everyone and everything, it's how we managed to fit in when it came to these cities and the social circles we were working with. He owned one of the hottest clubs downtown, called Centuries. His clientele consisted of New York's elite for the most part, keeping him overly informed and connected.

"The Autry's. Although the mothers last name is now Miller. She remarried Charles Miller a couple of years ago. One of New York City's biggest business tycoon. They actually share an interesting reputation." Elliot whispers, pensively.

"Do you know who the girl in white is?" I ask, praying he would offer me a clue about her.

"I would assume that's Rose Autry, since I haven't seen them here with her before. She went away for a while. I'm not a hundred percent sure why, but I can tell you that she's lived a pretty interesting life." Elliot explains, causing me to raise my eyebrows at what he could possibly be insinuating.

"Big party girl. Huge, in fact. I believe she's done more coke than all the rock bands in the eighties combined. When she resided in New York she was quite sought after. Two years ago, though, she fell off the map and went away, rehab or maybe school- it's unclear. The guy she was with at the time, Pierce Adami disappeared. Who knows what the fuck happened."

"How did I miss her?" I reply, keeping my gaze fixed upon her.

"I think everything happened, right before our arrival in the city," he explains. The people in the pew in front of us turn around to shush us as if our whispering was the worst sin to be committed in this church. Meanwhile, they had no idea that they were sitting next to two soldiers of Lucifer.

Chapter 3

ROSE

Church is long and boring, not to mention triggering. Every time I walk into St. Patrick's Cathedral, I can't help but remember my father's funeral. I also can't help thinking that God is going to somehow smite me for even walking into his house of worship after what I had done. Even though it was for my own survival, I don't really feel like I belong here anymore. Maybe, I'm too tainted. There really weren't enough Our Father's and Hail Mary's or any other prayers to save my soul from damnation. I had accepted that, but hearing the priest talk about divinity, God and the promise of peace and glory in the afterlife- made me long for something that no longer existed in my future. I didn't realize I was slightly shaking just from the thought of it, until my best friend Adeline placed her hand on mine. She gave me a reassuring squeeze and a sympathetic smile before we both refocused our attention back to the sermon.

Adeline Baker has been my best friend since we were in preschool. She has been the only person capable of talking me off a ledge, even when she didn't know why I was on there to begin with. We are the complete opposite of one another. She is the sweet, optimistic, fun-loving girl that everyone wants to be friends with. She honestly doesn't have a malicious bone in her body and can't recognize the evil in others even if it slapped her in the face.

She comes from one of Manhattan's most elite families. Her mother is one of the biggest, most sought-after attorneys in the city, while her father is one of the top Neurosurgeons in the country- but somehow this power couple managed to raise the kindest, most humble and caring individual I have ever been blessed to know.

While I, on the other hand, could literally be the poster child for every parent's worst nightmare. I have suffered from plenty of vices- smoking, drugs, alcohol- you name it- I have probably done it. My reputation for sleeping around is not a total lie and my attitude can be very off putting at times. Before I even got to college I was definitely known as one of the bad girls of the Upper East Side. They say bad girls have the most fun, and I can see how people might say that, but to be completely honest I was in my own personal hell... I kind of still am.

After the service and once outside my mother and stepfather mingle with some of their friends and acquaintances, while my brother Jason and his girlfriend Amanda Mathews walk over to greet her parents. Amanda or "Mandee" as we all called her, wasn't high on my list of favorite people. I was glad my brother had found someone that seemed to care for him, but Mandee and I had never really gotten along.

I walk over to the people that matter most- at least to me- my friends. Adeline, her boyfriend Collin Harris and my ex-boyfriend James Arthur- are all standing outside trying to figure out where we should go that evening.

"Do you guys want to go to Centuries tonight? I've been dying to go back after the animal night they threw a couple of months ago. The cages were a bit crazy but it's definitely a fun place."

Collin explains, hoping we would all go. His messy blonde hair shines in the sunlight as his light hazel eyes hold excitement for the possibilities of what tonight could bring.

I can't believe Adeline is still with him after all these years. I mean sure he was conventionally attractive, with his six foot two lean swimmers build and chiseled facial features, but his personality comparatively to hers was lacking. They had been dating officially since freshman year of high school, and he can still be the same asshole he was back then. Some things never change- and he was definitely one of them.

I always thought Adeline could do way better. I've seen what men are capable of and I've seen what Collin is capable of and it's not pretty. In his case though, I think modeling for the same New York City top modeling agency since junior year of high school has made him feel that he is God's gift to women. The crazy thing is that he never lets Adeline forget it.

"I've never been there. It sounds cool." I state. I can see Adeline's big blue eyes practically pleading with me to play nice.

"Oh, then we'll consider tonight a homecoming for you, and we'll get a table!" James exclaims throwing his big arms around me, in that all too familiar way. His steel like gray eyes stare into mine as he gives me that boyish grin that was completely irresistible. His body has gotten more muscular since I had last seen him. He looked good, and strong, not to mention his face had gotten way more defined. His cheeks were still rosy, and his lips still had that all too familiar kissable pout. I couldn't help but get sucked in by his beauty and charm every time.

James Arthur and I were high school sweethearts- well until I found out he had been cheating on me at a pretty consistent rate. I took him back each time and hated myself a little more with every restart of our relationship.

Looking back though, I've come to realize that I was never truly in love with him- not really, not in the way he had supposedly thought he was in love with me. I guess that's why we were better at being friends. I think we love each other as friends a whole lot better than as lovers- if that makes any sense. Besides, when I needed him the most, he had been there for me- no questions asked- which I will always be grateful for. He had been the one who had come to get me in Italy, when I called.

"So, Rose and I will meet you two there tonight? Around ten?" Adeline suggests, looking excited that our little group was finally together again.

Honestly, I felt excited too. They were familiar and it was comforting to be around people I knew and for the most part, cared about.

The boys agree to Adeline's plan before we all go our separate ways. Adeline and Collin have a lunch date with her parents and James is off to meet his brother Marcus for their weekly game of squash.

As I'm left standing alone outside of the church, I can't help but feel a little exposed. A strange feeling overcomes me, and I begin to wonder if I am being watched. I nonchalantly look around, when I spot the most beautiful hypnotizing emerald, green eyes I have ever seen. Our eyes lock- slaves to the others' attention. I can feel time suddenly stop- or at least that's what it feels like- as I stand frozen completely consumed by this stranger. Neither of us dare to look away, when he suddenly begins to walk over to me. The closer he gets, the more I realize who this mystery man is- Mr. Leonardo Lloyd- the city's most eligible bachelor. I had caught a glimpse of him earlier in the church, but I hadn't really gotten a good look until now. I could feel a shiver travel down my spine from his intensity.

Not only was Mr. Lloyd extremely good looking but he was the sole owner of Lloyd Enterprises. He was literally a self-made billionaire, adding more to the mystery of who he is. And it's funny because for someone who is so well known, no one really knew too much about him- which is strange as he is considered one of Manhattan's elite.

Mr. Lloyd finally makes his way over to me. I remind myself to breathe. His presence renders me utterly speechless as his captivating orbs stare right into mine. He was more handsome up close if that was even possible. The contrast of his dark brown hair and striking green eyes make me feel weak. I struggle with the idea of engaging my brain to my mouth and introducing myself. Instead, I fixate on his muscular arms, broad chest and impressive towering stature. He was at least six foot five if not taller. His face perfectly chiseled held the most beautiful lips and defined jawline I had ever seen. He was literally breathtaking- for a man.

"Hi, I don't believe we've had the pleasure to meet before today, but my name is Leo Lloyd." He smiles politely, his thick British accent holding me hostage. I snap out of my trance when he gestures for me to shake his hand which I hesitantly do. As soon as my hand touches his, I can feel an instant spark course through me. It felt *magical.*

"I'm... I'm Rose Autry. It's very nice to meet you." I finally manage to say. My eyes shift down his body and back up to his face. He is beyond handsome. He almost doesn't seem human. I can understand how others could be intimidated by his presence.

"A beautiful name for a beautiful woman." He grins, giving me the most heart stopping smile. I blush slightly from his compliment.

"I haven't seen you at Sunday services before." He states, although I can see the curiosity of his question dancing in his eyes. I look back up at him and meet his gaze. I feel as if he could literally see straight into my soul from the intensity in his stare. I can feel imaginary butterflies fluttering around my stomach. As cliché as it may sound, I can honestly say that I have never experienced any feeling or attraction quite like this before. It's absolutely exhilarating.

"I just got back a couple of weeks ago from California. I graduated from UCLA and decided to come back home." I manage to explain, still somehow mesmerized.

"UCLA, that's impressive." He replied, before continuing. "California is also a great state to be in. The weather is always enjoyable. You must miss it." He adds, waiting for me to reply. I couldn't think of what to say.

"The sun must have looked beautiful on you." He continues thoughtfully as I continue to stand there in silence. I let a small smile show as I place a couple strands of loose hair behind my ear. His eyes continue to pierce through me. I'd be lying if I said I didn't love the attention he was giving me. I welcomed the feelings he stirred within me.

"Yes, I loved it, but I had to come back. I have family and commitments to attend here in New York." I finally reply, trying to keep my response subtle enough so as to not seem like a total idiot.

"Ah yes, commitments, they always seem to hold us back somehow while also getting in the way." He states a bit cynically. I like it. Something about his demeanor entices me. I take notice that his eyes slightly darken when he speaks.

"I suppose, but honestly, I couldn't wait to come back to New York. I missed it here." I tell him, finally taking a hold of my emotions.

A warm breeze wraps itself around us as I take a step back. The summer heat was beginning to take over the day and Leo's presence was not helping, if anything it only made it that much hotter.

"Well, if it means anything, I'm glad you decided to come back home. Especially since it offered me the opportunity to meet you and ask you out to dinner or at least lunch." He grins, charmingly- almost throwing me off my game. The butterflies were now erupting within me as I considered his delicious offer.

"Well then, I'm glad I've returned." I smile shyly, trying not to throw myself on top of him. He then took the opportunity to offer me his business card and insisted that I call him to discuss our impending dinner plans. He even topped off the conversation by implying that he would be counting the minutes till my call.

I wanted to jump out of my skin. The idea of a man like Leo Lloyd waiting for me to call him, was enough for me to break a sweat. I hadn't gone on a date or even out to dinner with a man interested in me, in a very long time. Going out with Leo Lloyd though, was like jumping into the deep end headfirst. As much as I knew that I needed to take it slow, I wanted to drown myself in him. The feelings coursing through me were crazy. The attraction was insane. I actually felt awakened in a way I had never felt before.

"Hopefully, we will see each other soon, Rose." He grins, before giving me a light kiss on my cheek. I almost died.

Before I could even say goodbye, he walked away to where another man was waiting for him. I could not believe I had just agreed to go out with New York's most eligible bachelor. I guess in my own unprecedented way- I was back.

Chapter 4

ROSE

"Hey, I heard through the grapevine that you made a new friend, you wouldn't know anything about that would you?" Adeline asks playfully. She had decided to stop by my house a little earlier than planned to pick me up.

I try to hide my smile as I finish zipping up my dress for tonight's outing. It was a totally different look than what I had worn back at the church earlier this morning. It was tight, black, and low cut, making sure to accentuate my curvy figure. I paired it with my black strappy Prada pumps.

"I have no idea what you're talking about." I tease jokingly.

"You little liar, are you really going to act like you and Mr. Leonardo Lloyd didn't talk this morning? Everyone was gossiping about it at my parents' luncheon." She states enthusiastically. The curiosity glistened in her big blue eyes. She was dying for me to spill all the juicy details. And God help me, I couldn't wait to tell her. For the first time in what felt like forever I could actually confide in my friend about a cute guy that I liked. I hadn't been able to tell her about my relationship with Pierce in the past out of sheer embarrassment.

"Well, if the people said it happened then it must be true." I confirm, with a smirk.

"Rose come on; I want details." She begs. We managed to make it out of my bedroom and down the marble staircase before she stopped me.

"Nothing really major happened. We just talked and he told me he wanted to see me again." I informed her, as nonchalantly as I could without allowing myself to get overly excited. Adeline practically squeals with joy, at my confession.

"Rose, that's huge. Everybody wants him, you know. Catherine and Trina are always talking about him when I see them at the New York Society meetings. They are always talking about his parties and how he is apparently more than what meets the eye. There is even a rumor that he is completely covered in tattoos." Adeline dishes, causing my mind to wonder what they could possibly know about him that I had yet to find out.

"Well hopefully I'll know more when I meet him for dinner. But for now, I'd like to focus on going out with my best friend in the whole wide world and having fun." I state enthusiastically, hoping she'll drop the Leo talk, which she thankfully does.

* * *

Thirty minutes later, we pull up to one of the most popular night clubs in Manhattan- Centuries. The building is all black glass on the outside with two oversized metallic colored doors and large shiny gold handles. Two large bouncers stand outside monitoring the ropes, holding back the huge line of people waiting to get in. We both exit the car and are met by Collin and James who have been waiting for us. James whispers something to one of the bouncers and we are automatically allowed access, which earns us a couple of glares from the girls in the front of the line that seemed to have been waiting a long time. I guess two of them caught James's attention because he brings them in with us.

Once inside we all go over to the VIP section and sit at a corner booth. There is a chilled bottle of champagne waiting for us at the table. We immediately start to pour the gold liquid once we are seated. It feels like a lifetime ago, since I had last gone out to a club or even hung out with friends. I had been so sheltered and secluded in LA, that being here felt almost like it would be too much to handle. However, after the second glass of champagne courses through me I can begin to feel my anxiety lessen.

Once relaxed, I allow myself to take in the loud music that surrounds us and enjoy the evening. Adeline and I do most of the talking as James entertains himself with the two girls, he had invited in to join us, and Collin is busy on the cell phone talking to one of his "business" partners- code name for his and James's coke dealer.

He always tried to make it look like he wasn't fully involved in any drug related activities, but Adeline and I knew better. For God sakes, I was one of his best customers back in high school. Adeline always knew what he was up to but would turn a blind eye to it. When it came to Collin, she always had the, "out of sight, out of mind," mantra.

However, when it came to me, she never blinded herself. She was always there to kill my high or scold me for taking part in such a dangerous activity.

"Adi, would you care to dance?" Collin asks, after he finishes up his call. He quickly shoots a quick wink to James letting him know that their late-night order was on the way. I couldn't help but feel a little envious. It would be nice to do a line or two at this point in my life. I missed it as sick as this statement might sound. But I knew better than to get myself wrapped up into it again. That lifestyle can only bring problems, and I had enough of those on my own.

Adeline nods her head yes, then takes Collin's hand, but not before turning to me and making sure I am going to be ok with James and his two new friends. I of course give her a nod of encouragement and watch them walk off towards the dance floor. I serve myself another glass of champagne when I realize the bottle is almost out. I look over at James as his two new besties are literally climbing all over him. "Disgusting," I whisper to myself, when I suddenly get slammed with a flashback of Pierce. I remember how he had forced himself on me one night after we had partied a bit too hard. I shake my head slightly, willing the memory to leave, as I get up and leave James and his newfound pets alone to continue frolicking.

I walk over to the bar with the champagne bottle in my hand and sit. I pour the last drop out into my empty glass and swallow it quickly. My mood for the evening had been soured. It also didn't help that I was being forced to practically watch my ex-boyfriend be fucked by two random girls. As I set the crystal stem glass down the bartender turns to face me. He's probably around twenty-five years old. He is very tall and very handsome. He has dark black hair, beautiful whiskey-colored almond shaped eyes, and a large scar going down the left side of his face through his eyebrow to his under-eye area. The scar only added to his good looks. The old me would have made an attempt to flirt with him, hoping it would help me to feel better about myself but tonight I wasn't really in the mood. Besides, Leo's face was etched into my brain.

"I'd ask what you're drinking but I see you already have a bottle." He smiles. His British accent seeping through.

"I would like a vodka on the rocks please." I request, ignoring his cheesy comment.

"Coming right up. However, I'll trade you." He states looking at the bottle of champagne that is right in front of me. I push it towards him, and he grabs a hold of it, a bit shocked that it's empty. He then quirks an eyebrow as if both curious and impressed. Lots of mommy issues and trauma, is what I wanted to tell him, but instead I stayed quiet awaiting my drink.

"Well, someone's going through it. What is it my dear, boy problems...girl problems?" He asks, a slight smirk appearing on his beautiful face. This man is shamelessly annoying.

"You know you ask a lot of questions without even telling me your name." I state bluntly, becoming a bit impatient.

"Elliot, I own the club and Rose I wouldn't have to ask so many questions if you would allow yourself to be more open." He states throwing me off.

"How do you know my name?"

"Everyone knows who you are, my dear. You're the party girl. The legendary Rose Autry. You were a staple at every high-end establishment, before you disappeared two years ago." He states, before continuing.

"And I must say your reputation precedes you, you're even more beautiful than what I had expected." He smiles, before turning around and grabbing a bottle of Grey Goose vodka from the shelf.

"I'm going to make you a deal, you tell me what's on your mind and I won't let you drink alone." He smirks, leaning into the bar.

I look at him a bit unsure, then decide to take him up on his offer.

"Deal." I sigh, causing him to grin. He then grabs two glasses and pours the clear liquid into them.

"Bottoms up." He cheers taking his shot while I down mine not even fazed by the burning sensation in my throat.

"I believe you owe me an explanation for the sad look on your face. What happened to New York's party girl?" He smirks. I can't help but shake my head and let out a laugh.

"I see my name still holds some weight... but that was a long time ago and when a lot of dark shit happens to you, you tend to lose the party spirit." I explain giving him direct eye contact as I await my next shot, which he gladly pours for the both of us.

"Bottoms up." He exclaims as we both take our shots.

"Your energy tells me something troubles you, that there's something suppressing your light Rose... A darkness." His tone drops to a more serious note. He looks at me as if he could see right through me. I'm too faded to fully understand what he is trying to get at. I give him a weary look, not sure how to respond. The more I think about it the more I kind of want to laugh.

"God, so let me get this straight, you're a bartender who's a medium slash fortune teller...really?" I ask jokingly.

Elliot must have thought my accusation was funny as well, since he also lets out a laugh.

"Something like that." He mumbles then pours a third shot and downs it, slamming the glass down on the bar when he's done.

"So, tell me Rose what happened to you?"

His question triggers something inside me. I stop laughing and look down at my glass as I swirl it around and whisper, "death."

As the word leaves my lips, Adeline appears next to me. She looks happy. It's probably because she is the only sober one in this club, who is actually having a good time.

Before she even addresses me, I can tell something or better, yet someone catches her eye.

Elliot.

I couldn't help but notice how intensely they were looking at one another. It was as if they were magnets to one another's stare.

I couldn't help but giggle, causing Adeline to look away.

"Rose, are you coming back to the table?" She asks, still trying to steal a glance at the bartender who hasn't stopped staring.

"Yeah, why not, I think I paid my end of the deal, isn't that right Elliot?" I ask as I smirk looking from him to Adeline.

"Yeah, you're good, but why not one last shot? We can all do it together, what do you think..." he pauses, waiting for her to introduce herself.

"Adeline." She fills in with a smile, as she pushes a blonde lock of hair over her shoulder. He smiles back at the sound of her name. He then grabs the bottle of vodka and three fresh shot glasses and pours.

"Cheers- to new friends." He smiles, raising his glass. Adeline and I follow suit, before we clink our glasses and drink. Adeline is the only one coughing from the burning sensation. Elliot must think it's cute because he can't stop the small smile from forming on his face.

"Are you guys here with anyone?" Elliot asks, directing the question more towards Adeline than me.

"Yeah, a couple of friends." She replies. Her lack of truth makes me internally laugh knowing she had intentionally left out the part of her being here with her boyfriend. I make a mental note to tease her about that later if I can even remember to do so.

"Well, you guys are welcome here anytime. It was a pleasure meeting you...and Rose, you need to let your light shine through because whether you like it or not you have purpose. Don't block destiny because of the past." He warns, then walks over to the other bartender who seems to be overwhelmed from the amount of people requesting drinks. Adeline looks at me confused, "what's he talking about?"

"I have no clue." I lie, knowing exactly what he is referring to. I can feel my anxiety resurfacing as I rationalize with myself. He's a bartender. His job is to play therapist to sad depressed girls.

Like me.

"So, where's our *group*?" I ask her with a slight chuckle, unable to control myself.

"Shut up." Adeline mutters as we walk into the crowd of people.

Chapter 5

ROSE

The sunlight seeps through my long white curtains, managing to wake me up from a rare heavy sleep-like state. And for the briefest instance I feel peace, until my brain catches up and the room begins to spin. The sunlight burns my eyes as they adjust to my surroundings. I can't remember how I made it home. However, as I slowly start to look around my room, the conversation with the bartender from the night before slams into me.

It was just too fucking weird.

I take a much-needed breath before I attempt to sit up. The room finally settles, before my phone rings.

"Who the hell is calling this early..." I whine but stop when I notice that it's a New York City area code.

"Hello."

"Good morning, love." He greets, his voice deep and sexy as hell. It was like audio porn. His thick British accent makes me feel the need to clench my thighs. But that could also be due to, the fact that I had not been intimate with a man in the past two years.

"Good morning, Mr. Lloyd."

"Please call me Leo, love." He states, softly.

"Leo. Can I ask how you got my number?" I question, trying to keep my cool, as I take in the realization that it was currently ten am, and Leo Lloyd was calling *me.*

"I have my ways, love." He teases, only causing me to smile harder.

"Well then, Mr. Lloyd, what can I do for you?" I ask, my voice sweet and borderline cheerful. I haven't sounded like that in a long time. I just couldn't contain it, talking to him felt like the all too familiar feeling of a high.

"You can come have lunch with me this afternoon. I have already cleared my afternoon schedule hoping you would oblige me and meet me at Cipriani's for lunch?"

"I'd love to." I reply without even having to think twice.

"Good, I'll send a car for you. I look forward to seeing you, Rose." He states, making my stomach somersault. There is just something about the way he says my name that makes it feel like a promise of some sort. We quickly say our goodbyes, but not before I give him my address. The moment the line goes dead, I practically fling myself off of my bed. I go straight to my bathroom where I keep a bottle of aspirin and take two before I start getting ready. There was so much to do before our lunch date. Leo wanted me to meet him at twelve thirty.

I quickly get undressed and jump in the shower, feeling like I needed to scrub away last night's events and start my morning off with a cleanse so to speak. The hot water soothes me as I try to remain calm about today. I couldn't wait to see him again. I know it sounds crazy but something about our interaction had awakened the part of me that craved companionship and intimacy. I missed the feeling of wanting someone and them wanting me. It's been forever since I even looked at a man let alone gone out with one. However, I can honestly say there was no anxiety or fear when thinking about this afternoon. Only the feeling of excitement in terms of meeting up with a really handsome man that I hoped likes me.

The water begins to turn cold as I finish rinsing my body and I take that as my cue to get out. I wrap a white fluffy towel around my body as I use another towel to dry off my hair. Once I have it wrapped up and away from my face, I make my way over to my sink with my massive mirror that takes up the entire wall and I begin to brush my teeth. After I finish up, I decide to let down my hair and blow it out, leaving my naturally curly hair hanging down to my waist. For once my curls had decided to cooperate and they fell in beautiful waves down my back. Feeling more than satisfied I start in on my makeup deciding to go very light and natural. I stick with some neutral shades for my eyes and add a bit of glitter just for some much-needed sparkle in my life before applying a dark red lip gloss. Now that I look alive I make my way over to my closet.

I think out of everything, picking the right outfit for today was going to be the hardest decision. What the hell do I wear to a lunch date with a slightly older, sexy, successful billionaire who has an intriguing reputation? Oh, and who by the way, I wish would devour me whole.

I look through every article of clothing and start to seriously question my fashion choices until I come across my black mini skirt and a wine-red colored blouse. It was perfect. I pair it with my YSL slingback heels and matching bag. It was sophisticated yet sexy. Not over the top. Now feeling more than satisfied, I go back into my room and checked the time. I had approximately twenty minutes before Leo's car would arrive. I quickly place my Cartier bangles on each wrist before I make my way downstairs.

"Where are you off to?" My mother questions as I reach the last step.

"I have a date with Mr. Lloyd this afternoon." I answer, holding back my excitement in fear that she'll use it against me somehow. She assesses my outfit before cracking a small smile.

"Good. He's a very suitable option. Very successful and has a decent reputation. Although there seems to be a lack of information about him outside of how he conducts business. However, there's nothing wrong with protecting one's privacy." My mother reasons, as she leads me into the kitchen.

"I suppose we all crave privacy, especially with the way information travels around here. Mr. Lloyd seems decent. I don't think his mysterious nature is alarming. Unlike other men around here." I state, as my mother watches me intently.

"Well, I hope your date goes well. It's healthy to move on from the past Rose. Even though we have never talked about everything with Pierce and his disappearance, I think moving on with a man like Leo is a good idea." She assures me. I look over at her feeling a bit unsettled with her agreeability. Although her reasoning was rather transparent. She saw Leo as a means of gaining more equity in terms of social capital.

"I should get going, but I'll see you when I get home." I smile, before I make my way to the elevator. Once outside, I am met with a black SUV waiting for me. The driver is standing by the back door waiting to help me in. So far so good, is what I silently tell myself as the car begins to pull out into the New York City traffic.

***

We finally arrived at Cipriani's and Leo is standing out front wearing a dark grey suit with his hair perfectly gelled and parted.

He looked like he was posing for the cover of a GQ Magazine, and it took me a moment to compose myself before I even unbuckled my seat belt. However, I am pulled out of my trance when my door is pulled open and Leo makes his way over towards me, extending his hand in the most gentlemanly way. The moment our hands touch I can feel a fire ignite between us.

"Hello, love." He grins.

"Hi." I reply, feeling very much out of my element. It has been too long since I have been in the dating game. I feel like I no longer remember any of the rules. However, my worry begins to dissipate the moment Leo looks at me and gives me the most delicious smile I have ever seen. I knew right then and there that everything would be okay.

"Rose, you look absolutely breathtaking. Truly a vision." He whispers as he ushers me inside the restaurant. My cheeks burn as they turn bright red although the dim lighting helps me conceal my reaction. A hostess immediately recognizes Leo and begins to walk us to what is supposedly his regular table.

"You clean up rather nicely as well." I tell him when we are finally seated at a quiet table in the back. There were only a few other patrons besides us although they were all seated rather far, guaranteeing our privacy.

"So do you bring all of your dates here?" I ask, before my brain could fully think it through. Leo lets out a low chuckle from my rather blunt question before answering, "no, I've never actually dined with anyone here. I usually eat most of my meals here alone, since my office isn't too far."

"That must be very convenient for you, the food here is great." I state, on the verge of babbling. However, I try my best to contain my mouth not wanting to embarrass myself any further.

"Yes, it's pretty decent. But I don't want to talk about the food. I want to talk about you. Tell me everything there is to know about Rose Autry."

I nearly choked on the air I was breathing. What was there to tell? Especially, when the last four years of my life have been hidden behind the walls I had carefully constructed. However, I feel saved when the waitress comes and asks us for our drink order. I ask for a diet soda while Leo orders a Macallan neat. The waitress then walks away, swaying her hips a bit more than what is appropriate although Leo doesn't seem to notice since his eyes never leave mine- not even when ordering. He waits patiently for me to speak.

"There's nothing to really tell. I am a recent graduate of UCLA. I'm an aspiring writer. And I pretty much spend a lot of my time reading."

"A writer, what do you like to write about?" He asks, looking genuinely intrigued.

"Fiction. I enjoy writing romantic fiction."

"A romantic, I should have known. It's in your eyes." He smiles. His eyes darken to a forest green shade as he looks at me. My body warms from his gaze as my heart begins to pump a bit harder.

"What's wrong with being a romantic?"

"Nothing. In fact, I find it admirable. Romantics are tender and warm, everything that I assumed you would be." He tells me.

"Well, you're nothing like what I thought you would be." I state, once again not thinking before I speak. He raises a brow, as I scramble to think of words to elaborate on what I meant to say.

"You're less severe than I thought."

"It's a little early to make that assessment." He teases.

"Well, as of right now you're enjoyable to be around so I'm going to hold out hope." I laugh, as the waitress approaches us once more and hands us our drinks. Then Leo orders for the both of us. I didn't mind, I hadn't even bothered to look at the menu and everything he ordered was something that I would enjoy.

"So, Leo, would you say that you are also a romantic?" I question, once the waitress leaves us.

He takes a sip of his drink before meeting my gaze.

"You know, I never thought of myself as a romantic. However, I'm starting to see the appeal to being one." He states, causing my cheeks to once again burn bright red as I try to hold my composure. Well, it seems that Leo was not only successful in business but was also rather versed in charming this emotionally unavailable woman.

The rest of our lunch goes amazingly. The food is fantastic, and the company is even better. He tells me all about his business and a deal that he is in the middle of conducting. Not to mention he tells me about the Hemingway novel he is currently reading, which leads us into an hour-long discussion about who was the greatest American novelist of the twentieth century. The conversation was not only enlightening but hearing his ideas and perspective was also entertaining. I hadn't had this much fun on a date in a long time.

"You obviously love to read, Mr. Lloyd. You've just gained a lot of points on my end for that but what else are you interested in?" I ask, when our conversation begins to settle down, curious to know more.

"I like jazz music, and a good Bordeaux. I don't like to socialize much which is why you won't see me at social functions. I am very particular when it comes to movies since I usually stick with the ones that are in black and white, and I was born in France, but spent a good portion of my life in London, which is why my accent is so thick. And I am a victim of falling for a beautiful woman who is not only gorgeous but bloody brilliant as well." He grins, deviously.

"Well, it seems we have another thing in common besides our love of reading and our dislike of social gatherings. Since I am also a victim of falling for a very good looking, not to mention smart Frenchman slash Englishman that seems too good to be true." I whisper, as my eyes stare into his. I wish I could say my gaze was innocent, but I couldn't help but look for some type of warning. However, all I was met with was his intense jadelike eyes that also held a golden warmth to them. Almost as if the shades of gold and emerald decided to mix together to create a striking shade of green. The intensity that his eyes held was a mirror for what my own eyes were also displaying.

***

The rest of the lunch went amazing but sadly it was interrupted by a call he received informing him that he needed to get back to his office.

"I really hate that I have to go." He tells me.

"It's ok. Hopefully, we can do this again soon." I smile, even though I hated that we couldn't spend more time together. Our lunch date had lasted over four hours, and yet that didn't seem to be enough.

"Oh, we definitely will." He promises, as he leans in. His eyes look at my lips, like he wants to kiss me, but he holds back.

"Thank you for the amazing meal and company, Mr. Lloyd."

"You know when you say my name like that, it makes me not want to be a gentleman, Rose. And I am really trying to be on my best behavior right now." He practically growls, sending a shiver down my spine.

"My apologies, I didn't realize I had that effect on you." I tease, as I ever so slightly lean into him, my chest gently sweeping against his. He looks into my eyes with pure lust and desire as he holds my gaze.

"You have no idea what you do to me." He says, as he places a gentle hand to my cheek and pulls me in even closer, our lips are not even an inch apart.

"You are truly delectable, love. Everything about you is just enticing." He whispers, but then slowly drops his hand and lets out a small sigh of disappointment before he backs away, and as if on cue the car he ordered pulls up.

"I will see you very soon Rose." He promises, as he places a warm gentle kiss on my cheek before helping me into the car.

"I can't wait."

Chapter 6

ROSE

The car drops me off at home and thankfully the apartment is empty. I make my way up to my room and go straight to my shower. My brain is going a million miles a minute. Leo being the only thought that seems to be on rerun as I think about everything that had just occurred. I would have never imagined a date could go so well, almost borderline perfect. He was perfect. God, when his hands touched me, it made me feel alive, which was absolutely crazy.

When the water finally felt like it was at the right temperature I walked in and let the hot water soothe my aching skin. I soaped my body and rinsed off as my thoughts stayed with Leo, and everything I wanted to do to him. After finishing up, I quickly stepped out of my shower and dried off and changed into a pair of sweatpants and a camisole. I needed to go to bed and take a nap. I grabbed the book off my nightstand needing to settle my mind, but before I knew it my eyes began to close.

"Say it again." he growled.

I look up from my position on the floor where I am kneeling completely naked in front of Leo who is sitting on the edge of a bed covered in black satin. He only has on a pair of black slacks and nothing else. His toned muscles and black ink that covers his gorgeous glistening skin is on display for me to see.

"Say it." He repeats, looking down at me.

"I'm yours...Mr. Lloyd."

He seems pleased with my response as he lets a small grin show before he slowly reaches his hand toward my face and gently rubs my cheek.

"Good girl." He praises.

"Now, undo my pants and take what belongs to you." He commands, as I look from his beautiful face to his groin. I could see his pants straining against his raging erection. God, he must be huge. My assumptions are proven right when I unzip his slacks and pull down his black designer box- ers.

"You're so big, Mr. Lloyd." I tease, as I wrap my hand around his mas- sive member and lick a strip of his smooth velvety skin. The tip is already glistening with precum. I lick it up and moan from the sweet taste of him.

"I might be big love, but you can take it. You belong to me after all. You were made for me." He states. No words needed, I lick him once more before I put him into my mouth and begin to bob my head up and down. Leo grips my hair as he continues to use me. I wanted to please him more than anything. He only pushes my head down further, causing me to gag as I continue to take him into my mouth.

"You take me so well, my beautiful Rose." He praises, before thrusting up into my mouth even rougher, my eyes watering as I try to keep up. Af- ter a few more thrusts he releases me and lets me come up for air.

"Get on the bed." He commands, his voice even deeper and darker than before. I do exactly as I'm told. I lay completely naked on his bed as he looms over me and takes in the sight before him. Once his eyes meet mine, he begins to stroke himself.

"You're fucking gorgeous, love."

"You're not too bad yourself." I agree, licking my lips at the sight of his abs contracting as he continues to stroke his massive dick in his hands.

"Open your legs baby, I'm fucking starving." He demands, kneeling before me. He begins to feast on my obscenely wet sex. My lips release the loudest moan as I call out his name. His tongue continues to lick me as he uses his beautiful lips to suck on my overly stimulated clit. His teeth tug at it gently as I move my hands to his hair and pull ever so slightly.

"Just like that, please don't stop." I beg, as I grind my hips against his beautiful face.

"I wouldn't dream of it." His voice drops, sounding a bit different, although the voice replying seemed familiar. I tug his head up ever so slightly and that's when I see those vibrant violet eyes staring back at me.

"Let me finish Doll, I'm starving." The mystery man says against my soaked sex, hiding his face from me.

I wake up, sweating and frustrated, as I look around the room. It was just a dream. Nothing more.

Although who the hell is the man with the violet eyes?

Hours must have passed, and my mother and Charles must have finally gotten home, because when I look at my clock it's eleven o'clock at night. Right as I am about to roll over and go back to sleep, I hear my mother calling for me, I slowly get up and make my way downstairs. When I finally reach the last step, my jaw practically hits the floor. A hundred long stem red roses are displayed in front of me.

"Oh my God."

"They're for you, from Mr. Leo Lloyd." She smiles, as she hands me the small note card.

To My Rose,
I look forward to when I can see you again.
-Leo Lloyd

"You must have made quite the impression on Mr. Lloyd for him to have sent these." My mother states, as she grabs one of the roses and hands it to me. I nod silently as I look at the thoughtful gesture and breath in the beautiful aroma.

"I should go thank him." I state, before making my way back upstairs. The moment I close my door; I rush for my phone and notice a missed call from Leo from two hours ago. It must have been on silent.

I quickly call him back, hoping that he is still up. After a few rings he picks up.

"Hello love." He greets me with a raspy voice. I must have woken him up.

"Did I wake you?" I ask, feeling a bit guilty for interrupting him.

"No, not at all." He assures me as he tries to regulate his voice. I can tell he's lying.

"I just wanted to call you, to say thank you for my flowers. They are absolutely beautiful."

"Roses for *my* Rose seemed appropriate, love. Besides, I need to make sure I leave you with a lasting impression so that you'll agree to have dinner with me this coming week." He explains sweetly.

"*Your* Rose?" I ask teasingly.

"Yes, mine or at least I hope you will be in the near future. I want you Rose and I usually get what I want." He rasps, causing my body to shudder.

"Is that so... Mr. Lloyd?" I question back, loving the conversation.

"Absolutely. And the moment that you are, I am going to show you just how crazy you make me when you say my name like that." He growls, his voice dropping into a deeper raspier tone. The sound of him getting turned on, is enough to make my body quake.

Although, when paired with the memory of that dream, I feel like I might just explode.

"Really?" I mock seductively, urging him on, curious to see how far he would go.

"Yes. I rather like how it sounds rolling off that tongue of yours. I can't help but picture those beautiful lips calling out my name-over and over again." He replies, making my breath hitch.

"Well, you're a bit cocky." I giggle into the phone, breaking the very thick sexual tension.

"When your name is Leo Lloyd, you can be cocky." He states, although I can practically hear him smirking.

"You keep dreaming...Mr. Lloyd." I tease.

He lets out a low laugh as we continue our conversation late into the night. Talking mostly about the problem that came up at his office and more about my adventures in California. Family, friends and relationships- he finds my life fascinating. I think it odd since all I've done the past few years is go to school, write and drink coffee. I guess keeping a low profile, isolating oneself and embracing loneliness is the new cool.

"Weren't you lonely out there, all by yourself?" He asks, as I reflect back on how I would spend my days when I wasn't at a lecture or studying at the library or one of the many cozy cafes.

"Not really, I actually really liked the loneliness that came along with being so far away from everything and even everyone. Don't get me wrong I missed my family, but I also savored my time alone." I explain, hearing how cold I must come off to him, although he surprises me when he agrees.

"One's own company can sometimes be better than being surrounded by those who don't feed our soul."

"I couldn't agree more. I moved out there looking for a new source of nourishment and having those two years, essentially to myself, was necessary for my sanity and well...soul. I started taking my writing more seriously and stopped partying and if I'm being honest, I took the time to learn who I was at my core and not who I was trying to be in order to serve the expectations of those around me." I explain, saying way more than I mean too, but not minding since Leo seems to make me feel comfortable enough to talk too. We continue to talk, and Leo even gets me to divulge a little more information on my book that I'm currently writing. I tell him it's a fictional novel about a tumultuous relationship that sets the female protagonist on a journey to self-discovery, that may or may not have a happy ending, which he seems interested in. I feel bad not telling him more, but as of right now those extra details are only for me to know. And as if he couldn't get even more perfect the conversation turns into one about classical fiction which I am absolutely obsessed with. I love that he can converse about topics like classical stories and weighted subject matters rather than the cookie cutter nonsense some people rather talk about. This guy had layers. I mean, honestly no other guy had ever gone into such deep detail and discussion on how Pride and Prejudice- for example- is such an influential romance novel. The fact that he thought that the age of romanticism is probably the most exciting era of writing- almost blew me away in the best way. And to top it all off, he is a huge Jane Austen fan!

I was in love.

As our conversation touched on Darcy's character and society's quick judgment on him- including Elizabeth's- it got me thinking. Are the rumors that circle Leo too judgmental as well? Are people too quick to judge him? Would he judge me?

"Mr. Lloyd, would you consider yourself a good man?" I ask. He pauses for a moment on the other end of the line.

"It depends, what if I'm not a man at all, how could I consider myself to be good or bad?" He questions. I can't tell if he is joking or not. I mean the remark is a bit absurd, of course he is a man.

I wasn't sure how to answer him. He takes this as an opportunity to add more clarification.

"I would consider myself a man who can no longer see the difference between what's good or what's bad anymore."

"I can understand that, sometimes those lines can become blurred." I add, as I let out a small sigh.

"I don't think someone like you could ever blur those lines, your soul is too pure." He says, his tone light and sincere.

"I don't think my soul can be considered pure." I whisper, then quickly ask, "What about you, would you consider your soul clean?" He takes a minute, and I can't help but sit up, with anticipation as I wait for him to answer. He replies quietly and in a sorrowful tone, "a man like me doesn't have a soul."

"I can't imagine that being true." I reply, as our conversation slowly shifts to other, lighter topics. I couldn't help but feel a sadness towards him and his view of himself.

Neither one of us really wanted to hang up or for our conversation to end but unfortunately, my exhaustion took over. We pleasantly said our good nights and planned on getting together sooner than later.

The next morning came fast and unforgiving, since I was awoken with a million text messages and missed calls. I couldn't believe my eyes when I saw what was on my screen. Mr. Arthur, James's father, was dead. He was found late last night in Central Park, brutally murdered. My immediate instinct was to call James but instead I decided to call Adeline.

"What the hell happened?" I ask, before she even had a chance to say hello. She nervously explains to me everything that she was able to find out since the news broke.

"Rose, can you meet me at my place? Collin is coming over. Hopefully, he has more information." She reasoned. I told her to give me twenty minutes and that I would be right over. As I rushed around my room getting ready, I felt almost like I was on autopilot. Everything seemed surreal.

After tying my hair up into a high ponytail, I quickly ran down the stairs and grabbed my purse before being met with a pot full of Mums. My heart fully stops as I look down at the flowers. They were a dark crimson color and were in full bloom.

I look around the room, wondering who the hell had left them here, when Charles appears from the living room, absolutely scaring the hell out of me.

"They arrived here earlier this morning, they're addressed to you." He explains, walking over to the small table by our entryway and handing me the folded note. A part of me was praying it was more flowers from Leo, but somehow, I knew better.

I cautiously open the note and practically feel my body freeze when I see the words written perfectly on the paper.

To symbolize our love. Remember Rosie, there is always beauty, even in death.
-Your lover

"*In my culture mums symbolize death. It's kind of morbid but I always liked when my mother would plant them. It also reminds me that there is beauty even when we are gone.*" His words rattle in my brain as they echo the words written in the note. My hands begin to shake as his voice overtakes my mind. I crumble the note and toss it into the small garbage pail near the elevator. Charles takes a step to-ward me, a bit of concern etched into his face, as I proceed to press the button to the elevator. I needed to get outside. I needed air.

"Rose, are you alright? You look like you've seen a ghost." Charles questions.

"No, but I definitely just heard from one." I whisper, as I step into the elevator, reassuring him that I was fine. Once the elevator doors closed, I let out the frantic breath I was holding in. I couldn't believe he was actually alive, and he was coming.

Pierce was coming for me.

Chapter 7

LEO

"Elliot, can you do something about these bloody lights!" I practically growl, from my annoyance. My heightened sight struggles to deal with the constant flashing from the newly purchased strobe lights that had just been installed in the club.

"Not to mention, this God-awful music," I continued. But honestly who in their right mind would even consider this to be actual enjoyable music. I pick up the drink in front of me.

"Sorry Leo, but you'll just have to suffer your way through it as you enjoy your O Positive neat, since we are the only establishment that serves that specific vintage." Elliot smirks, as he rounds the bar and leans against the counter to people watch. There was no denying his pleasure at watching all these strangers enjoying themselves around him. I could never quite figure out his fascination when it came to them. I knew I was tainted in that department. Humans were nothing more than a meal to me- in most cases.

"If it was at least fresh I could be less of a whiner." I argue, taking another sip. Elliot cracks a smile as he makes his way back over to me.

"No feeding on the customers Leo, besides I thought you were going straight?" He inquires, lifting a brow. I can feel his judgment permeating the air around me. He hates that I feed straight from the source rather than use a blood bag, what he doesn't understand is that I need to sometimes. I crave the release.

"You know I like to switch it up every now and then, besides I'm hopeful that my luck will change, and I'll be able to sink my teeth into someone a bit more permanent." I explain, relishing in the thought. I craved nothing more than Rose. I wanted to feast on her warm soft flesh, feel her pleasure as I satisfied my own. The thought alone caused my hidden fangs to emerge. I quickly stop myself.

"Rose, I take it?" Elliot asks. I nod my head.

"She came in here the other night. She's a troubled little soul that one. If I were you, I would keep my distance, now that you've decided to settle here more permanently."

"A little trouble never hurts, but it depends- what kind of trouble are we talking about?" I question curiously, his warning definitely piqued my interest.

"I'm not exactly sure, but something dark haunts that little trust fund kid." He states, then moves back behind the bar. I turn in my seat and right as I'm about to ask another question, I feel a strange presence, someone is approaching.

Another vampire.

Elliot scans the room, his calm and aloof demeanor becomes alert and guarded, I follow his line of vision to a young guy who couldn't have been more than twenty years of age. He was definitely a vampire, a newbie.

He confidently strides towards us.

"Leonardo Lloyd, I presume?"

"Yes, now who in the bloody hell are you?" I state agitated as I place my drink on the bar.

"A messenger. Michael asked me to deliver a message to you. Personally. He would like me to tell you that he is looking forward to seeing you again." He smiles, maliciously. I straighten my composure. Michael Aldrich, I hadn't heard that name mentioned in quite a long time. I could feel the chaos begin to unravel. Michael always had a knack of finding me when my life seemed to be going at its best.

"One of Michael's errand boys I see." Elliot scoffs, coming around the bar to confront the arrogant little fuck still wasting our time.

"You know, I have a message for Michael as well...if he so much as comes near one of us, I will not hesitate this time." Elliot growls, as he steps closer, snapping his fingers, causing time to slow down around us. I get up from my seat and straighten out my suit jacket. This stupid little asshole had no idea what he was doing. He needed to understand who he was fucking with.

He continues to stand his ground.

"I'll make sure to give him the message." He smirks, as his eyes narrow in on us. Without a glance I grab him by the throat and slam him into the bar.

"I'm only going to ask this once, what is your name?" I demand.

"Pierce."

"Did Michael turn you?"

"Yes.

"For what purpose?" I snap, applying more pressure to his throat. I could smell his fear.

"I'm supposed to find Rose Autry." He growls, his cowardice evident in his face now.

"Why her?" I question much more sternly. My patience running thin.

What the fuck could Michael want with her, but before I can continue questioning this asshole, Elliot lets the spell go and time returns back to normal. I retract my fangs and slowly remove my hand from his neck.

"Tell Michael, if he touches one hair on her head I will rip him apart, but not before ripping your heart out first. You reek of ignorance and inexperience. Be careful, as those traits can cost you your existence." I sneer, he nods his head reluctantly, before he takes off.

Elliot's face seems confused and even slightly fearful.

"What the fuck is going on?" I ask, angrily.

"I can't explain it here, but there are some things we need to talk about later." Elliot states dismissively, as he goes back to tending the bar.

"Elliot..." I begin, but he cuts me off. I knew he wouldn't budge. I decided not to waste any more time and make my way out of the club. If he wasn't going to offer me any answers, then I was going to have to find them out on my own.

***

I left Centuries and decided to go to Rose's apartment. I needed to make sure she was ok. I couldn't dismiss the feeling in my gut that told me something was wrong. I didn't like the malicious way that the newbie had mentioned her name. I should've ripped his fucking head off right then and there. And I definitely didn't like that she was on Michael's radar. After all this time, you would think he would stop fucking with me and leave me and my romantic conquests alone.

As I made my way up to her apartment, I couldn't help but feel slightly nervous. I honestly couldn't remember the last time I felt any form of anxiety. When the elevator finally reached her apartment, Rose was waiting for me in the open foyer. She looked gorgeous. She was definitely a sight for sore eyes. She wore tight fitting blue jeans and a black tight top which accentuated her very full chest. My eyes scanned her- head to toe. She was absolutely beautiful.

"Hello Rose." I greeted her, controlling the slew of emotions I was somehow feeling. I was a little taken back, since I wasn't used to having any, but it seems this human girl has managed to bewitch me somehow.

"Hello to you too, Leo, to what do I owe the pleasure." She smiles.

"I was in the area, and I thought I would stop by to see you. I apologize for dropping in so unexpectedly, but to be honest I just couldn't resist seeing you again." I explain as I silently wait for her to invite me in.

"I'm glad you came. Please come in. Your visit is definitely the highlight of my day, especially with everything that has happened." She confides, causing a spark in my unbeating heart.

"I'm sorry your day wasn't better. Is everything okay?" I question my curiosity getting the better of me. I wonder if Michael or Pierce had approached her yet.

"I'm not sure if you saw the news today, but Mr. Arthur, a friend of the family, was found brutally murdered. I'm good friends with his son and emotions have been very high today- to say the least. This loss was not only unexpected but has caused my own feelings of loss to resurface. Feelings that I haven't felt in a long time." She explains, her expression showcasing a glimpse of the pain she is feeling. I wish I could ease her, help her. I would give anything to remove any hurt or sorrow from her life. Kill anyone who would cause it.

However, within seconds her expression shifts, and a smile returns to her beautiful face. Her instant moment of vulnerability is now gone. I follow her into the living room.

"Please have a seat." she suggests, as she sits across from me. The white leather sofas lay centered in the middle of the massive room.

"Can I offer you anything?"

"No love, just a few moments of your time." I grin, as I stare into her big brown eyes. They were the definition of warmth and vitality. It made her feel more welcoming, and I wanted nothing more than for her to allow me access inside.

We spent the rest of my visit talking about the most mundane things, her life now that she was back in New York, her plans, and even about her father and his premature death.

"That must have been really hard for you to lose your father at such a young age." I point out, causing her to nod her head in agreement.

"I never knew my mother; she passed away during my birth." I reveal to her, surprisingly. I never talked about my mother, not even when I was human. However, seeing Rose made me want to tell her everything, which was dangerous.

"I'm so sorry. That's horrible Leo. Were you and your father close while you were growing up?" She asks. My body stiffens as I remember the man that could only be considered a father through blood.

"He was present." Is all I can bring myself to say.

"I see, my mother was also a *present* parent." She explains, her usually warm and sweet voice was now coated in bitterness. And for a moment our eyes meet. No words need to be exchanged in order for us to understand one another. However, trying not to rehash the past I shift the conversation.

"So, on a lighter note, what have you been reading my darling Rose?"

She takes a moment to comprehend the shift in the conversation and keeps the questions I can see in her eyes to herself. She knew better than to pry, probably because she herself didn't want to drudge up her past as well. As much as she wanted to keep her secrets buried, they were staring right at me in her eyes. And I knew I'd get her to open up to me, but only when she was ready.

"I'm doing a re-read of Pride and Prejudice. Our conversation the other day kind of sparked my need to pick it up again." She beams, obviously happy to talk about this topic. This girl really loved to read. She could not have been any sexier than she was to me right now.

"Very good! I feel like we've discussed books so much during our time spent together, I feel like I can make some assumptions about you." I point out as I give her a devilish smirk.

"Oh really, like what?"

"Well let's see Jane Austen is your favorite author, Bukowski is a massive red flag although you enjoy reading his perspective even though you hate it, and you absolutely devour Edgar Allen Poe's poetry." I state, enjoying her shocked expression, knowing fully well that I had been right.

"Well, it seems that you are a quick study Mr. Lloyd."

"It's easy to be when the subject matter is as interesting as you, love. You know, Annabel Lee is a personal favorite of mine." I tell her, loving the awe in her stare as she takes in my words.

"Annabel Lee is my favorite poem too. There's something so enchanting about a tragedy." She explains, before continuing by saying, "The way that their love was so eternal that even in death they knew they'd be together. That's real romance."

"So, you believe that there is romance in tragedy?" I question, curiously anticipating her answer.

"Well yes, in a way. Tragedy emphasizes the existence of the love that was shared between both lovers. Not to mention it creates a romance that is more compelling and consuming. Love should consume the lovers to the point that they can't even breathe without the other. Therefore, solidifying that the love two people share is tragic since nothing lasts forever. However, there is romance in the idea since not even death can separate a match that is destined to be together. I know that might sound a bit severe, but love should be flawed and even messy because if it feels too perfect and clean cut then something is very wrong." She explains. I can see a flash of a past full of pain slam into her before she pushes it away.

"I agree, love should be messy and intense. Your souls should be synched and there should be no lines of separation. Two hearts beating in perfect synchronicity. Two souls bound for eternity. There should be no question in either lover's mind that the person they claim to love is theirs, because their name is already etched into their very being. And if they both are meant for one another then their love alone should be able to transcend the boundaries of death and immortalize both souls." I add to her already dark yet truthful idea of love. I find myself pondering my own words after voicing them, wondering where that had all come from. The last time I felt a love like that was actually- never.

She remains silent as she contemplates the words I laid before her, before she looks up at me with a slight smile, obviously pleased with my view.

"Well, it seems we're on the same page Mr. Lloyd, yet again."

"Would you like to have dinner with me this Friday?" I ask, unable to control myself. I need to spend more time with her. Understand this attraction, this connection.

"I can't, Mr. Arthur's services start on Friday. And...I don't know if us going on another date right now is such a good idea." She explains, her voice soft and quiet, like she was saying something she didn't truly feel but rather felt obligated to say.

"Can I ask why?"

She takes a moment to think about her answer, and it's as if I can see the conflict in her mind through her eyes.

"I like you Mr. Lloyd- a lot. But right now, I have a lot going on. A lot of things I need to take care of before I can take you up on that offer."

"I understand. Yet I cannot take no for an answer." I reply boldly.

"Unless, and please be honest Rose, is there someone else? Is it me?" I ask, playfully hoping she would come clean.

"It's just dinner. We already had fun at lunch, I have a feeling dinner will be even more of a thrill" I add, fully knowing that I should respect her boundaries, but I couldn't help myself. I needed to take her out, get to know her, have her get to know me and then I needed to make her mine. I wanted to brand her with my name and mark her with my fangs.

"No, it's definitely not you, and there is no other guy, but I do have an ex that just came back into town and might become a problem. I need to square things away with him first before I involve you into my life. I like and respect you too much to have you in the middle of any craziness that might take place." She explains, worriedly. I can sense her fear. Whoever this guy was has her scared.

"Rose, is there something happening between you and this ex? Something that might be scaring you?" I ask, my voice surprisingly soft as the anger of someone hurting her courses through me. "Because if there is, I can help you." I add.

"No, everything is fine. Look, it's no big deal. I'll be fine." she replies, I can tell she's lying to me.

"Very well." I reply, controlling myself.

"It is getting late, and I do need my beauty sleep." I reply playfully, lightening the mood.

"It is getting late, and I have an early day tomorrow." She begins, her relief noticeable, that the subject has been dropped. I begin to get up. She follows my actions but as she starts to lead me to the elevator, I stop her by placing myself right in front of her so that she can see the seriousness in my face.

"I will wait however long you need, because I want you, Rose. I want to take you out on a proper date, I want to have dinner with you, get to know you and work for the opportunity for you to allow me to make you mine. But, if there is someone who is somehow getting in the way of this, who is hurting you or making you feel scared, I just want you to know that you can tell me and believe me when I tell you I will take care of it." I offer, sincerely. I can see it in her face- the struggle. It takes all of me not to compel her, but I can't stand the idea of doing that to her. She doesn't say a word, but nods- slowly acknowledging my words. I give her a tight smile before I turn around and walk to the elevator. The doors immediately open when I press the button, and I get inside.

"I hope to hear from you soon."

Chapter 8

ROSE

The next morning came rather quickly. I barely even slept. Leo's words stayed rattling around in my mind all night. God, it took everything in me not to crumble last night and tell him everything. I can't explain it but something inside makes me feel like I have known him forever and that I can trust him. I wanted to trust him more than anything and I wanted to leap into those big arms of his and let him claim me as his own.

I wanted to be his and I wanted him to be mine.

Trying not to hyper focus on these thoughts all day, I decide to get up. I needed to get a dress for tomorrow's church service for Mr. Arthur and I also needed to get out of this house. When I left the apartment yesterday after receiving those mums, it took every bit of strength to come back home. But I knew I couldn't hide from it; he was alive, and he had found me.

I make my way to my bathroom and place my hair in the highest ponytail I can achieve, and get my day started. After finishing up, I make my way downstairs, thoughts of Leo fluttering my mind. I can smell the scent of freshly cooked bacon, as I enter our kitchen. My mother, Charles, Jason, Caroline, and Mandee are all sitting at our breakfast table eating and wrapped up in conversation.

"Rose, how nice of you to join us. Your sister is home." My mother smiles as she gestures to the empty chair beside my sister Caroline who had flown in from Georgia the night before. I walk over to my sister and give her a hug, feeling happy to see her, before grabbing a clean plate off the counter and making my way over to the table where I'm met with our regular breakfast spread. I serve myself a bagel with cream cheese and some fruit.

"Well, isn't this nice, everyone back home and together." My mother smiles as she looks at her kids and Mandee- Jason's girl-friend, who she probably loves more than me at this point.

"How is James?" Jason asks not acknowledging our mother's previous statement. Him and James were good friends, and I could see the concern for him in his eyes. Even Mandee looked at me waiting for a response.

"He's as ok as can be expected, considering everything that's happened. He was very close to his father." I explain, then proceed to take a bite of my bagel. Nothing beats the taste of a freshly baked New York City bagel.

"I need all of you to be extra vigilant when you are outside of this house at least until they catch whoever did this to poor Mr. Arthur." My mother tells us, her voice stern but laced with con-cern.

"Of course, mom." Jason assures.

The rest of breakfast is spent talking about business and poli-tics. After we all finish up, I go back upstairs, the scent of roses trailing me as I make my way back to my room. They really are beautiful. Maybe I should call him and schedule a date. The idea alone makes my fingers itch to text him, but I know that I can't or at least shouldn't. I can't risk putting him in the middle when it is very clear that Pierce has an agenda, and I am top priority on his list.

***

Trying not to spend my day fixating on boys, new and old, I decide to head over to Fifth Avenue and do some minor shopping. I walk over to my closet and put on a pair of black ripped up skinny jeans and a black cropped tank top, pair it with my black leather Alexander McQueen heels and a matching bag.

Before leaving, I stop by my sister's old room to see if she wants to join me. She looks up from her computer and nods her head in agreement, then quickly gets herself ready.

After what feels like forever, she finally emerges dressed, literally embodying Jackie Kennedy. Her long dark brown hair styled perfectly straight complimented her tweed mini skirt and chiffon short sleeve top and Chanel flats. She was truly my mother's proudest creation. And even though our style could not be more different, she was still the best big sister a girl could ever ask for.

We quickly say goodbye to everyone before heading out the door. Once outside we make our way to Ben, our personal driver. He is usually on call for both my mother and Charles to use but since they both decided to stay home, we had him all to ourselves today. He greets us each with a warm smile as he holds the door open for us.

"Where to ladies?" He asks once he makes his way back to the driver's seat.

"Bergdorf Goodman." My sister states as she smiles kindly at the young driver. He was new, and if I'm being honest very cute. He nods his head, letting us know that he heard our request as he begins to drive.

"Well, this is nice, we haven't spent a day together like this in forever." Caroline smiles as she looks out her window admiring the surrounding buildings as we drive along.

"I know, with you being in Georgia and me in California we really haven't had much time for sister bonding." I reply, as I think back to when she moved to Georgia to be with her fiancé Trey, right around the time I left to go to California. A part of me was so grateful, since it took a little bit of the heat off of me. My mother was so busy helping my sister and her politician future husband to be, that she didn't have the time to focus on her problem child.

"So, what made you want to come back to New York?" She asks.

"I missed home." I state simply, then avert my eyes to the window next to me.

"You left so abruptly I was so sure you were never coming back." She confesses. I feel horrible that I made her and I'm sure the rest of my family feel that way, but when your survival instincts kick in, all you care about is making it out alive.

"Well, that writing program came up and I didn't want to miss out." I lie. Although, at this point it's starting to feel more like the truth.

"I get it, it was just surprising to us. I mean you leaving and Pierce disappearing. It was just a lot of change in a short period of time." She explains, causing my heart rate to accelerate.

"We're here." Ben informs us, saving me from having to come up with some bullshit response. The car pulls up to Bergdorf's iconic main doors. Caroline mumbles a quick thanks as I barrel out of the car, desperately in need of fresh air. I feel like I'm suffocating.

"Are you, ok?" She asks as she comes around the car. I nod my head and begin to walk.

"I'm sorry if bringing up Pierce is a sore subject, I didn't know there were still feelings there." She explains. I know she means well but hearing his name snaps something inside me.

"Just fucking drop it, Caroline!" I snap, more harshly than I intended to, which causes a couple of New Yorkers to look our way. Feeling more than embarrassed I quickly walk into Bergdorf Goodman and begin walking around, Caroline follows behind me, probably confused and a bit hurt from my outburst.

I try to walk further ahead hoping to avoid her confrontation on what my problem is, but I am defeated when she grabs a hold of my arm and pulls me towards an empty section of the women's department.

"What is your issue?" She insists. I avert my stare to the floor, avoiding having to look into her eyes. I can't keep lying, it's killing me, but the truth would kill her. So, I settled for a compromise. I bravely look into her blue eyes and tell her, "Look Care, I'm sorry I really am, but I just don't want to talk about Pierce, it is a very touchy topic for me."

She gives me a small forgiving smile and hugs me.

"It's ok Rose and I'm sorry too, I promise for the rest of the day I won't bring him up."

I thank her, as we both begin our expedition of some much-needed retail therapy. We take the escalators to the desired floors, and we end up separating by the time we get to the massive shoe department. As I'm looking at all the beautiful shoes in front of me, I spot someone familiar not too far away. Upon further inspection, I realize it's Pierce. As soon as he realizes that I have taken notice of his presence, he winks at me- emphasizing his amusement. I stand there frozen as he remains perfectly still watching me, like a predator strategizing their next move.

It takes me a few seconds to register what is actually happening, before I run to find my sister so we can get the hell out of here. I can't believe Pierce is really back. His presence confirmed it. A big part of me wanted to believe the mums had been a sick joke and that he truly was dead. Apparently, I was not only a failure when it came to my life decisions, but I also sucked at killing someone too. Every part of my body burned with anxiety as I barrel through the department store. Until, I finally make it to the designer handbag department, finally spotting Caroline. I run straight towards her.

"We need to go!" I demand, pulling her towards the elevator.

"Rose what's wrong, what happened?" She asks, worry taking over her once relaxed demeanor.

"If you don't come with me right now, I'm leaving." I warn her, trying not to waste time or come up with another lie.

She puts back the bag she is currently holding and follows me to the elevator and out the store.

Once outside, I am in complete panic mode, I feel like I'm going to pass out from the impending panic attack threatening to unravel. Caroline looks absolutely confused. We continue to walk aimlessly in my attempt to get as far away from the store as possible. This was a mistake, me coming back here, I should have stayed in California, I scold myself as I continue to walk.

As if that would have made a difference.

After Caroline and I walk a block in complete silence, I mentally break down. She grabs my arm and pulls me to the side.

"Rose, what the hell is going on, you're scaring me." She exclaims. I can see the fear in her eyes. I'm scared too. When I feel this way, it terrifies me more than anything. I want to tell her that I'm fine and that this is nothing, but I am too far gone to lie to her.

"I...I saw him." I whisper as I feel the tears begin to roll down my face. She looks confused by my cryptic response. I have never been more thankful than I am right now to live in New York where a crying girl in the streets isn't some big deal.

"Come on, I'm calling Ben to pick us up, you can explain everything in the car." She tells me, concern gleaming in her eyes. I nod my head, not fully able to respond. I couldn't believe my worst nightmare had returned.

Caroline calls Ben our private driver and we wait for him to arrive. It doesn't take very long since he is actually nearby. I'm shaking as Ben pulls up in front of us. Caroline opens the door and lets me go in first before following behind me.

"Hello girls we're to?" He asks.

"Home." Caroline instructs him. I want to protest but I'm too distraught to even form a coherent sentence. Ben looks concerned but doesn't say anything.

Caroline, now feeling a bit more secure with our surroundings, looks over at me waiting for an explanation. I look over to the opening between us and Ben and she takes this as a signal to put the divider up so we can have some privacy.

"Now speak." She demands once Ben is out of earshot. I nod my head and gulp down my fear. I had to tell her. I couldn't hide it any longer.

"I saw Pierce." I blurt out.

"What? Where?"

"In the shoe department. He was there." I tell her, panicked as I fight the urge to cry.

"Rose, he's been gone for over two years, are you sure it was him?" She states, only making my mind race faster as my heart pumps harder.

"Yes, it was him." I assure her, knowing that I could never mistake those cold blue eyes. Those were the eyes that still haunted my nightmares. I try to calm down.

"Pierce is the reason I left New York, not that stupid writing program." I confess.

"What?" She asks more intrigued into what happened, especially since the situation has always been a hazy topic.

"Look you need to swear to me that you won't tell anyone anything that happened today." I beg. She nods her head as her eyes fill with curiosity as she agrees to my terms.

"Rose what happened between the two of you?" She asks, her voice soft as if realizing that she's in the car with a ticking time bomb that's about to go off.

"Look, all you need to know is that Pierce is not a good person. Now, let's please just drop this and never speak of him again." I ask pleadingly. Hoping she understands just how serious I am about this. She nods her head once again and is silent for the rest of the drive.

Once we are dropped off, we thank Ben for the ride and exit the car. We both rush into the building.

"Did he do something to you, Rose?" My sister finally questions, as we enter the elevator. Every bone and muscle stiffens in my body, she takes notice answering her own question.

"That bastard." I could hear her mumble.

"Please, you promised we wouldn't speak about it." I remind her. I know she only wants to help but all I want is to just forget.

The elevator doors finally open and I immediately go towards my room leaving Caroline alone. Once upstairs, I close my door behind me and lock it as if that could save me from what might come next.

Pierce really is back in the city. I really thought I could be brave, even though the fear that thought instilled in me crippled me- I hoped he would go away.

I let out a breath of relief finding comfort in my room and my belongings. I drop my bag and take my shoes off and walk over to my dresser where one of the roses Leo sent me had been placed. I take in the beautiful scent from the flower and try to block out all of the crazy feelings whirling around my head. For a split second it works.

As I try to gather my emotions, my phone dings- it's James. I know I should pick it up and talk to him, but I can't. I send it to voicemail and throw myself in bed and let the feeling of sleep consume me. Sleeping is the only time I can truly feel at peace.

Chapter 9

LEO

Days have passed, and still Elliot has not come home. He's been avoiding me ever since that fucking idiot vampire came barging into the bar. I know Michael has always been a sore topic...for the both of us, but fuck, what the hell could be so bad that he's avoiding me? And how does Rose fit in with all of this?

The more time that he stays away the more anxious I grow. I hated this feeling. It was too human for my own comfort. However, for some reason, when it comes to Rose, I couldn't help it. Everything about her made me feel on edge, it was like a fucked up high that never ended. I knew my obsession with her wasn't healthy- insane even. Trying to get out of my own thoughts, I roll out of bed and throw on a white t-shirt and loose gray sweatpants. One of the better perks of the twenty first century- lounge wear.

I make my way downstairs to a silent and empty penthouse and grab a blood bag. I rip it open and drink. If Michael was coming, I was going to need all the strength I could get. I hadn't seen him since the late sixties back in Spain, but it seems that time has caught up to us. My body physically tenses when I think about all the pain and hatred the thought of him stirs up within me. I truly wanted nothing more than to rip his bloody head from his body. And now that he was coming after Rose, I wouldn't hesitate. He had already taken one lover from me; I would not allow him to take another.

I finish the last drops of blood and throw the bag away, before heading to my study to look through some paperwork I had found earlier on the living room table that Elliot had left behind. It was essentially useless, at least to me. The words it had been written in were like a foreign language. It was probably written in some type of dead witch lingo.

Throwing the papers to the side, I lean my head on my hands and let out a frustrated sigh. Right as I was about to call it quits, I heard the elevator ding, signaling someone had arrived. I practically jumped from my chair and used my vampire speed to meet whoever was there, but once the scent of bourbon and leather reached me, I knew Elliot had come home. As he approached, I could smell the scent of his own blood on him as well.

Once he comes into sight, my eyes drop from his bloodied face to his ripped clothes.

"What the hell happened to you?" I ask, as I follow him to our living area, where he grabs a bottle of bourbon from the bar cart and serves himself a glass. He makes me wait for a response as he takes a drink, letting the alcohol burn through his system.

"I had to go see an old friend."

My eyebrow arches, as I take in his cryptic response. Who the hell did he even know around here that he would consider a friend besides me? Elliot had plenty of acquaintances that he had made during his many years of existence and through the night club but not friends, in fact I'm pretty sure I was his only one.

"Some clarification would be extremely welcomed right about now." I grumble, growing more and more annoyed. Elliot only lets out an amused chuckle before he finishes the rest of his drink. He sets the glass down, avoiding my stare, before walking towards the couch and sitting. I remain standing, as I cross my arms across my chest and wait for him to speak.

"We have never really discussed the entirety of our pasts, during our many years of friendship, and I for one, have always appreciated that. We've never needed too. It has always been a mutual agreement that our past would not define our future. However, it seems that the past really does come back to haunt us when we least expect it." He states, before pausing to take a contemplative breath.

He was nervous.

"I am over seven hundred years old, and during that time I have made my fair share of mistakes, but none as big as the one I made, that landed me this pretty little scar you see on my face." He explains, his face growing remorseful as the memory resurfaces.

"The person I went to see today is an old warlock from back home, by the name of Andrei. Seeing him has made me realize that I need to be honest with you. Michael is here on a quest to rectify a mistake him and I made over five hundred years ago. Cain wants Rose and he wants Michael to bring her to him. He is willing to exchange her soul for Marie's."

As I let his words register, my whole body goes rigid. Marie was dead, there was no bringing her back, not even Cain could do that. He was a leader and held a tremendous amount of power over our society, but he was not Lucifer or even Alukha.

I try to argue, these points to Elliot but he just shakes his head, as if I'm the one not thinking clearly. He stops me short in my reasoning when he pins me with a sympathetic look.

"She was never killed Leonardo; she was taken as a hostage by Cain. Look, I have tried to shield you from the politics that take place in our world all of these years, but the time has come." He begins but stops himself as he gauges my reaction. I stay perfectly still as I await this new information, that I have never been privy to. I always knew that there was a system in place for the creatures of the dark world, such as vampires, witches, demons, gypsies, and even werewolves, and whatever else Lucifer had decided to conjure up, but I tried to keep myself distant from all of it. I had zero interest in politics when I was human and I had even less interest in them when I turned, but now that Rose is involved, that changes everything.

"A very long time ago, hundreds of years before you were turned, Michael and I had become very close friends. I would even go as far to say we were practically brothers, until Marie. Michael and Marie desecrated a belief that is considered sacred to our order. One of the only major rules that our elders enforced back then and would even use the penalty of death as punishment for those who would dare break it." He explains, as he tries to settle his anxiety from having to dig up the past.

"They severed one of the oldest rules known to our kind- they severed a soul tie. And believe me when I tell you, you can't come back from that sort of thing." He finishes explaining, anxiety turning into anger.

"What is that?" I ask, still standing as I watch him shift uncomfortably.

"A soul tie is a bond so powerful that nothing could sever it, unless one's heart stops beating. You see, a very long time ago, way before my creation Lucifer made a deal with a very small but powerful clan of gypsies- offering them his blood in exchange for certain gifts. I'm unclear how this deal came to be but all I know is that through this deal some of them gained one of three powers. Hellfire, Darkness, and Chaos and all of them gained the gift of knowing. With these gifts they became the watchers of the soldiers of Lucifer. They helped Lucifer to grow his army, preparing them for war.

However, what no one not even Lucifer himself counted on was the fact that by providing the women in this clan a drop of his power, that a loophole so to speak, would be created giving these women the ability to procreate with vampires. No one knows how it was possible but through these new children, ties were formed between the very lively soul of a gypsy and whatever remnant of a soul was left behind in a vampire. They became bonded. But once Lucifer became aware of these so-called children and how distracting they had become to both the gypsies and the vampires- he slaughtered them.

A few managed to survive, which made the tie become much rarer and more sacred. As time moved forward and with Lucifer out of the picture in our world- the elders stopped the hunt for these ties as they had become far less within our kind- diluted through the centuries."

"Are you telling me it is possible for vampires to sire an heir through blood?" I ask, my mind spinning with the possibility.

"No, not exactly. Not every vampire can procreate; it has to be a decision made by some higher being. Talks of vampires and gypsies conceiving have dwindled in the last thousand years since Lucifer began eradicating their offspring. So that it's possible yes, but that it's likely probably not."

I stay silent for a moment as I try to take in what Elliot explains to me and then decide to focus on the issue at hand. So, I shake off my fleeting disappointment and ask the question that I should have asked first.

"So, Michael and Marie broke their soul tie?" I ask, as I try to process this new information.

"No, not exactly. You see Marie was promised to Cain, and Michael turned her so that the tie would break, hoping they could be together. He stupidly thought she had truly chosen him over Cain. That she loved him. He was so in love with her that he couldn't see her for who she really was, a narcissistic, selfish little bitch.

So, as you can imagine, Cain did not take kindly to their betrayal. In his eyes Michael had committed treason. He threatened to kill them both. Desperately, Michael sought me out for help. He needed me to try to save them, so I intervened on my friend's behalf- little did I know who I was helping. I bartered a bargain between them. I used my magic to save the bond, removing it from Marie and suspending it for another connected to her bloodline. But that wasn't enough. Cain demanded that Marie remain with him until he received his new soul tie." He explains, his eyes finally meeting mine.

"The scar on my face is a reminder of my willingness to help a trader, since not only did Michael break that law but he also ran off with Marie after the deal was struck. Not to mention aside from this lovely scar I also had to suffer the consequence of being stripped of some of my magic." He states, getting up from the couch and motioning for me to follow him into his study. His words weigh heavy in my head. Elliot was the most powerful witch I knew; I can't imagine just how much more powerful he would be at full strength.

When he opens the door to his private office, my eyes widen from the absolute mess that surrounds me. Books and papers were everywhere. He's been looking for something. He walks over to the ancient grimoire that is opened on his desk and grabs it. I stand beside him as he scans the page and points to some strange drawings and words written in the book.

"I had done a very old and ancient transfer spell, essentially trading Marie's soul for another's."

"What does all of this have to do with Rose?" I ask, as I scan the symbols and letters in the book, not understanding how Rose, a very human girl, got mixed up into all of this.

"I don't know." He whispered, making me clench my jaw. He was lying to me. Elliot never lied to me.

"Elliot, we have known each other for centuries, do not pick right now to lie to me. When it comes to Rose, I seem to be very unstable, and I do not wish to ruin this friendship because of that." I explain, my words sharp, as my features harden. Elliot's shoulders stiffen as he puts down the book and lets out a defeated sigh.

"I don't know anything for sure Leo. But, if I had to guess, Rose is the descendant that Marie's soul tie got passed down to. Although, it seems as though fate has a sense of humor since you are also the very lucky recipient of having a connection with her as well."

Silence filled the room, as we both let his words sink in. I had a connection to a human and she was destined to be the general of Hell's soul mate. I really did have fantastic luck in the love department.

"Rose has gypsy blood, coursing through her?" I ask, as I take in everything that Elliot just threw at me.

"It would appear so."

I decide to move that piece of information to the back of my mind, since finding out that her and I are soul tied takes precedence in my brain. Not to mention Cain, our general, a leader of Hell has a claim on her as well.

"What do we do now?" I ask, not knowing what else to say or even how to feel. I wasn't used to caring for anyone else- all these feelings- they were foreign to me. In all honesty, if I didn't have this over exaggerated need for this silly human, I would have gladly stepped back and let the chips fall as they may. However, it seems this soul tie has brought forth a consciousness that had long been forgotten. I needed to save her, protect her, especially from Cain. He was not to lay a hand or even a finger on her- if anyone was going to have her, fuck her, it would be me.

As if reading my thoughts Elliot is quick to shake his head, "You interfering would be a suicide mission Leo. He's coming for her, and he *will* kill you."

"He can't kill something that is already dead. I will not stand by and let him have her." I growl, my anger coursing through me.

"What you want in this case, will not matter. When Cain comes for her, Leo, and he will come. I promise you; the carnage and chaos that will follow will be enough to damn all of us." Elliot replies.

"Set up a meeting with that witch friend of yours, him and I need to talk." I instruct, before moving to the bar cart and pouring myself a glass of bourbon.

***

Not even two hours later, Elliot and I were sitting in his office at Centuries, when a tall, pale, man walked into the room. He looked to be somewhere in his mid-thirties, but his eyes told me he was much older than that. His hair was the color of blood, as it hung down his back.

"Andrei, thank you for meeting me again today." Elliot, mutters.

"You must really enjoy the feeling of my fist against your face Elliot, for you to call me back so soon." He states, not even acknowledging my presence.

"Well, what can I say pain has always gotten me off, just ask your wife." Elliot retorts, somehow thinking that picking a fight with this man right now was the best thing to do.

Andrei's face reddens with anger as he takes a step towards Elliot.

"Andrei, is it? We didn't come here to fight; we actually need your help." I state simply, as I shove myself in between both men. Andrei takes a step back as he looks at me, assessing who and what I am. Vampires and witches didn't have the best track record of getting along.

"You must be Leonardo Lloyd, the vampire Marie liked to play with back in the day." He says his voice deep and gravel like. I nod my head, holding back my aggravation.

"Yes, look I need information on Cain. I need to know how to stop him. I will be indebted to you for any piece of information you can provide me with." I state trying to hide my desperation. I hated the position I was in, but I couldn't let anyone, or anything come between Rose and I. I needed to protect her.

"Relax lover boy, I don't need you owing me anything. The only thing I ask, is that after this meeting neither one of you ever fucking contacts me again." He states, then moves to sit on the edge of Elliot's desk where he faces both of us.

"There has been talk that Alukha wants Cain dead and has been looking for the weapon to do it. Therefore, solidifying there is a weapon capable of killing him." He whispers, as if the walls surrounding us had ears.

"Who told you this?" Elliot questions his voice shaking, as his body goes tight with unease.

"My source does not matter. What matters is that there is a weapon out there that can take care of this problem you and your friend are in." He states, before getting up.

"Wait, what is the weapon that we need?" I ask, as I practically jump out of my chair, desperate for the answer.

"That I do not know, but one does exist." he answers as he begins to walk towards the door. "I believe I have provided you with enough information to get you two started on this suicide mission." He continues before turning to say, "just know this mystery weapon has been missing for almost a thousand years. Good luck finding it." He states as he opens the door and walks out of the room.

Elliot and I look at one another in silence, as we let the information process. Elliot finally breaks the silence.

"War is coming. I fear that Rose is just the beginning of what will lead us into chaos."

"That might be true, but from where I'm standing Rose is my chaos and I will do whatever I have to do to protect her; everything else can burn for all I care." I could hear the anger and hatred in my own voice, realizing no truer words could've been spoken.

Chapter 10

ROSE

Death is a funny thing, especially in Manhattan. A burial for a member of one of the elite in the Upper East Side isn't just a place for mourners to mourn the dead, it is rather a sanctuary for probable business deals, talks about assets and even at times fights over the unread will. Death in our society attracted more vultures than the norm.

Today was a reminder of that.

Most of the people in attendance were more interested in clout and having their photos in the paper than anything else. Status-proving to those around them that they were high enough on the social ladder to be acquainted with the deceased- meant more to them than the dead person themself.

You do however, on occasion have a true mourner attend for the right reasons. In some cases, it might be the children of the deceased, their spouses, or extended close family. In most cases, however, grief towards the deceased could manifest itself through the mistresses since their cash cow was now six feet under in a very expensive mahogany casket and maybe their business partners- elated that the business deals were now possibly solely theirs to handle and profit from. It was a sad and entertaining thing to witness.

I stand next to Adeline at Trinity Cemetery, when I notice through my thick black sunglasses, James holding his poor mother as she tries her best to keep her composure. She is an older woman, who looks absolutely incredible for her age. Her figure and hair always kept perfect. She truly did love her husband; they were a true Upper East Side, New York love story. Their marriage was one of true love, which is a rarity around here.

The priest continues his sermon as everyone tries their best to listen. James stands tall next to his mother and to the other side of her holding her hand was James' older brother Marcus. Cheryl Arthur was a good mother to both of her boys. She, unlike the other mothers around here, was actually present and involved in her children's lives.

Collin stands next to James in support of his best friend. He truly loved James. He considered him almost like a brother. I know that this loss was hard on him too.

Mr. Arthur had taken him in when Collins' own father had abandoned him. Collin was like another son to Mr. Arthur. I know Adeline was most grateful for the love he had shown Collin through the years, especially when he needed it most.

Collin had a very rough and strained relationship with his own father. He had basically abandoned Collin and Collin's mom after realizing domestic life just wasn't for him. He fled back to his home country Australia- leaving his family blowing in the wind. It was a shitty situation all the way around but thank goodness Collins mom was no idiot and instead stepped it up taking advantage that her husband was no longer in charge of the businesses, decided to run things herself. No one would've guessed it, but I guess when life gives you lemons, choosing wisely can make you a boss bitch. Sometimes, when Collin and I were kids, he would tell me how he wished his father had died instead of my own.

As I stand here trying to pay attention to what's happening and suppress the flashbacks of my own father's funeral, I spot two familiar faces on the other side of where I'm standing. Leo and Elliot. Adeline notices my attention is directed somewhere other than the solemn scene in front of us and moves ever so slightly to get a better look.

"I didn't realize they knew each other." Adeline whispers.

"Me neither." I reply. I mean I guess it makes sense for Leo to know Mr. Arthur since they probably ran in the same business circles, but I do find it strange that he's here with the club owner from Centuries.

I am so caught up with Leo and Elliot and figuring out how they know each other, that I didn't even realize that James was delivering his last words to his father. His voice is shaky and strained. You could tell he had been crying but was trying to keep it together.

"I will find out who did this. My father's death will not be dismissed and forgotten. Whoever is responsible will be held accountable." He proclaims, before placing his hand on the casket.

"I love you dad. I will make you proud like you did me."

His mother looks up at him and holds his hand as a gesture of support and gives him a small assuring smile. Marcus then speaks as everyone listens to what the oldest Arthur son has to say. His speech is short and sweet, much like his brothers. Once he finishes his last few words on how he will miss his father everyone says one last prayer before we all begin to start walking back to our awaiting cars.

Everyone is invited back to the Arthur's house for a luncheon and to pay their respect to the family personally. Adeline and I get ready to follow the rest of the crowd when I feel a pulling feeling directing me towards Leo. It's as if my body is subconsciously craving him.

I look over as I try to find him when I notice the crowd of family and friends that wouldn't be attending the reception over at the Arthur's home, offering condolences before leaving. Suddenly, flashbacks of my own father's funeral surface. I quickly dig through my purse for a cigarette which I light as soon as I'm able to grab one, ignoring Adeline's judging stare and silent protest.

"Rose seriously?" She asks, shaking her head trying to display how disappointed she is with my continuation of this wretched habit. I can't help it. It's one of the only things that helps to suppress the feeling of running and hiding in a small corner, away from everyone and every reminder of what I've been through. Sounds pretty dramatic I have to admit.

"I need something to help with my nerves. I'm sorry." I explain, as I take a couple of puffs before throwing it to the ground and stepping on it.

"I get it, it must be hard being here and seeing all of this." She tells me, placing her arm around me, supportively. I smile. Adeline stands next to me silently waiting to see what I do next. I can tell she wants to ask me something but refrains from doing so. I pop a piece of gum in my mouth then without another word I begin walking. However, we both have different ideas of where we're going because I begin walking towards Leo and Elliot who I finally spot while she finds herself walking in the opposite direction towards her car.

"Where are you going?" Adeline asks when she realizes we are not on the same page anymore.

"I have to talk to Leo. Come with me." I tell her, I need her to distract Elliot so I can speak to Leo alone. Adeline follows behind as if silently agreeing.

"We have to be quick. I promised Collin, I would meet him back at the house. James is going to need all of us today." she explains. I nod my head in agreement.

We walk over to where Elliot and Leo both stand conversing with one another under one of the many trees lining the outside of the cemetery grounds. Leo's eyes light up as soon as he sees me walking towards him.

"Rose, Adeline." Elliot greets, happy to see us or should I say happy to see Adeline.

"It's nice to see you again, Elliot." I smile then look over at Leo.

"You as well Leo."

"Rose, it's always a pleasure, and it's very nice to finally meet you, Adeline." He smiles tightly, moving his hand forward as a gesture for her to shake it.

"Yes. It's nice to meet you as well Mr. Lloyd, if only it was under better circumstances." She replies while shaking his hand. They pull apart, as Leo gives her a tight-lipped smile, acknowledging her words. Elliot takes this moment of silence to push his way into the conversation and grab Adeline's attention.

"It's lovely to see you out in the daylight instead of in the dark. A woman as beautiful as you deserves to be fully seen." Elliot tells her, his British accent only adding fuel to the feverishly hot flames his kind words ignite. Adeline blushes like a schoolgirl as she tries to hide a smile. Leo and I simply glance at one another then look at Elliot amused by his boldness.

"Rose, why don't you and I take a walk, and let these two talk. I actually have some things to discuss with you." He suggests. I look over at Adeline for permission to leave her, which she gives me by nodding her head obligingly. Something tells me she wants alone time with Elliot as well. Leo offers his arm for me to grab which I gladly do, and we begin to walk further away from the cemetery.

We walk to the next row of trees up ahead not too far from where we previously were, but far enough that we can talk in private. Tomb stones can be seen in our line of view as we stand by the entrance gate. We take in one another's presence, like we did the first time we met. He gazes into my eyes like they're somehow a safe haven holding secrets he can't wait to unravel.

"I'm sorry I haven't spoken to you much these past few days." I apologize. I feel guilty for not pursuing him and ignoring his text messages. It's just that I needed time to sort through everything. Pierce coming back from the dead wasn't on my list of worries when I decided to come back to New York. Seeing him, alive and well, the other day had me literally spiraling inside. I needed to figure out my next move, before I got involved with anyone, even Leo.

"Rose, it's ok you have had quite the full plate. You being there for Mr. Arthur's son is admirable." He praises, his words soft and gentle.

"I'm glad you think so, I mean I had to be there for him, he's been there for me more times than I can count." I respond.

"Well, you seem like very close friends," is all he says. I can't help but internally laugh, if he only knew all the shit we had to go through before we could become such close friends.

"Look Leo, I just wanted to tell you that I really like you, and that I want nothing more than to go out with you, but certain developments in my life recently won't allow me to act on my desires." I explain, wanting to be truthful and not string him along. I'm sure there are plenty of other women who he could be pursuing. Even though the very thought of that made me cringe and even feel unreasonably angry. I can't even stomach the thought of him with someone else.

"Rose, excuse my boldness but I have to ask and please be honest with me, is this ex you mentioned the last time we spoke becoming a problem?" He asks, his eyes boring into mine, looking for my candor.

"What? What makes you think that?" I ask, my eyes growing a bit wider. I need to control my emotions and not show any fear.

"You seem nervous. You're trying to hide it, but I can see it in your eyes. I just want you to know that if he is doing anything that is scaring you, you can tell me, and I will help you." He explains, his eyes glimmer with genuine intent. The crazy in me wanted to tell him everything. I couldn't help but feel that he would understand. However, the part that was still being dictated by fear made me hold my tongue.

"I'm handling it." I explain, my voice low as my eyes look out into the distance unable to face him. I knew he would see through my lie. The connection I felt between us felt scary yet endearing. I felt more connected to Leo who was practically a stranger than I have ever felt with anyone else in my life.

"Let me in, Rose. I can see this is troubling you." He pleads, stepping closer as he reaches for my hand. When his fingers intertwined with mine, I can't help but let out a breath of relief. I needed his touch more than I needed air. It calmed every overactive nerve in my body. My eyes meet his and I nod my head, surrendering to his want to help me.

"My ex was not a good person, and well, he's back in town now. Going on a date with you will only make the inevitable confrontation between all of us more severe and I don't want that for myself or for you. The last thing I want is to drag you into my mess." I finally admit, as my eyes begin to water. I fight back the urge to cry. Leo looks at me sympathetically.

"Let him try to come near us, Rose. He can't do anything I swear to you." He proclaims, his words so confident that I almost believe him. Leo pulls me towards him and then wraps his arms around me.

"You and I are going to dinner this Tuesday." He whispers as he holds me close to his chest. Feeling completely secure wrapped in his essence, I make the crazy decision and agree.

"I think we should get back to Adeline and Elliot, we have to get going." I frown slightly as I pull away from his embrace. For a split of a second, I can feel his disappointment of having to let me go. It mirrored my own. Leo nods in agreement then grabs a hold of my hand as we make our way back to our friends.

As we approach them, I can tell they are in the middle of discussing something that I can't quite hear until I get closer.

"Mademoiselle when you drop that boyfriend of yours, give me a call." Elliot informs Adeline before gesturing to Leo that it was time for them to leave. Leo looks at me and says goodbye placing a small kiss on my cheek.

Elliot stops mid stride as he is leaving and looks back at both Adeline and I, "come by the club anytime ladies." He shouts looking at Adeline specifically, "remember what I told you." before he starts walking again, trying to catch up with Leo.

"What was that about?" I ask curiously.

"I don't know, I never even told him I had a boyfriend." Adeline informs me, still looking shocked. I shrug my shoulders, not giving it a second thought. He probably knows she is spoken for by the way she isn't throwing herself at him. He is probably arrogant enough to think that. We both walk silently back to the car.

Adeline starts the car as soon as we get inside and then drives off to James's mother's house.

"So how did your talk with Leo go?" She asks, arching her brow.

"It was enlightening. What I want to know is how your talk with *Elliot* went?" I smirk, putting more emphasis on Elliot's name. I can see her shift uncomfortably in her seat.

"Interesting... Elliot's an interesting man."

"Interesting?" I question her choice of words.

"Interesting." She repeats then continues to look out towards the road, "besides I have a boyfriend, so interesting is an appropriate response." She states, trying to convince herself that he isn't way hotter and not to mention more interesting than her current boyfriend.

"Don't take this the wrong way Adi but don't you think you and Collin have been dating for far too long, like don't you want to try something new?" I ask. I wasn't trying to be that bitch of a friend, but I always thought Adeline could do better than Collin and I see the way Elliot looks at her and I see the way she wants to look at him. Collin couldn't give two fucks about Adeline, he only cared when it was convenient for him.

Yes, Collin is the son of an Australian entrepreneur and is incredibly rich, but he could also be a tremendous whore. I don't know for sure if he ever cheated on her, but I've seen too many ugly moments in their relationship to rule that possibility out. Adeline was way too good for him, and he knows it.

"I found my soulmate young." Is all she says. The idea of a soulmate was such a foreign concept. How could anyone truly be designed for someone else? I don't even fully believe in the concept of love let alone the concept of being someone's perfect match.

"Do you believe in true love?" I ask, not even fully comprehending what I'm asking her until it comes out. She glances over at me, her eyes a bit saddened by my question.

"Is love even real, like honestly. I read about it all the time in these books and novels, but it's hard to imagine that someone can love someone that deeply. That they would die for them, give up everything for them. I don't know, the whole thing just seems like a hoax." I explain, curious to know her thoughts. Adeline analyzes my words before responding. She can be what Charlotte from Pride and Prejudice would consider a fool in love. I would definitely classify her as a hopeless romantic. In the past I would've considered myself one as well. Nowadays it just seems more realistic to read about love in stories rather than live it. Pierce had jaded me. Love never seems to end well when it comes to me. My life just didn't seem to be meant to have a happily ever after.

"Rose, you will meet someone one day who is going to completely change your outlook and then those novels that you love so much won't be just fiction anymore." She states sternly. She was hopeful- at least one of us was.

"I don't know. I guess I'll have to see."

"Rose just with Leo you're already living a fantasy I mean just look at him he's like something right out of those pages you read. He's tall, bruting, complicated, and a loner. I mean he's either a serial killer or a starter pack for a Charlotte Bronte romance novel character."

I can't help but laugh at her thoughts on Leo. I guess in a way she wasn't wrong he definitely has the brooding, dark mysterious thing going for him. He is gorgeous and from what I can tell quite the gentlemen. He really seems like a character straight out of that era.

Adeline continues her point by saying, "sometimes you have to make your own story, and who knows maybe Leo is going to be the main character in your epic romance."

I hope with everything in me he will be. I really like him, and we haven't even had a proper date yet. I can't explain the feelings that surface when I'm around him, but I'm happy they're there. They seem to be more than just a distraction.

The rest of the car ride I sit in silence allowing my thoughts to take me captive and let the idea of love be the only thing that runs through my mind. I want to believe in it, desperately, but how can I believe in something when I have never felt it, let alone really seen it. I have nothing to compare it to except books.

Chapter 11

ROSE

When we arrive at James's house, the three-story brownstone is filled with visitors offering the family their condolences and remembering Mr. Arthur. Most of those who had come back to the house had truly liked and cared for him.

Adeline and I weave our way through many of New York's elite members until we spot James standing by the staircase. His face is void of any emotion, as he takes in the reality around him.

"Rose, Adeline, thank God you're here." He says looking away from the scene around him. "I'm really sorry about your father, James." Adeline apologizes. James nods his head as a silent thank you.

"That means a lot Adi, Collin is upstairs if you want to go find him." James states. I could tell he wanted to talk to me alone.

Adeline hugs James before making her way up the stairs.

"Your speech was very powerful." I commend. James gives me a sad smile, before looking at me, concern etched into his face.

"Rose, I'm not sure if this is the right time to tell you this, but Pierce is back."

Everything fades as I take in his words. Yes, I was already aware but hearing it from him made it feel that much more real.

"He was on the list to come, but I made sure to have him blocked from all the services. Him and his family. If he's back Rose, you aren't safe. We've never talked about what happened to you back in Italy. I've never wanted to ask...." James continues but before he can finish his thought, we are interrupted by his mother insisting he join her conversation immediately.

Hesitantly, James excuses himself and goes over to his mother, leaving me alone with his words rattling in my head. Trying not to panic, I decide to push it to the back of my mind and instead go and find Adeline. I walk up the stairs and down the long hallway but stop when I hear yelling. It's Adeline. I hurry down the rest of the hallway calling her name until I finally arrive at the scene that I would've never expected to see- at least not here.

Collin is naked while Adeline shouts and tosses everything and anything in arms reach. Meanwhile, the girl he had been hooking up with is scrambling to put her dress on- mortified by the scene unfolding in front of her.

"You liar! I hate you!" Adeline screams as she flings a small vase at him nearly hitting his face.

"It's not what it looks like Adi." He pleads. His words bring back some disturbing memories of how James would feed me the same line, whenever I would catch him.

"It's not what you think.... I'm sorry.... Please forgive me, it was a mistake." The starter pack phrases for cheaters. It's funny to think back on those days. I was younger and the thought of him desiring someone else in place of me, I guess hurt my pride more than my heart. His disloyalty to me was what hurt the most.

"Adeline." I yell, as I try to refocus her attention before she kills Collin. I approach her grabbing her arms

"You were right Rose; Collin is an asshole." She laughs cynically. I could tell she had finally lost it.

"The worst part is I used to tell you to leave James, that he was never going to change, and I couldn't even take my own advice. Because this is not the first time, he couldn't keep his privates to himself." She cries while laughing at her own words. I try to push her out of the room.

"Finish getting dressed then leave...Now!" I state firmly looking at the boxed blonde-haired girl who continues to look absolutely terrified.

"Let's just go." I sternly tell Adeline, as I finally get her out the doorway. I know once we leave, she will calm down.

"Adeline, I'm sorry." Collin continues to shout. She looks at him with such anger and hatred that if looks could really kill- he would be dead.

"You're not sorry Collin you never are." She wipes her tears as she collects herself. "We're over. I never want to see you again. Do you understand me! You can keep your cheap whore but never call or look for me again!"

As he stands there still fully naked and in shock, I couldn't help but feel pride in the way Adeline handled the situation to a certain degree. I couldn't help but smile. She had finally found the courage and the strength to dump him. He looks at me, angrily.

"What are you smiling at?" He asks, bitterly.

"That you just allowed her to be happy." I reply

His face fills with confusion as I walk out of the room and find Adeline in the bathroom down the hall sobbing. I make my way inside and comfort her.

"You'll find someone better." I assure her.

Adeline and I have been friends since preschool, and I don't think I have ever been the one to hold her while she cried; she was always the one doing that. This was definitely new territory for me.

I didn't mind though; heaven knows I owed her for all the shirts I've stained through the years with tears, mascara, and regret.

After Adeline manages to get her feelings under control and collect herself, she splashes some cold water on her face as she waits for the puffiness and redness to disappear from her porcelain-like skin before walking out of the bathroom. I follow close behind. We both agree that we have had enough death for one day and decide to leave earlier than we probably should have.

We both walk down the stairs and head towards the elevator. I tell her to go ahead without me and that I will meet her at the car once I say goodbye to James. I luckily found him by the foyer.

"Hey, I was looking for you." He states walking over to me as I approach.

"Look I'm sorry but Adeline and I are leaving. I'd tell you why, but I have a feeling Collin will fill you in later."

"That stupid fucker." He mumbles, knowing what I'm alluding to.

"Yeah, go, please make sure she's ok." he encourages.

"You're not missing much here." he says reassuringly. And as if on cue, someone in the other room begins to yell about the reading of the will.

"Let the games begin." I state cocking my brow. James raises both of his brows and tightens his lips as if acknowledging that of course this would happen. Nothing says Upper East Side funeral like the fighting over the reading of the will.

"And Rose, we need to finish our conversation. Pierce being back is not a coincidence. Keep yourself safe and let me know if he causes any problems. I'm not letting him hurt you again." He states, before wrapping his arms around me holding me close. It feels nice being in his arms, his warmth is familiar and much needed.

"We'll talk soon." I whisper as I hug him goodbye and make my way to the elevator. Once on the ground floor I find Adeline in her car ready to go. We drive over to her apartment; she seems ok or at least as ok as she can be from what she had just experienced. We both agree in the car that we will have a full-blown breakup-palooza as soon as we get back to her place. Sweatpants, ice cream, and sappy movies.

***

We pull into Adeline's apartment garage, and she parks in her usual spot. Once inside her sanitary white apartment that I adore so much she immediately throws herself on the couch and just lets out a breath of what I can only assume is relief. Relief from the pressure of being with Collin, possibly. Adeline always comes across so put together and whole, the truth is she is one fake smile away from suffocating herself. She is constantly pushing herself to be perfect- but honestly at what price?

The next few hours are spent eating ice cream and watching stupid rom-com movies. We were in the middle of making fun of the cheesy storylines when my phone rang. It's Leo.

Adeline throws popcorn at me to scold me for keeping my phone on when we were supposed to be in the movie zone. However, I give her an apologetic look moving her legs from on top of mine, so that I can get up, which earns a mocking booing sound to emanate from her. I can't help but let out a small laugh from her childish antics. I walk into the other room and answer my phone.

"Hello."

"Rose, it's lovely to hear your voice." Leo greets me. I can barely hear him through the sounds of loud music and people in the background. It sounds like he's in a club, which I guess wouldn't be a shocker since Elliot owns one.

"Thank you...I can barely hear you......are you out?" I ask curious to know where that loudness could be coming from.

"What no. Elliot decided to throw a party." He explains, annoyed that Elliot would do something like that.

"Hey, would you like to come over and join me? It's not really my scene as the kids say these days but it would be more bearable with you here keeping me company." Leo asks, causing me to giggle. I felt like a schoolgirl.

"I'd love to, but would it be ok if I bring Adeline too?"

"Of course. Here let me text you the address..." Leo replies before we hang up.

I make my way back into the living room to talk Adeline into going. I know pushing her to go to this party is maybe not the best idea, but a part of me really does believe that it's better to have her distracted with fun than to sit in this apartment and watch sappy movies and cheesy rom-coms all night. As I enter the room, I see her stuffing her face with chocolate chip ice cream while screaming angry nonsense at the TV as The Notebook plays on the screen.

"Hey, as much as I love this look for you, we are going out tonight." I tell her, deciding that giving her the choice to decline is out of the question. She needs this. Maybe her spending more time with Elliot will be a good thing. Boost her confidence a little bit. And maybe even loosen her up.

"What?" She asks confused, placing the container of ice cream down on her marble coffee table and wrapping the blanket around her tighter.

"Leo called; Elliot is throwing a party!" I exclaim, hoping she will also get excited. She takes a moment to process the words I just said and looks from me to the ice cream container and the TV as if weighing her options for the night. After a couple more seconds of silence she nods her head in approval of my idea.

"Let's go." She states firmly as if on a mission.

She picks herself off from the sofa and walks straight to her bedroom. I follow behind her, curious to see what she has in mind. Her first step is to go through her massive walk-in closet. She is meticulous and thoughtful as she sorts through her clothes. Finally finding what she's looking for. She pulls out two dresses. She tosses a short cocktail dress that is black with silver chain straps over at me. Then she pulls a light pink dress for herself, deciding that it would be the perfect dress for tonight.

I go into the guest bathroom while she gets ready in her bedroom. I changed from my previous black dress into this one which is more tight fitting and much shorter than my funeral attire. Keeping my heels on from the service and leaving my hair as it is, I straightened it in the morning, and it has managed to keep itself in check. My makeup is light, nothing too crazy, however, I remember that I always keep a red lipstick in my bag and decide to go and grab it. As I walk out into the living room, Adeline is putting on her shoes. A white pair of designer pumps, in true Adeline fashion. She has thrown her curled hair into a high ponytail and touched up her makeup since it had been washed away by her tears from earlier today. I grab my lipstick and use my phone as a mirror. After smacking my lips together and making sure it is perfect, I walk back to where Adeline is sitting.

"Ready?" I ask. Although not entirely referring to the party.

"Yeah, let's go." She smiles. I could tell she was a bit excited and wasn't completely faking it.

"It's going to be fun." I reassure her before calling for a private car to come and pick us up. We both grab our bags and walk out the door. Once outside we are met with the black SUV waiting for us. We step inside and drive off.

Leo's apartment is located in the very chic Baccarat Hotel, which just screams luxury and elegance. The chandeliers hang beautifully as we make our way inside. My nose is immediately met with the smell of roses, as I look around and notice all the beautiful bundles and bouquets scattered around the place. Adeline and I quickly find the elevator, both of us eager to see the apartment and make our way up. For the first couple of seconds the only thing that you can hear is the numbers dinging as we pass each of the floors, as we start reaching the top floor, we begin to hear music. Adeline and I look over at one another as we get closer.

"Elliot can really throw a party." I laugh. Then before Adeline can reply the doors open to his floor. There are hundreds of people moving around in the massive apartment space.

"Yes, he can! I think I'm going to go find him and tell him what I think about this glamorous party." Adeline smiles excitedly. Giving me the reassurance that I had been right about bringing her here.

"Good luck with that!" I smile as she saunters off into the room of people, getting lost in the crowd. I stand by the elevator entrance, taking in my surroundings. Lights keep flashing as the music continues to blare and the guests are dancing and kissing, some look to be even fucking. A party without rules, I think to myself as I search the area around me for Leo. I couldn't help but feel out of place, this was no longer my scene, I actually felt uncomfortable surrounded by so many unfamiliar faces. I couldn't believe I enjoyed this when I was younger.

I stop as someone taps me on the shoulder causing me to slightly jolt.

"Did I scare you, love?" His British accent took my breath away. I turn around smiling.

"Never." I yell over the music.

He lets a low chuckle escape his lips as he looks into my eyes and moves a piece of loose hair behind my ear, "you look absolutely beautiful."

I blush.

"Thank you, Mr. Lloyd. You don't look too bad yourself."

Leo smirks without speaking and grabs my hand walking me over to what I can only assume is the living room since I can't really tell where the rooms start and end with so many people covering the space. As I sit down on the dark blue velour sofa, Leo looks over at the other couple sitting opposite to me as they both immediately get up and move somewhere else. He always seems to get what he wants- hopefully that applies to me as well.

"Do you want something to drink?" he asks.

As I am about to answer I can't help but notice the strippers prancing around, dancing between the guests. I smile remembering a time when my friends and I thought it would be fun to take a strip dancing class. It's truly an art form.

"No, I'm good for now thank you. This is a.... nice party you have going on here the strippers add that much needed touch of class." I joke.

Leo lets out a laugh, sitting next to me on the sofa.

"Believe me this is not my kind of party. This is all Elliot's doing."

Elliot definitely looks like he likes to have a good time- complete opposite of Adeline to a certain degree. I think they might be good together. I think she needs someone like him.

"He's very extravagant." I say looking around at the craziness surrounding us- topless waiters, exotic dancers besides the strippers and God knows what else I haven't seen yet. I was pretty sure an orgy was happening in the other room.

"You're telling me. He once threw a party and got real life tigers. Can you imagine real life bloody tigers, sorting that out with the association of this building was a nightmare." Leo explains. I have been to some very crazy parties in my life, but I have to say Elliot has truly outdone himself here tonight.

"I can only imagine. Although I'm sure since it was you, they looked the other way."

Leo smirks at my comment knowing I was right. There is just something about him that you can't help but say yes too.

"Well, how could they not? I do think, however, it has more to do with fear than anything else. And of course, a little persuasion. People seem to fear me for some reason here." Leo jokes although there is pride evident in his tone, that he is able to bring out that reaction to the surface in most people.

I can see how people would be afraid of him. He is very intimidating. I still get a little nervous every time we talk. However, I actually feel safe with Leo Lloyd. It's kind of ironic poetry.

"You can be an intimidating and overpowering man. No one really knows a lot about you- on a personal level. People fear mystery. People need to know everything about a person and you Mr. Lloyd are the only thing that they can't seem to figure out." I explain thinking out loud.

Leo moves in closer and pulls me in with those green eyes of his.

"What about you? Do you fear mystery?"

I can't help but let out a small nervous laugh from his question. His stare is so intense, as he looks from my eyes to my lips. His face moves ever so close to mine, trying to figure out whether he should kiss me or not.

"No." I state, trying to sound unaffected by his eyes.

I don't fear the mystery that lies ahead, I want to embrace it and let it consume me. I can't explain it. I feel like I'm going insane. I barely even know this man, yet I feel like I've known him forever.

He leans in closer, causing me to move back. I end up hitting the back of the sofa with my figure as he hovers above me. His designer cologne taking a hold of my senses.

"You think you have me figured out Rose?" He questions teasingly although I can tell he is genuinely curious to hear my reply. I don't think I have him figured out, but I do think I have a pretty good clue as to who he is. A mask wearer can always spot another mask wearer.

He stares at me, the intensity rising. My breath starts to quicken as I try to think of what to say next.

"We're all mysteries, some of us are just better at being one than others. But when it comes to you, I think I have a good idea." I respond in an almost nervous whisper.

I'm dizzy from his scent and his breath against my skin. God help me.

"I'm glad someone has a clue. You, my beautiful Rose, are the only mystery I want in my life. You drive me absolutely crazy. There's just something about you...that I can't figure out."

I can't help but shutter at his cool breath tantalizing my ears. I swallow the lump in my throat that is currently holding back my words.

I allow a small smirk to show when he lands his eyes back on me. He straightens himself up, sitting back in his original position. Feeling a bit more bold, I respond back, "if you think I'm driving you crazy now just wait until I get you in bed."

I have never wanted to connect with a man on a sexual level the way I want to with him. I want to explore everything about him. I want to feel his hands explore me. I want him to claim me as his own.

Leo's eyes travel down my body relishing my words.

"That can be arranged rather quickly." He smirks. I become excited by his suggestion. However, in the back of my mind I know we need to take this slow. I need to be smart when it comes to him.

So, deciding it would be best to let the flames of this conversation simmer I respond, "how about for now... Mr. Lloyd, we enjoy the party. You know, I took a couple of classes in exotic dancing."

His eyes go a bit wide, probably from the unexpected reveal.

"What?" Is all he manages to ask as he licks his lips at the possibilities of me wrapped around a pole giving him a show.

I slightly shrug my shoulders before explaining, "about three summers ago, me and a couple of my roommates decided it would be fun to take a couple classes. It was surprisingly fun...and made me quite flexible."

I can't help but laugh internally as he adjusts his tie and shifts in his seat trying to keep his composure.

"You must show me."

I shrug my shoulders before nodding my head in agreement. Giving a lap dance seemed less serious than having sex. At least that's what I'm telling myself in order to justify my next couple of moves.

"Ok, Mr. Lloyd...But first alcohol."

Chapter 12

ROSE

I'm either the bravest or the stupidest person at this party. When did I gain the confidence to do this with a man like Leo Lloyd? I can barely look at him without keeping myself together. However, not allowing my nerves to get the best of me I get up from the comfort of the couch and pull Leo along with me. He doesn't look that excited about joining the party. However, the moment he wraps his arm around my waist as we make our way through the drunk crowd, I can feel just how excited he is to get a private show from me.

We both grab a shot from the trays, one of the shirtless waiters is walking around with and clink glasses before downing them. I feel confident enough to grab his hand which is surprisingly cold and walk us over to the dance floor. Leo looks uncomfortable as he scans the room and takes in the rather vulgar scene.

"You don't like to dance?" I ask, screaming over the loud music.

"Not really. This isn't my type of dancing." He confesses. I stay silent and flash him a wicked smile, as I turn around and begin rubbing my body against his, swaying my hips, creating friction between the two of us. I grab both of his hands and place them firmly on my hips. After a few uncertain moments, I feel Leo loosen up. I can feel his hands on me, his fingers gripping at my skin through my dress.

As we let the music move us, we both dance in sync with one another. I feel a sense of safety in his arms, something I haven't felt in a long time. My mind is completely turned off and the only thing I am focused on is him. He has invaded all of my senses, and there isn't any room for anything else.

Once the music changes to a faster paced beat, I decide to take a risk and make my move. I dance myself out of his grasp, turning to face him and grab his hand, leading him forward. He offers me a questioning look. I ignore it and continue to drag him through the crowd of people.

"Where's your bedroom?" I ask, as we move into a less crowded area. He motions towards the stairs. I take the opportunity to get the show going and position myself in front of him as we make our way up the stairs- swinging my hips the entire way up.

"You teasing me Rose, isn't going to end well." He growls in my ear before tossing me over his shoulder. I yelp in excitement as he strides down the hall and pushes his bedroom door open. The decor is dark and modern. The windows around his large bedroom are covered with black drapes. The walls are covered in mahogany wooden bookcases full of beautifully new and aged leather-bound books. He places me down, and I am able to get a clearer view of all the little details housed in his bedroom.

His bed is placed in the middle, and it's covered with black satin sheets and a black comforter, not really a shock. I walk over to the wall of books that takes up a good portion of his wall space. I look over at him making sure it would be okay to peruse the books on the shelves which he grants, by walking over to me and holding my hand as he guides me to a particular section. The first thing that catches my eye is the first edition Pride and Prejudice book on the shelf.

"Is this a first edition?" I ask, having a difficult time believing it.

"Yes. I collect old books. I actually just got this one." He states, walking closer to me. He was perfect- my perfect match.

"That's incredible." I exclaim still in awe of the book's presence.

"Pride and Prejudice is one of my favorites." I tell him as I continue to scan the shelves.

"Really, I thought you were more of a Bronte lover." He replies, playfully.

He grabs the book off the shelf, causing me to flinch.

"Be careful!" I caution, as he hands me the book.

"It's yours." He smiles. My jaw drops to the dark wood floors. He can't be serious. No one in their right mind would give such a treasure away. I can almost feel myself begin to cry from the thought of it.

"What?" I ask, still processing.

"The other night during our conversation, you spoke very highly of dear Jane here and her book, when I saw this, I wanted you to have it." He smiles.

I could feel my body become engulfed in the heat of his sincerity. No one had ever done anything quite like this before for me.

I hesitate to grab the book, before gently taking it from his grasp. Our fingers ever so slightly touch.

"This is incredible." I whisper. I can feel a tear roll down my face. Leo steps closer and moves his hand to my cheek to brush the tear away.

"I thought the book would make you happy, love, not sad." He frowns a bit.

I quickly shake my head then look up at him with a smile on my face from pure happiness. I haven't felt this way in so long.

"No, I'm incredibly happy, thank you." I assure him, wrapping my arms around his neck, pulling him closer. His arms immediately engulf my small waist as he pulls me in and kisses me. My body relaxes in his embrace. It's as if I've kissed him a thousand times before. Our lips move in perfect synchronicity. I can feel sparks within me. This moment has in some way brought me back to life.

After a couple of long minutes, I remember why we had come up to his room in the first place. I release my hold of him and walk over to his bed as he follows close behind. The dim lighting in the room and the moon light gently seeping through his windows illuminates his beautiful face.

"You're perfect." I whisper.

He smiles at the compliment as I push him back onto the bed. I place the book down on his nightstand before standing in front of him. He sits on the edge of the mattress while I play with his hair contemplating my next move. I have never given a man a lap dance before.

"Are you ready?" I ask seductively. Pulling his hair slightly so he is looking up at me. Leo lets out a low sinister growl, "I am as ready as I'll ever be, love."

I look more intensely into his eyes and smile, "let's get to it then."

His eyes lock with mine as I slowly take a small step back and turn around, so my back side is facing him. I sway my hips gently before sitting on his lap, grinding lightly as the music from down-stairs guides me.

Thankful, that I am not facing him, I bite my lip. I can feel his length against me as my face heats. He is definitely large and ready to go. I try to mentally prepare myself that this would only be a lap dance. A tease for him although it seemed to be for me as well.

Over the clothes only!

I can hear his breath hitch every time I move on him. He seemed hesitant at first on what to do, before deciding to move my hair away from my neck and kiss it. I can feel his lips dancing up and down my neck before he ever so slightly bites, tugging at the skin before sucking it harshly. I wince as the pleasure mixes in with a bit of pain- when he begins to lick the spot, he had previously assaulted. The mix of sweet and rough causes a soft moan to escape me. His lips trail down as his hands move to my breasts. He gently grabs them, feeling them through my dress. I can see his large muscular hands moving over me.

"Leo." I whine, continuing to move seductively while he explores my body. He ignores my whine as he trails his kisses down to my shoulder where my birthmark is. When he suddenly pulls away to admire it, before releasing his hold on me all together.

"What's wrong?" I ask, as I stiffen, still sitting on his lap.

"Nothing, love." He dismisses as he places his arms around my waist and begins to kiss the back of my neck. I can tell he's lying; however, I decide not to push.

"A woman of many talents I see." He smirks.

"You have no idea." I reply as I detach myself from him, causing a small groan to escape his lips. Then move my hips slowly in front of him as I turn around and wrap my legs around his torso. Still grinding but this time his lips attach to mine. His tongue is dominant as we explore each other's mouths. I bite onto his bottom lip giving it a slight tug. He groans, sending vibrations throughout my entire body. His hands explore my back before moving to my ass and giving it a rough squeeze which makes me moan out in pleasure.

His eyes never leave mine as he continues to move his hands. The intensity of his stare has me rocking back and forth trying to create more friction between us. He smirks realizing my disparity. He then proceeds to slide one hand up my thigh and between my legs as he begins to tease my clothed sex.

"Leo." I plead, before dipping my head into the crook of his neck, kissing his cool skin.

"You're properly soaked, love." He growls, before applying a bit more pressure. I continue to moan as his hand continues to move and his lips attack my needy skin.

"Do you think of me, when you're alone at night, and you feel the need to pleasure yourself?" He asks, only making me more desperate and needy.

"Yes." I answer truthfully, before he applies more pressure bringing me closer to my climax. His mouth finds mine and he kisses me so roughly and so passionately, that I can feel his desire for me through his delicious lips. Between his kisses Leo whispers, "you know Rose, you're nothing like the other women that I've come across. It's been a while since a woman has enticed me the way that you have."

I hum in response as I go in for another kiss. His lips are addictive. The more I taste him the more I want. I push us down onto the bed and he pulls his hand away and we intertwine fingers as I deepen the kiss. My hips continue to grind on him desperate for more.

"Rose!" He groans, detaching his lips from mine.

"I want you." I whisper, completely forgetting my want to take things slow, I go back in for another kiss, but before our lips can attach Leo grabs my wrist touching the bracelet that covers the reminder of how weak I had been. Memories of my past resurface, throwing me off. I quickly back up and fall off the bed by accident. Leo is quick to his feet.

"Rose!"

I grab the wrist he touched and look down trying not to let my insecurities show. I hate that I'm on the verge of letting my past ruin this.

"Rose, are you ok?" Leo asks crouching down and gently placing his hand on my chin to move my face up to look up at him. I nod my head and try to muster up the best smile I can.

"Rose, what happened, talk to me." Leo pleads now sitting across from me, giving me the space I needed but also giving me the closeness I craved.

"It's nothing, I promise." I tell him, looking into his worry filled eyes. I can tell he's not buying any of it. The sound of my heart pounding overtaking the space. His green eyes pleading with me to confide all of my darkest secrets to him.

"I'm fine Leo, seriously can't we just rewind and go back to what we were doing?" I ask, in an attempt to undo the past few minutes. However, based on the frown on his face, I knew he wouldn't let this go.

"Rose, you're...special to me. I'd like you to trust me enough to tell me what's going on but if you don't, we can just sit here in silence. You don't have to try and distract me especially when you don't really want to engage in the activity you're proposing" He explains understandingly. God, he was mature, sexy, and understanding. How the hell did I manage to get his attention?

"You must think I'm really screwed up." I say, as a stream of silent tears spill.

"No, I think you're scared, and haunted. I just don't know from what? Is it me? Did I do something wrong?" He asks.

"No of course not, God you're perfect. Why would you even think that?" I ask. I never would have thought tonight would have turned out like this. Leo and I sharing our vulnerabilities with one another, seemed way more intimate than what we were about to do.

"Because my pure beautiful Rose, I am a monster, who has caught the eye of a princess." He explains, his eyes riddled with pain. I can feel it. I move closer to him slowly hoping to see his face more clearly. His eyes are now closed, he looks ashamed as he avoids my stare.

I slowly move my hands to the sides of his face forcing him to look at me. I inspect his face side to side looking for the monster he is referring to. Realizing there isn't one- believe me I would know.

"You are no monster, Leo. Trust me I have been around enough monsters in my lifetime to tell the difference."

Leo looks down, probably trying to understand why I would say that when he runs his thumb over the scars that are exposed on my upper thighs. He then gently grabs my hand and runs his thumb over the fading scar on my wrist. He looks up at me, his eyes revealing he understands what my previous weirdness was about.

"Did a monster do this?"

Trying not to climb back into my shell I decide to be truthful. "Like I said, I have known many monsters in my life. I'm not the type of girl to usually land the hero."

Leo lovingly takes my face in his hands and looks into my eyes.

"My beautiful Rose, I will kill any monster that touches you. I might not be the hero in your story, but I will never allow another monster to ever hurt you again."

A small giggle escapes my lips after hearing his promise. Not because of him, but because the idea that someone wants to protect me instead of harm me, is foreign to me.

I needed to lighten the mood, "I didn't take you as the cheesy type." I say with a slight smile.

Leo smiles at my words then grabs both of my hands bringing them to his lips and places a gentle kiss on them before slowly kissing my scars.

"It might sound cheesy, but I mean every word. You're no damsel Rose. You're tough and strong. But I would still burn the world down for you if it means saving you. A hero would try and save everyone. I would only care about saving you. I will always choose you."

I let out a nervous laugh from his bold confession. It feels too soon for him to say those types of things. Even though I can't help feeling like this isn't our first lifetime together. I wonder if he feels that way too.

"Isn't it a little soon to be telling me that...we haven't even gone on a proper date yet?"

I get my answer when he replies, "I can't explain it, but I mean every word of it. It might seem strange to hear but I do feel as if I have finally found the one missing piece I have been searching for my entire life."

I couldn't help but smile. He makes me happy. Truly happy. I have always been surrounded by tragedy and deceit. However, when I look at Leo all of my disappointments are replaced with a sense of hope. I would even go as far to say that I genuinely trust him.

"I think I know what you mean. I can't really explain it either. When I'm with you I feel as if we've been together before, in another lifetime perhaps." I confess.

"I understand. It's quite rare for me to have such a strong attraction and connection with someone. I hope you know I mean every word I say."

I lean forward and place a kiss on his lips then pull away and whisper, "I know you mean those words but what if I'm not worth you burning down the world for? What if I'm meant to burn along with it?" I ask, confessing my truest, darkest thoughts. I sometimes felt that maybe I did deserve the monster, that maybe that was how my life was supposed to be- tragic.

Leo moves slightly back so that he can face me directly.

"You are more than worth it Rose. You are luminosity at its finest. The brightest of all the stars. Your purity is blinding. I crave it and will always come back for more."

Not knowing how to respond to that, I lightened the conversation with a bit of humor, "and here I thought it was my lap dance that had you."

Leo lets out a small laugh then moves a stray hair behind my ear.

"You are more special than you will ever know Rose."

"So are you. You're a good man Leo Lloyd; I can feel it."

We lean into one another once again and kiss. This time the kiss isn't rushed or rough, instead it's soft and passionate. I can feel my body and soul burning with desire. I somehow feel alive. I never want to disconnect from him. Kissing him makes me feel whole.

***

The music can still be heard coming from downstairs as the party rages on. Leo and I decide to just linger and enjoy each other's company- in a deeply understood silence. I lay my head on his chest as I try to listen to the sound of his heartbeat. Unfortunately, the music doesn't allow me to hear it.

I close my eyes as I take in the moment. The old Rose would have jumped at the opportunity, to run downstairs and join the party. The alcohol and the drugs alone would have been enough to lure me away from this perfect moment. Instead, I opt to lay here- wishfully forever. I loved that he much rather be here with me as well. I felt safe- a very new feeling for me to experience. I kept re- playing all the beautiful things he had said to me earlier. No man had ever said anything even close to what he had shared. Our con- nection was insane. It felt so natural to be here with him.

I lay on his chest hoping the moment wouldn't end when he lifted his finger to my chin signaling me to look up.

"What are you thinking about?" He asks.

"Do you believe in love?" I ask for the second time today.

"Yes, I do. What about you?" He replies. I can see the curiosity on his face.

"I don't know. I've never been in love before. So how can I be- lieve in something I've never felt?" I respond. It's the truth, I always felt like something was holding me back, like a piece of the puzzle was missing. However, as I lay here with Leo, I can't help but won- der if maybe he's been the missing piece all along.

"Well, I intend to change that, if you will allow me the honor of doing so mademoiselle." He speaks softly, looking at me with those amazing eyes. I turn over, placing my leg over him as I lift myself up to sit on top of his groin. He automatically places his hands up my thighs.

"And if I don't?" I tease. He offers me a devilish smile and with- out any warning he flips us over, causing him to hover over me.

"I really like you Rose- in case I wasn't clear before and I want the opportunity to show you." he whispers as he slowly caresses my neck with his lips. "I know we haven't known each other long but there is something undeniable between us." he adds.

"I am willing to give myself to you, body and soul." he continues as I gently pull my head back giving him better access. "And I ask the same of you in return. I want you, all of you. But I need to know that you will only be mine."

I can feel my body shutter. They were the most beautiful and enticing words any man had ever said to me. How could I refuse? I couldn't.

"I need you to tell me that you're mine. The thought of you with anyone else...." his voice trails, "I'm too selfish of a creature." he finally adds, looking straight into my eyes. I can feel him peering into my soul. I gently touch the side of his face with my hand, "I'm yours Leo, but only if you are mine."

"From this moment forward Rose, I only belong to you."

Chapter 13

ROSE

I look over to my side and see Leo fast asleep next to me. He looked so peaceful. I couldn't help but smile at the sight of him.

He lays in a white t-shirt with his arms exposed showcasing his beautiful tattoos. All the black ink in different shapes and sizes swirling all over his big muscular arms. I stare at him admiring his beauty. He was unlike any other man I had ever seen. As my eyes linger longer than they should, I notice a few more tattoos under his shirt. I shift slightly, giving myself a better view to see them. One in particular catches my eye.

It's an angel.

The tattoo has a year written under it, 1789. I wondered what it meant. It seemed like an odd thing to ink on one's arm.

"Morning love." He says sleepily, as he begins to open his eyes slowly. His voice is raspy. Even when he's half asleep, he is still able to make my heart race.

"Morning." I whisper.

"You see something you like?" He asks, beginning to shift to where he is laying on his back. His eyes solely fixed on me as his head is propped up on his pillow.

"I didn't realize you had so many tattoos." I say hoping he'll either show me more or tell me about them. I sit up criss- crossing my legs as I wait for him to respond.

"I do. I'm assuming you were looking at the angel and the date?" He asks. I shake my head slowly trying to figure out how he knew.

"It's a weird date to have as a tattoo." He states nonchalantly sitting up, then placing his arm out in front of him.

"The angel symbolizes a loved one and the year is the year the French Revolution began." He chuckles. Probably laughing internally at how weird it sounded. It's such a random thing to have tattooed.

"Are you like a history nerd or something?" I ask.

"Something like that."

Before I can look further, he retracts his arm and gets out of bed. He stands by the side of the bed in his white t-shirt and gray sweatpants, looking absolutely delicious. The man looks like a statue, carved by the gods themselves. His six-foot five frame towering over the bed as he faces me.

"What would you like for breakfast?" He asks, innocently.

I look him in the eyes as I fight the urge to answer him- you.

So, before I reply, I shake all those naughty thoughts out of my head and take a breath. I don't think any man has ever asked me what I wanted for breakfast after a night spent together but, I guess Leo wasn't like any other man.

"Breakfast?" I ask.

"Well, you stayed the night so it's only fair. I mean you didn't stay over the way that I had hoped you would. For one thing I thought it would involve a lot more nudity." He jokes. I can't help but let out a small laugh and then throw a pillow at him. He catches the pillow with superhuman reflexes then lets out a low chuckle, as he places the pillow back on the bed.

"Do you remember last night's conversation?" He asks in a more serious manner.

"Yes." I reply.

"I meant every word." He states, staring at me as if waiting for my reaction. I move over to where he is standing and kneel on the bed in front of him.

"I'm willing to give this a try Leo. Just don't hurt me, ok? You have to pinky promise."

Leo lifts his brow not understanding what I mean. I push out my hand and place my pinky out, as I try and hold back the big smile threatening to take over. He quirks his brow but pushes his pinky out anyway. I can see the amusement in his eyes. I wrap mine around his and let the smile I was holding back show.

"This is a serious promise Leo, you can't break it." With a small chuckle he looks down, tightening his pinky around mine then kisses me.

"Never."

After kissing me one last time he makes his way downstairs. I take this as an opportunity to get out of bed and look for my dress. Leo had given me a t-shirt and shorts to sleep in the night before, which I think helped to give me the best sleep of my life. Although my experience could also have been influenced by the very large, tattooed man holding me all through the night too.

He laid out a pair of gray sweatpants for me this morning which I gladly put on and tied the string as tight as possible. After feeling somewhat content that the sweatpants wouldn't slide down my waist, from there fit on me, I make my way into his bathroom. I immediately notice the towel and brand-new toothbrush he's set aside on the counter for me. I look into the mirror trying to not be absolutely horrified that this is the face he woke up to this morning. I decide to just wash my face with water and wipe off last night's makeup with the wipes he has on his counter. Now looking at my natural face I feel a bit more at ease. I try to salvage my hair by throwing it up in a big bun and finish off this mini morning routine by brushing my teeth.

After I feel more human, I make my way downstairs and hear familiar voices along with Leo. Then I remember... Adeline.

I walk faster into the kitchen where I am met with a smirking Leo, a laughing Elliot, and a very red and mortified Adeline.

"What's going on here?" I ask, coming up from behind Leo. Adeline immediately makes eye contact with me. Her eyes are wide, and her cheeks are flushed with pure embarrassment.

"It seems we were not the only ones to have a sleepover." Leo informs me.

"Nothing happened." Adeline quickly adds, looking up at me.

"Well, we did sleep next to each other, love. Some might argue that's more intimate." Elliot teases.

Adeline turns her head glaring at Elliot for adding fuel to the fire.

"Then I guess Leo and I are very well acquainted." I state, trying to make Adeline feel like she isn't alone. Leo looks over at me while Elliot looks at him.

"Will you excuse us? Adeline, can I talk to you?" I ask, walking over to her and gently grabbed her arm, not really giving her the option to decline. We quickly walked outside the kitchen and into the living room. Once out of earshot I immediately turn on my detective mode.

"Did you sleep with Elliot?" I ask. She has never done anything like this before. She's only ever dated one other person, and she waited until practically college to sleep with him.

"No, I mean we slept in the same bed together, but we didn't you know…" She explains before looking me over realizing I wasn't wearing my dress.

"Did you sleep with Leo?" She asks.

"No, we talked and then ended up passing out." I explain. She looks a bit shocked, probably remembering the old me that would have jumped at the first opportunity to sleep with him. However, this is a new and improved Rose, and I am happy that Leo and I had a deep conversational filled night. It felt more fulfilling than I think sex would've been.

Right as she is about to comment, her phone rings. She pulls her phone out from her pocket as James's name displays across the screen. We both look at each other knowing exactly what he wants to talk about.

Collin.

"Should I pick it up?" She asks. I would have answered no, but given the circumstances surrounding James, I nod yes, just in case something is actually wrong.

"Rose and I slept over at a friend's house last night…we went to a party…I'm fine, tell him I'm no longer his concern…yes, Rose is here with me… I have to go." She states, then hangs up.

"You know he's going to tell Collin, right?" I comment.

"Not my problem." She states then walks back into the kitchen.

"Everything all, right?" Elliot asks as he places a couple of strips of bacon on a frying pan. Without responding, Adeline walks up to him and wraps her arms around his waist and kisses him. I think that answers his question, because they continue to have a small conversation while he cooks.

I on the other hand walk into Leo's office where he is going through paperwork, trying to give Adeline and Elliot their privacy.

"So, does Elliot cook for you too?" I ask jokingly.

"Yes, and he cleans. He's basically the maid." Leo laughs.

I walk further into the office with my brows raised, Leo only laughs harder, "I usually cook too, but Elliot does cook very well." He responds.

"Is that why he lives with you?" I ask, still unclear as to why and how Leo knows him.

Leo lets out a small laugh as if I have said something funny.

"No, Elliot is my oldest friend. We've been friends for centuries, or what feels like it anyways." He explains then starts rummaging through a pile of papers on his desk.

"Found it!" He exclaims then places it at the top of the stack and walks over to me.

"He's a good man, don't worry about him and Adeline."

I hope he's right because I do like the idea of them, but I also know he's a man and men can be stupid. I nod at his words and we both walk back into the kitchen.

Breakfast has been served. We sit at the dining room table and eat while also making small talk. It feels nice having breakfast and enjoying early morning chit chat with everyone. It is definitely the most fun I've had in a while.

After we eat, Adeline and I decide it's time for us to go. So, after grabbing our clothes and our bags we say our goodbyes and leave. Kissing Leo before I walk to the elevator feels amazing. Who knew saying goodbye could feel so good.

Adeline and I ride the elevator down, still dressed in the guy's clothing. I have to admit Leo's clothes are extremely comfortable and huge, but I have no plan on returning them. I like feeling close to him. The shirt I'm wearing still smells like him which gives me a sense of comfort.

As we exit the elevator and are walking out of the lobby a tall man approaches me. He is of a lean build with jet black hair that is a bit wavy, cut just below his shoulder, with dark brown eyes. His features are sharp and cold. His eyes are slightly sunk in as his cheekbones sit high on his somewhat beautiful face. However, there is a chilling energy that radiates off of him.

"Marie?" He asks, hesitantly.

"No, I'm sorry." I say as I slow down, somehow intrigued by him.

"Sorry Madam, you just seem familiar. Apologies." He says, before continuing to walk over to the elevator.

"What was that about?" Adeline asks.

"I don't know." I say, thinking about what that man had called me.

Marie.

Where have I heard that name before? I question myself before deciding not to dwell on it. We continue to walk out of the building and decide to go back to Adeline's apartment. As we wait outside for our car to pick us up, I can't help but feel that we are being watched.

Chapter 14

ROSE

The ride back is filled with laughs and talk about the night before.

"Elliot is nothing like I had expected. He's sweet and funny. All he wanted to do last night was cuddle. Don't tell Leo I told you that." She laughs.

"I'm glad you had a nice night with him." I smile. I know her and Collin just broke up, but I think this can be the beginning of something great.

"So, you and Leo just talked?" She asks, glancing over at me from where she sat.

"Yes, although I did give him a lap dance." I explain, as if giving Leo Lloyd a lap dance was the most normal thing in the world. Adeline's surprised expression was enough to make me actually giggle.

"You gave Leo a lap dance?" She asks, her jaw practically hitting the car floor.

"To be fair it was a short- lived lap dance." I smile, trying to control my laugh. Adeline went on to say something else, but my mind replayed last night's happenings instead. The feel of his hands sliding up my thighs and his perfectly soft lips brushing the skin on my neck.

"Rose?" Adeline asks, snapping me out of my thoughts as I turn to face her.

"What?"

"So, you and Leo, do you think you guys will start something? Maybe something serious?" She questions, as we pull up to her apartment building.

"I think so. For the first time in a really long time, I'm actually hoping this turns into something really serious. I mean I really like him, and I think he really likes me." I ramble, as we make our way out of the car.

***

We take the elevator up to her apartment but stop before entering, when we notice that her door is slightly ajar. We both look at each other as if silently asking one another what we should do.

"Did you lock the door before we left last night?" I whisper.

"Of course. I always lock my door, Rose." She practically squeaks, from the fear coursing through her.

I gently push her aside and peek my head in first. I don't initially see any sign of danger. Therefore, I very cautiously open the door fully and slowly walk in. Adeline follows closely behind me. As we finally walk further into the apartment, we realize the culprit for the open door is Collin.

Adeline and I both take in a large breath of relief.

"Collin, what the hell are you doing here?" Adeline snaps, her tone glazed with annoyance as she glares at him.

"I had to come over and see for myself that my girlfriend really is whoring herself around New York City." Collin barks. These days not a lot gets me angry. I've mellowed out a lot the past couple of years, but hearing Collin yell those words snaps something inside of me. Too many flashbacks resurface for my liking.

"Shut the hell up Collin and get out of here. Who do you think you are talking to her like that!" I growl, practically baring my teeth, catching him off guard and causing Adeline to snap her head in my direction.

"Rose, I can handle this." She says softly, as if realizing he struck a nerve, then moves closer to Collin.

"You need to leave. You are no longer my boyfriend which means I am no longer your concern. If you want to believe that I am the biggest whore in New York City, well that's your prerogative but you need to leave. Now!" She states firmly, leaving no room for argument. I watch as Collin's jaw practically drops. I can't help but feel an overwhelming feeling of proudness towards Adeline. She was finally sticking up for herself in the most Adeline way possible, with grace and elegance.

"Adi, come on, why can't we work through this?" He begs, causing my eyes to roll at his pathetic attempt to get her back. However, based on Adeline's poised and unaffected stance, it seems to roll right off of her.

"Because as you just said, I'm the biggest whore in New York City, now please go." Adeline replies, slapping Collin with his own words. She walks over to the door and holds it open, signaling for him to leave. Collin stands there for a moment, probably in shock. Finally, after what felt like an eternity, he walks towards the door. Before he leaves, Adeline stops him and holds her hand out.

"Keys please."

Collin looks hurt but reaches into his pocket and drops the keys into her hand.

Adeline closes the door behind him, before she can retract anything she said. That took every ounce of strength within her to do.

Once the door finally closes, she leans up against it and slides down to sit on the floor. She holds her head in her hands as she takes in a couple of small breaths. I frown at the sight, hating to see her upset. She doesn't deserve this. I walk over to her, sliding my back on the wall next to her until I'm sitting down too. Silently letting her know that I am here for her.

Time passes and we finally settle in after Collins's performance. Adeline goes to her bedroom to sleep, although I know she just wants time to process what happened. Collin's words had really gotten to her and I hated him for it. Men, seem to not understand the repercussions they have on the women that love them the most. I know that as much as Adeline claims to be moving on, a part of her will always love him. Much like a part of me will always have a soft spot for James. They were our firsts. The first introduction to what a relationship could be like. Granted, my relationship with James should have been a sign for me to move to a convent and never look at men again but that is neither here nor there.

I linger in the living room and sit in front of Adeline's computer and open up the file to my private memoir. I allow myself to just let my mind go crazy expressing everything I'm feeling. I need to see it on paper, I need to know that what's going on in my head isn't just fiction. I need to see that it's real.

I once believed that love was a scientific concept. Nothing more than chemicals being released in our brains that give us that warm feeling when you're around that one specific person. However, science doesn't have a beating heart or a soul. What happens when you throw science to the wind and really experience what love is? A gut wrenching, heart aching, bliss, caused from being with that one person who understands you fully and who you're fully in sync with. Who can make you feel completely insane but can also make you incandescently happy. Love can make you feel more alive than you've ever felt in your life, but it can also kill you. Love has a crazy effect on people and can be the cause of mass destruction. Knowing that, how come we allow ourselves to fall in love? Are we all just masochists or are we dreamers– who dream of that fairy-tale romance? I know with Mr. Lloyd, I'm allowing myself to become a dreamer, to dream of a moment where he and I can live out our fictional romance story. Maybe he can be my Mr. Darcy. Dark, brooding, and complicated. After all, I never did like anything that came easy.

As much as I would have loved to stay at Adeline's apartment for the rest of the night, my mother calls me and informs me that I have to get back home. Apparently, I had a visitor waiting for me. I thought this was strange since she wouldn't tell me who it was. I waited until Adeline felt better and moved from her bedroom to the sofa. She promised me that she would call if she needed anything.

I then took a cab back home, dreading every moment in the elevator as I made my way back up to my apartment. I hated being here. I really needed to find my own place.

As the doors open, I walk inside and see no one in sight. I walk further into the apartment when I hear people talking in the living room. I hear both my mother and Charles laughing along with a stranger's familiar laugh echoing through the house. As I walk closer, I realize who it is. I stop dead in my tracks as I feel my blood run cold. My first instinct is to run, but it's too late. His eyes meet mine, and I swear on everything that I believe in, that for a second, they suddenly glowed red.

"Rose you're home, look who came to visit you!" My mother exclaims, snapping me out of what I can only assume is a mind trick. There's no way Pierce's eyes had glowed red, but that still didn't mean he wasn't a demon trapped inside a human body.

My mother's smile is large and bright as I take in the sight of all three of them. Everything inside of me is screaming at me to run, that it's not too late to escape. However, my feet seem to be planted firmly to the floor. I can feel the color drain from my face, as I see his cold eyes staring directly at me. His sadistic grin plastered on his face, knowing I still feared him. He knew he still had power over me. Although, somehow, he seemed different, more evil...even *sinister*.

"Don't just stand there, come say hello." My mother smiles. She always did love him; he was wealthy and had status. I think my time with Pierce was the only time in my life where she was truly proud of me.

If she only knew.

I practically drag myself over to where my mother is standing. For once in my life, I feel grateful for her presence.

"Pierce, it's nice to see you." I say, robotically. His name feels like poison on my lips. I can barely look at him, as I wait to see what he says next. My mother and Charles, both give me a questioning look but decide not to comment. I feel numb from the internal terror I am fighting within, as I try to hide my fear.

Pierce, with a twisted grin on his face, walks over to me, "Rosie, I've missed you."

Just the sound of that stupid nickname makes me want to vomit. However, my stomach truly starts to twist when he wraps his arms around me. I can feel my heart beating more rapidly against my chest as my anxiety reaches an all-time high.

After what feels like forever, he finally pulls away, staring up and down at my body, which only makes me feel like setting myself on fire. I hate that he knows what lays underneath my clothes, as his eyes linger, undressing me with his stare. He wants to see me squirm. He enjoys it.

"Charles and I are going to leave you two alone. You probably have a lot of catching up to do. Pierce, I am so glad you came back to New York. I know your parents missed you while you were gone." My mother announces, as if he hasn't been on the missing persons list for the past two years.

I didn't know what to say as my brain screamed for my mother and Charles not to leave the room. However, my silent pleas remain unheard as they smile while heading up the stairs to their bedroom. Once out of sight Pierce walks over closer to me. I can feel myself becoming small, even defenseless.

He made me feel pathetic.

He moves his hand over to move a piece of my hair away from my face, causing me to flinch. Memories of what happened- the abuse- come flooding back, each one slamming into me more viciously than the previous.

A cocky smirk appears on his smug face, which only worsens my nausea.

I hate that he touched what Leo had just touched this morning, ruining the feeling of Leo's gentle touch.

"How are you even here, I left you..." I state, trying my hardest to keep the tremble from my voice in check.

"For dead. Yeah, I know, but you see it appears I have a higher purpose in life Rosie, one that I have waited for all these years to finally do. You don't know how hard it's been staying away from you." He explains, as he leans in and breathes me in, causing me to take a step back. His presence was suffocating.

"What do you want, Pierce?" I ask, trying to steady myself although my attempt was pointless. The shakiness in my voice was inevitable. All the walls I had built to keep him out of my mind came crashing down. A part of me wished that Leo would storm in and save me but the truth of what I had lived through with Pierce was too embarrassing. I would never want anyone to know the cruelty and abuse this animal before me made me endure.

"I want you, Rosie. You left in such a hurry in Italy." He frowns, as he moves closer allowing his large frame to tower over me.

"I had to leave; you were a monster." I whisper, feeling whatever little confidence, I had left slip away.

"Rosie, you didn't leave though, did you? You fled, after killing me." He frowns mockingly.

"Well almost killing me. I was given a second chance, which is a good thing too because now I can finish what I started." He growls, placing his hand on my cheek. His skin is ice cold and his once piercing blue eyes turn black.

"Poor Mr. Arthur had to pay the price for his son's foolishness of helping out the girl that could never really love him. I wonder who will be next? There are so many to pick from." He whispers as he draws his face closer to mine and smirks.

"I've waited so long to find you Rosie. It was so cute watching you hide, wondering when people would start questioning what really happened. Well now everyone will know what a conniving little bitch you really are." He states, as he wraps my hair around his hand and pulls causing me to yelp.

"You bastard." I seethe in Italian, as I try to hold on to any composure I have left. Pierce only seems to be amused by my use of the language he fluently speaks.

"I see you picked something up from our trip in Italy." He snarls as he releases my hair, then grabs my arm with such harshness that I could already feel the bruises forming under my skin. He pulls me towards him. My nose practically crashes into his as he leans down to meet my gaze. I wince in pain but manage to hold back my cries. I didn't want to give him the satisfaction.

"As I remember, your mother was so proud of you when you and I decided to take that trip. I wonder how she would feel if she knew what you did." He whispers, still grasping my arm and using the other to caress my face. I can feel tears begin to brew within my eyes at the reminder.

"You mean what you forced me to do. Besides, I wonder how everyone here would feel, if they found out what type of monster you really are." I spit. My threat only makes him laugh.

He was enjoying this.

"Oh Rosie, you don't even know what kind of monster you helped me become." He smiles, the most wicked sinister smile I had ever seen.

"Go to hell!" I grind out through clenched teeth, as his fingers continue to bruise my arms from his grasp.

"Oh, we will both be on our way there soon enough. But I just wanted to let you know that I'm back and that I will be seeing you very soon." He smiles, before releasing his grip as he then proceeds to walk over to the elevator. I stand in place- shaking. I can hear the elevator doors open and close, signaling that he had finally left. Before I could even move, my mother comes down the stairs as if on cue, eager to hear all about our reunion. However, she looks confused once she sees my face. I couldn't move as the tears began to run down my face.

"Rose." My mother rushes over to me. She places her hand on my shoulder startling me, all my defensive instincts rush back.

"I have to go." I state manically, "I have to get out of here." I insist, not knowing what else to say or do.

"Rose what's wrong? What just happened?" She asks, concern evident in her voice. Without giving her an explanation, I step back from her and turn around. I needed to leave and get as far away from this apartment as possible. I wasn't safe here. I begin to walk to the elevator, ignoring the million questions my mother kept asking.

"Mom, I can't talk about it!" I yell, ignoring her questions. All the while thinking that I should've been better prepared. I should've known he wouldn't leave me alone. He's going to kill me this time, and I know for a fact I won't be able to stop him.

"Rose." My mother yells trying to get my attention, but I am too far gone.

"I have to go." I repeat one last time, then press the elevator door button, the doors open immediately. I rush inside and before she can come after me, the doors close. Once in the elevator I can feel myself slowly fall apart. Not knowing where else to go or what to do, I hail a cab once I'm outside and ask to be driven to the only place I know will understand what is happening.

The cab drive is short, thank God and the driver doesn't seem to care about my mental state as I silently cry in the back seat. Once he pulls up to the all too familiar brownstone, I pay him his fare and walk over to the front door. I knock a bit frantically when he soon appears. I could tell I had awoken him.

"James." I cry before completely falling apart in front of him. I fall into him and completely crumble as I practically choke on my own sobs and tears. James quickly pulls me in and shuts the door.

"Rose what happened?" Concern in his voice, as he holds onto me firmly.

"He's found me and he's going to kill me." I explain.

"Who?" James asks, panic lacing his words.

"Pierce." I state.

James falls silent as he hears the devil's name leave my lips and continues to hold me tighter. I never gave James the full details of what had transpired during that summer in Italy. I never told anyone. However, James is the only one that knows Pierce's return is a very bad thing.

When I called James that day in Italy, I had informed him that Pierce had been abusing me and that I needed to leave. There was no need to give explicit details, because that alone was enough for him to come and get me. He chartered his father's private jet and dropped everything he was doing to come pick me up. The flight home was silent. I never talked about what happened, even when he tried to ask. And when Pierce was considered a missing person after we came back, he stopped asking questions all together.

My phone buzzes as we sit inside. I know it's my mother, but I don't want to talk to her. I don't want to talk to anyone. I slowly feel myself drift off, after we stay there for what feels like hours. My body and mind finally shutting down from all the anxiety and adrenaline pumping through me.

***

I wake up the next morning in an all too familiar bed, with last night's memories replaying. I'm still dressed in Leo's clothing from the day before.

"You're up." James smiles, sitting beside me.

"What happened?" I ask, not understanding how I made it to his bed.

"You passed out in my arms yesterday, probably from all the anxiety of seeing Pierce." He explains. I wince at the sound of his name. Now fully awake, I manage to sit up and look down at my wrists where I see the all too familiar black and blue bruises.

James takes notice of the bruises as well and his eyes burn with what can only be described as pure rage.

"He did this?" He asks, as he clenches his jaw. I nod my head slowly.

"Rose, you need to go to the police." He demands. I know he means well but going to the police is completely out of the question. Everything that happened in Italy would be known, and I can't have that. I don't need people knowing what happened- what I had done.

"I can't." I respond coldly.

"Why not? He's a fucking monster, Rose. Look at what he did to you." He says harshly, as he grabs my arm and brings it up for me to see. I pull my arm from his grasp and look at him defeated.

"James, I can't. People will know things; things I don't want anyone to know."

"What can be so bad that you don't want him locked away? Look at what he's done to you! I mean Jesus Rose, is it that you don't want people knowing he abused you?" He asks, trying to understand.

"There's more to the story James." I say, realizing it was time for me to go. I didn't want to spill more secrets than I needed to. For one thing, I knew who killed his father, even though I wasn't about to announce it. Especially, since it came out of Pierce's mouth. I need to leave and clear my head. The moment I begin to remove myself from his bed in an effort to leave, he begins to protest.

"Rose don't go. Look I'm sorry, I just want to understand." He pleads.

"It's not your issue James. Thank you for being here for me once again, but this is something I'm going to have to deal with sooner or later...on my own. Look I'm going to head out, but I'll call you." I promised.

"Where are you going? He knows where you live, stay here it's safer here than in your house." He tries to reason.

"I'm not going back to my house. I'm leaving the city for a little while. I just need to clear my head."

"I'll go with you." He offers, practically begging me. But I knew that I needed to be alone. He would only get caught in the crossfire if I let him follow me.

"I'll call you." I promise as I move swiftly, grabbing my shoes and placing them on my feet before he can say anything else. I then begin to make my way down the stairs.

"Rose." James begs.

"I'll be fine." I assure him before walking over to the front door and opening it. He watches me as I walk out, and leave.

Without even having to think of where I would go next, the perfect place where I could hide comes to mind. Somewhere no one would ever even think of looking for me, not even my mother. I hail a cab rather quickly and tell him the address.

"To Jersey it is." He agrees, after he makes me promise that I will pay whatever the fare is plus a little more. I sit in the back of the cab, looking out the window watching as I leave my beautiful city behind once again.

* * *

The ride into New Jersey is longer than expected. Traffic leaving the city is always ridiculous. However, the taxi soon pulls up to a nice white house located in a suburban town called Franklin Lakes in northern New Jersey. The house belonged to my father. My mother never enjoyed it and rarely visited it, since she didn't believe in leaving the city. However, my father used to bring me here almost every fall and spring when I was a little girl before he died. He loved seeing the wildlife surrounding the property bloom and change in seasonal colors every year.

I paid the taxi as promised for the inconvenience of leaving the city. I watch him leave, before I walk over to the house. Memories and thoughts of my dad overwhelm me as I approach the front door.

I stand outside taking it in, realizing the last time I was here my father was still alive. I was literally a kid- no worries in the world. It felt surreal at how much time had passed and how much things had changed.

I walk up the stairs and move the plant that died a long time ago to reveal the spare key he had left in case of an emergency. Before unlocking the door, I look at the house, noticing that its white paint is now looking more cream colored showcasing the years that have passed. However, the yard looks freshly cut. Jason must still be keeping tabs on the house. He also loved coming here with our father too. Any chance to escape the reality of our household back in the city, was always welcomed.

Chapter 15

ELLIOT

The air is cold as the winter wind cuts my face. The streets are dark and damp from the snow melting, but I continue my descent because he needs me. He is giving his soul over to the demon inside of him because of me. I continue walking the cobblestone path, when I finally get to the old brothel located in a small village just outside of Paris. The windows are covered as a few drunks hang around hoping to get invited in. I make my way to the door, and I am immediately approached by the madam of the house.

"Sylvie, it's been a long time." I smile, as I wait for her to let me in. She grins back, genuinely satisfied to see me. I was, after all, her best customer for the last hundred years. Sylvie was one of the oldest vampires in France and had decided to have an eternity of great sex, at least that's what she would tell me, every time I paid her a visit.

"Always a pleasure Elliot, are you here to see me tonight?" She asks, although based on her raised brow, I can already tell she knows my true intentions.

"Show me to him." I sigh, not even trying to hide the true purpose for my visit. With a silent nod she steps aside to grant me entrance then leads me down a corridor. The house was dim, mostly lit by candlelight as the sounds of pleasure were heard all around. This brothel was one of the most

exclusive establishments in the area. Especially since it was the only place vampires could feed and not be fearful of being caught.

"In all my years as a vampire, I have never come across one that enjoyed the kill so much. His pleasure is insatiable when it comes to draining those, he finds sufficient enough to fulfill his needs. His demon is much darker than most." She explains. I nod my head, acknowledging her assessment as I try and think of a way to garner his attention in the hopes of helping him.

As we pass by each door in the corridor, the more my anxiety grows. My idea seemed crazy- to save the one she turned just to help manage my guilt over all the destruction that has occurred over the years. Finally, Sylvie leads me to the last door at the end of the hall. But when she opens it, for me to look inside, my stomach drops. I have seen the worst of the worst in all my years existing on this earth, but none were as savage as him.

"I thought we were promised privacy." The man growls, wiping the blood from his face, as the naked girl leans over his shoulder extending her wrist. She was completely covered in bite marks and blood as another girl kneels in front of the bed, he is currently sitting on taking him into her mouth. It was then that I noticed the blood stains on the walls and floors and the two other fully naked women pleasuring themselves as blood dripped from their necks.

"Leonardo?" I ask, as I step in, leaving Sylvie to close the door behind me and walk away.

"It's Leo. Now, what do you want?" He snaps, as he continues to push the girl's head further down his shaft.

"I came to find you; you and I have some business to discuss." I state, trying to concentrate on my mission and not the bloody fuck fest happening around me.

"Oh, really and what serious business do we have to discuss?" He asks, before throwing his head back, as he cums in the prostitute's mouth. It's *then that I pull her off of him, along with the other girl and pin Leo to the headboard as I wrap my hand around his throat, using a spell to bind him, so that my lack in strength could at least match his overabundance of it.*

"Your way of living stops now! You and I are going to get revenge Leo. Michael is coming for us; do you not want to avenge what they did to your precious Marie?" I ask, my voice dropping to a menacing tone. I remain cold and serious as I silently pray that I stirred his curiosity. I did want revenge on Michael, but I also needed a way to extract Leo, so that I could start helping him clean his soul.

"When do we leave?" He asks, his eyes now blazing with rage. I drop my hand trusting he won't fight me anymore and let a wicked grin take over my face.

"Now."

The memory of what kickstarted my friendship with Leo plays like a movie in my head, before I'm yanked out of the memory by my alarm clock. I hate modern technology. In the good old days, you didn't feel the pressure to set an alarm to be responsible. I slowly opened my eyes and spread my arm out to the cold side of my bed that remained empty. To think just yesterday my blonde-haired angel had been wrapped in my arms. Her beautiful laugh replays in my head as I think of how she reacted when I kept pulling her towards me as we tried to sleep. I was hooked from the very first touch all the way to when she kissed me. I was completely thrown back but relished every second of it. I couldn't believe it when she told me that her boyfriend had cheated on her, who would need anyone else when they had her. She was everything.

Hundreds of years, I've spent wandering this earth, yet no other woman, man or any other supernatural creature has compared to her.

Adeline is special and beautiful. I almost find it strange that she would want something to do with a man like me. I mean she has no idea who or what I am, or what I've done. In her mind I'm just an arrogant club owner who is very good looking. I have never once questioned myself because of a lover. I guess this only proves my point that she really is special. However, in the end when she finds out the truth, she will only despise me.

As I am deep in my thoughts about the blonde-haired angel that had left my bed yesterday morning untouched, might I add, I am ripped away from her memory by Leo, who storms into my bedroom.

"Leo what's wrong?" I ask, my senses on high alert from the troubled look on his face.

"Rose, she had this mark on her shoulder. And at first, I didn't think anything of it, but I started looking into the ancient symbols. I remembered seeing it before." He explains.

"Ok? Lots of humans have birthmarks Leo, maybe it's a coincidence." I point out, although deep inside I knew it was something more.

"No Elliot, this was different. I've seen this mark before. And now she's not picking up her phone."

"What did the mark look like?" I ask, more intrigued by the worry brewing in his eyes.

He walks over to my bed and hands me a piece of paper that has a drawing of a crescent moon. My stomach absolutely sinks as I take in that horrid mark. It was too late; he's already laid his mark on her.

It feels as if the end is upon us, and I can feel that demon's hand wrapping itself around my neck.

Cain.

"It's an ancient symbol, something pertaining to..." He stops before he can even finish. His face suddenly morphs into the one Lucifer picked out for him.

"Leo..." I begin but I'm cut short when Leo takes off. I quickly jump out of my bed and run down the stairs, only to be met with the last person I ever wanted to see.

Michael.

"Just the two I was looking for." Michael laughs, as he walks further into the apartment.

"No need for the face Leo, put your fangs away," he states, walking past him to sit down.

"Michael, what a pleasure." I greet, with a tight-lipped smile as I walk closer to Leo's side. Michael's eyes look me over as they glimmer with evil.

"Nice to see you, Leo's bitch, is it?"

He really does know how to get a fire going under any one of us. I mutter a few words of an incantation under my breath and immediately Michael falls to his knees screaming in agony. His pain doesn't seem to last very long because he soon turns his screaming into a fit of laughter. This only makes me angrier. I hit him harder with a more severe spell which makes him shake to his very core as his eyes and nose start to bleed. Still the sadistic son of bitch that he is, he plasters a condescending grin on his face displaying his blood covered teeth. I twist him a bit more hoping to make him suffer, the way he has made both Leo, and I suffer throughout the centuries.

"I am nobody's bitch." I spit as I throw another incantation at him causing him to lay on the floor screaming.

"Your power is not what it used to be old friend." He laughs, as he flinches from the pain.

"Elliot, that's enough." Leo commands, growing tired of our forever back and forth. I can't help it. He truly does bring out the worst in me.

"Oh, come on Leo we're only having fun. Right, Michael?" I sneer.

Michael lets a low chuckle slip past his lips as he now kneels and wipes the blood from his face.

"What brings you here?" Leo asks, stepping between Michael and I. His demeanor is strong and unshakeable as he tries to establish dominance. It is a futile effort because as strong and as fast as Leo is, he is nothing compared to Michael. Vampires as old as him are more powerful than one can even imagine.

Michael being the cynical bastard that he is, answers Leo's question sarcastically, "I missed my old friends."

"We were never friends. Now how did you find me?" Leo questions trying to remain calm, but I could see the fire in his eyes. He wanted nothing more than to beat the shit out of Michael.

"What makes you think I came here for you?" Michael asks, deflecting Leo's question.

Leo lets his vampire face show as he rushes towards him using his vampire speed and slams him into the nearest wall. The dry wall shatters and dust coats everything around us.

"You won't touch her." He seethes as he grabs Michael by the throat, lifting him off the ground, then slams him into the wall once again. Michael somehow finding pleasure in Leo's attack allows it. He really is a sadistic bastard, and Leo is a fool for allowing him to get under his skin like this. Not that I should talk.

Michael only laughs at Leo's threat. However, after a few minutes of Leo using him as a vampire rag doll Michael begins to grow tired of him. He quickly grabs a hold of Leo's hand and turns it in a way, forcing him to remove it from his neck. He then grabs a hold of Leo's neck and slams him against the wall. Leo shows his fangs and hisses as he tries to release himself from Michael's grip. However, Michael doesn't yield. I'm ready to intervene when Leo shoots me a look to stay put. This is between Michael and him.

"When are you going to learn that I'm older than you, meaning that I am stronger than you. Do not push me Leonardo because I will rip your heart out so quickly that you won't even get the chance to think of that pretty little blood whore of yours."

It must've been the derogatory term Michael used against Rose because in all my life and years of knowing Leo, I had never seen him this enraged. He somehow managed to channel all of his anger as he threw Michael across the apartment, into our living room like he was nothing more than an annoying ant. Michael crashes through the study door and falls into our living room table. Leo and I walk over to see the damage. Michael lays on the floor covered in cuts and glass. Cuts that instantly heal as he manages to lift himself up using his speed to grab on to Leo once again pushing him into the living room wall where the bar cart is. All of the bottle's fall to the floor, and shatter from the impact.

"She's really pretty Leo; it's a shame Cain is going to be the one to enjoy her. I mean, I almost broke protocol and had a taste of her myself yesterday. Wouldn't be the first time both of us lusted after that blood line. I guess we all have our kinks."

"Shut your mouth." Leo growls.

Michael dusts the glass off his shirt.

"I wanted nothing more than to taste her. Her scent is all too familiar- just like Marie's. I mean fuck, she must taste just like her and I'm not just talking about her blood." He laughs. "I found it difficult to restrain, so much so that I had to follow her yesterday which almost ruined my big evil plan." Michael states, his fangs appearing. Leo glares into Michael's eyes and allows his true vampire face to take over once again.

Leo charges towards Michael knocking him to the floor and grabs a hold of him. Glass crashes all around them. There goes my vases from the Emirates.

"I will fucking kill you if you lay a hand on her." Leo roars as he punches Michael in the face, the crunching of bone echoing.

"Oh my, what a funny little plot twist. Your soul is tied to hers, isn't it?" Michael asks, as he pieces the puzzle together for himself.

"That's enough!" I boom, before I cast a spell causing them both to pull back and cry out in pain. I felt guilty for hurting Leo, but they both needed to be checked. Once there is a bit of distance between them, I release them and turn to Michael.

"Enough! Michael, you need to leave before I kill you myself." I growl, my own frustration snapping as I look at him.

"Now, why would I leave? Especially when Leo has the opportunity of asking me the questions that have been burning through his mind?" He points out. It's as though I can see the evil intent practically glowing in his eyes. Before Leo can intervene, I manage to get the three of us to sit at our dining room table, in an attempt to make sure nothing else in the house breaks.

Michael and Leo are both covered in each other's blood currently engaged in a staring competition with one another as they sit at the farthest ends of the table. Finally, after what feels like an eternity, Leo speaks,

"Why is Rose being summoned? Why can't Cain just come here himself to take her back with him?"

"Oh, you poor bastard, Elliot appeared to have left out the best part of the story. Rose isn't just being grabbed Leonardo; she has to be sacrificed to our dear general so that she can preside over hell with him. And this is all being done to rectify a very old promise that was made to him by your dear friend Elliot." He explains as he looks directly at me. Leo stiffens but doesn't take the bait. Michael wants to sever our united front to make this whole thing more painful than it needs to be.

"Cain will never lay one fucking finger on her." Leo states flatly, his emotions completely void from his tone. His demeanor is scary. I have been Leo's right hand for centuries and till this day there is something about him that terrifies me, not that I would ever tell him that. A darkness lies within him that I know one day will consume him.

"You can't stop him, Leo. Cain will get what he wants" Michael explains.

"Obviously not, since he didn't get Marie and the three of you are still breathing." Leo points out, causing a thoughtful silence to preside over the room.

"Believe me, Cain got what he wanted in the end, he always does." Michael states, his eyes showing a flash of pain, which quickly vanishes.

"And what did he get, except a shady fucking deal and the headache of hunting you and Marie down for centuries and then dealing with you after capturing her just to bid his time until the next viable soul tie?" Leo growls, his patience thinning. Michael purses his lips as he sits silent for a moment then leans over the table and pins Leo with a very serious look.

"Leo, in all your years on this earth you have never turned someone. Am I right?" Michael questions. Leo leans back as he looks intently at Michael.

"Yes. I would never damn someone to this life, the way that I was. A soldier of Lucifer I would never put someone through that." Leo argues. I know he hates what he is, but I also know he doesn't let it cripple him like other vampires we have come across. He embraces it for what it is. Just like I have with my powers and immortality.

"You obviously haven't fallen in love again either. You see I had never turned anyone either- until I met her." Michael explains.

"Witch make yourself useful and pull out this memory for us all to see."

I shoot him a glare before I mutter a few words to transport us all into Michael's memories. Suddenly we were all standing in a familiar grass field. We're back in what modern times would call Romania, our home. The place that bonded Michael, Marie, and I forever.

Standing next to Michael and Leo, Michael begins to walk forward and speaks, "She was a beautiful, young woman in a long white dress. Running barefoot through the field outside of Transylvania. I was on my way back home and I sensed her. I knew right then and there I had to know her."

We follow behind Michael as he continues to walk, both Leo and I throw each other weary looks. Then we see her. Leo's eyes go wide, and he runs using his vampire speed towards her. However, she is oblivious to his presence. It's a memory after all. Michael and I catch up to Leo. Leo's face reflects disappointment and sorrow as we notice a younger version of Michael appear. He approaches the young woman who is the human version of Marie. We stay silent as we let the memory play.

Marie had been running in the empty field, her white dress contrasting with the green blades of grass. Her long caramel hair is identical to Rose's, it's flowing in the wind. She seems innocent and young. Nothing like the Marie I met after he had turned her.

Michael appears to her in his true form. I can see out of the corner of my eye Leo's composure stiffen. He must think this is when

Michael turns her, if only he knew, what he did was actually much worse.

As Michael approaches her, Marie stills her movements and looks over at him. Her face shows no signs of fear.

"How did you find me?" She asks. Her voice is gentle and kind. Very human, although she wasn't truly mortal. Michael stalks closer, like a predator circling its prey.

"You're not frightened my lady?" He asks, ignoring her previous question. I look over at Michael who is standing next to me, fixated on the sight before him.

"Why would I fear you? You wouldn't hurt one of the watchers." She giggles.

Michael lets a smile of amusement play on his lips from the lack of sense the girl seemed to have. She needed to run. I can sort of see how he would've found this to be amusing. It was something different. Vampires are usually not very often surprised, yet this human girl had managed to do so. She was different.

Michael gives her one last look before putting away his vampiric face. He steps closer to her. She remains calm and unbothered to be in the line of sight of a killer but rather shy and intrigued.

"What is your name?" Michael asks. She looks down, blushing at his question.

"Marie."

Michael grabs her hand gently, placing a loving kiss on it as he breathes her in. Marie lets out a light laugh at his foolishness.

"Marie, that is a lovely name for a lovely girl. They call me Michael."

Marie looks at Michael's face with a smile then steps closer and gently places her hand to his cheek.

"Well Michael, what brings you out here?" Marie asks, as she inspects him further.

"I'm on my way back home, what about you? It's not safe for a young gypsy such as yourself to wander the fields alone." Michael states, waiting for her to reply.

"I got bored. I'm tired of hearing the same stories of my people. Personally, I don't truly understand why as watchers we have to be responsible for the soldiers of Lucifer." Marie says as she walks towards the trees in the field and sits by the largest one. Michael chuckles at her bluntness and proceeds to sit down next to her.

"That's not a very gypsy attitude. I mean there's more to your power than your bleak view." Michael tries to reason.

"Not for me. I'm not even my own person. I've been promised to another, on my twenty-second birthday my freedom will be over. And that day is fast approaching." She whines, as she looks up at his face, her eyes brimming with tears.

"Soul tied? Well, aren't you a rare one?" Michael states intrigued by his new revelation, if only he knew the trouble it would get all of us in.

"Yes. Michael, can you help me? If you could change me, turn me into one of your own, then the soul tie will be broken." She pleads, grabbing onto his shirt forcing him to look at her. He seems amused by her plea.

"Marie, I can't do that, and you know why. I would be breaking a sacred rule." She lets go and leans back against the tree looking utterly destroyed. Michael sits contemplating for a moment.

"You know you are the only person on this earth who does not fear me." He confesses. Marie lets out a small laugh.

"Why would I fear you? You have not yet tried to harm me. You seem like you have a pure soul, Michael, you're obviously an honorable man."

"I would not dream of harming you, my lady." He states, sincerely, looking at her beautiful face.

"I'll make you a deal, I'll change you if you promise to let me court you. When is your twenty-second birthday?" Michael asks.

"In fourteen days." Marie responds, more animated than before, from the hope of being freed from her potential suitor.

"Well then my love, in fourteen days' time, you will be a free woman." Michael grins. Marie practically tackles him to the ground from excitement and kisses him.

"An honorable man you are, Michael. "

We are all flashed out of the memory and put back into the dining room. Leo looks like he's going to kill someone. I know it is a lot for him to take in. Seeing their meeting, seeing her so human, so in love with someone else, and most importantly seeing her innocence being taken by Michael.

I can sense the pain coursing through my dear friend's eyes.

"Marie was like no other woman I had ever met. She was warm, kind...special. So, granting her this favor seemed justifiable." Michael explains, somehow trying to justify his actions.

Leo's anger finally comes to the surface, his true face now out on full display. He stares at Michael then seethes, "Until you turned her into a demon, just so you could break a sacred soul tie."

Michael very calmly takes a breath then looks at him, with a small knowing grin of acknowledgement. He seems proud of what he did to her.

"That was never my intention Leonardo. For the first time in five hundred years, I had fallen in love. I didn't want to lose that feeling and I knew it would only be a matter of time before her promised match got in the way. So, I turned her. She begged me to."

"You turned a gypsy girl Michael!" Leo argues. The veins on his neck protruding from the anger that was coursing through him.

"She was more than just a gypsy girl. She was as ruthless as me once she got a taste of real power. My perfect match. Although, none of it mattered since in the end Cain got what he wanted. Cursing us to an endless abyss of unhappiness."

"What I find most amusing about this story is that you're about to have the same fate with your precious Rose." Michael teases.

"Rose and I are nothing like you and Marie. And unlike you I will protect her." Leo growls. His fangs looking larger than normal. He is seething with rage.

"You're right, you two have nothing compared to what Marie and I had. However, if you think for even one second that you're going to be able to protect Rose from her fate you are sadly mistaken. Cain will rip out your heart before you even get the chance to touch her. Face it Leo, you are doomed just like I was. Your last lover concealed the truth from you and your new lover will ultimately leave you." Michael laughs at his own cruelty. My fingers twitch with the need to cast an incantation that will shut him up, but Leo beats me to it. He jumps out of his chair and uses his vampire speed to tackle Michel to the ground once again, catching him off guard as he swiftly pushes his hand through Michael's chest in an effort to pull out his heart.

"Marie never lied to me and Rose will always choose me. I will destroy any other option." He seethes.

"Marie never loved you, Leo. You were only a chess piece for her to do with as she willed. She was never capable of true love. I was there the night you were turned Leo; I saw what she did. She tricked you, took advantage of you, your desire for her is what led to your damnation and her ability to toy with you for all of eternity. You meant nothing to her. And once Cain gets his hands on Rose, you'll mean nothing to her as well."

I knew Michael was unhinged; I just didn't realize he was suicidal. I could see the pain flash in Leo's eyes before he tightened his grip around Michael's heart centimeters away from yanking it out of his chest.

"Give me one good reason why I shouldn't just kill you right now?" His eyes go completely black, the demon within taking over.

"Because then you'll never know how to save Rose from her doomed fate."

"Rose is Cain's soul tie. Not his true one but she was promised to him all those years ago. When I met Marie, she left out the fact that her promised soul tie was to no one other than Cain. Once I figured it out, I knew I would be hunted. I also knew I needed to find a way to escape his wrath. So, I went to the only person I knew who could help me. The only person, who at the time I could trust." He begins as he looks over at me before continuing.

"Elliot, being the loyal friend that he was, tried his best- which in the end earned him that nasty scar on his face. A scar given to him by the blade of Cain."

His words rattled in my mind, as things suddenly began to click. We had options. Of course, the blade of Cain could be the weapon needed to finish this once and for all. However, the weapon Andrei had spoken about was something else, something that was still missing. whereas the blade of Cain was still in use.

"Why are you telling me this?" Leo asks, as he squeezes his fist even tighter around Michael's heart.

"Because your love or lust for her has consumed you enough to try to kill Cain yourself. And if there is a chance that you can pull it off, I'm all for it." He confesses.

Leo finally let's go of Michael's heart and pulls his hand out of his chest as crimson blood drips all over the floor.

Michael stands up composing himself before walking over to the entrance of the apartment.

"Well gentlemen, as fun as all of this has been, I think I really should be on my way before things continue to go south between us." He smiles as he heads over to the elevator and leaves.

"I need to find Rose." Leo states, his voice hard and serious as he races up to his room.

"I'll start a locator spell." I mutter before going into my office.

We met up after a couple more minutes. Leo freshly rinsed and changed into a clean set of clothing as I continued to locate the little gypsy girl Leo can't seem to live without.

"We'll find her Leo," I emphasize, hoping he would eventually forgive me for my part in all of this.

"Once we find her, you and I will begin our true journey. Killing Cain."

Chapter 16

ROSE

Two days have passed since I've been here. I've only left the house once to get the necessities like clothing and food. I just needed enough supplies until I could figure out what my next move would be. I need to be smart; Pierce is never going to stop looking for me. My stomach twists as I think about how manipulative and calculative he is. I can't believe I ever let myself get involved with him. If only he would have stayed dead when I tried to kill him the first time.

Jesus how fucked up am I! What has he turned me into? My mind questions, as my own darkness rises to the surface.

Thinking back to that day still sends shivers down my spine. It started off as a petty argument. I wanted to go back home to the states. I had already taken so many hits both physically and mentally- which had already caused me to end up in the hospital for a week, from my desperate attempt to escape him.

However, that night after mentioning my want to go back home, things only got worse. He didn't want me to leave, he thought he would lose control over me, so during a heated argument, he pushed me causing me to fall to the floor.

"You're so unappreciative." He boomed as he proceeded to throw a glass at the wall beside me. The glass shards pricked me as they exploded from impact.

"I'm sorry...please." I cried, afraid he would unleash more of his anger on me.

"You're not fucking sorry! Stop fucking lying to me! If you were, you wouldn't have brought it up to begin with. I mean Rosie, do I not treat you well? I take you out, I buy you expensive things and I love you, Rosie." He ranted, continuing to throw anything he could find as he walked over towards me. I tried pushing myself back in fear, but it was no use. That night wasn't the first time he raped me, but it was the last.

I laid there silently crying while he laid next to me passed out, still sleeping off the drugs and the high that came with them. I remember praying for someone to save me. I was desperate for a savior who would kill the beast and take me far away.

I quietly got up and walked over to the kitchen. I had finally had enough. I grabbed my phone and called the police. I needed help. Except right as the poor woman answered the phone the line was cut dead. Pierce grabbed my arm and slammed it on the side of the counter. My phone shattered when it hit the floor.

"Who are you calling, Rosie?" He asked. I wanted to die, more than I had ever wanted anything else. I wanted this to be over with. However, suicide wasn't an option, I had learned that the hard way a couple of weeks before. I had to think about another factor, not just myself.

"You fucking bitch. You're lucky I don't kill you right here and right now. The cops aren't going to help you because you'll already be dead by the time they arrive." Pierce threatened. It's not like he hasn't teased me before about putting me out of my misery. He once came close to it while he was having his way with me. He wrapped his hands around my neck so tight, practically bringing me to the brink of death, but sadly never let me fall off the edge.

"You won't do it." I counter, as I try to hold back the tears that so desperately wanted to fall. Pierce's features darken, as he challenges my words.

"Excuse me?" He walked over, backing me into a wall as I tried to keep my distance. He wrapped his hand around my hair and pulled trying to show his dominance. I knew right now he wanted me dead and this time he wasn't going to hesitate. I had questioned his authority. So, in order to save my life and my baby's life too, I played the only card I had left...the truth.

"You won't hurt me, because I'm pregnant... with our baby."

I snap myself out of the most horrific memory I possess and try to calm my nerves from the remembrance of it all. I place my hand over my stomach and mindlessly rub it, as if there is still someone in there.

Staring out as the rain hits the glass, my phone buzzes. It's James.

I have been ignoring his calls along with everyone else's these past two days, because anything that comes out of my mouth is going to be a lie. And I was really tired of lying- it was exhausting. However, I remember how worried James was when I left his town house, and I feel compelled to answer his call.

"Rose thank God, where the fuck have you been? Your mother just stopped by looking for you." He explains, his voice aggravated and worried. A pang of guilt churns within me. I didn't want him to worry about me especially when he already had so much shit to deal with.

"I'm fine, James. I just needed to get away. What did you tell her?" I ask.

"I told her that you and I haven't talked since the service. I've been feeding that lie to everyone. Everyone is worried about you Rose, you need to come back, and I promise you that I will hold your hand through all of this." He pleads. I felt bad for stressing everybody out, especially him but I didn't want to go back. I couldn't.

Call me selfish, but the only thing that mattered to me right now was my survival. Nothing else. I needed to figure out how to escape him, but I know if given the opportunity I wouldn't be that lucky again.

I stayed silent for a moment, before promising James that I would be back soon. I just needed a little more time to process everything and regroup.

"Where are you staying?" he presses.

"James, I can't tell you. Just tell everyone I'm fine and that I left town because some friends of mine from LA invited me to their cabin, somewhere in upstate New York." I instruct, figuring it would be believable enough. It would definitely have been something I would've pulled years before.

My mother, though, had witnessed the beginning of one of my panic attacks the night Pierce had appeared. She had physically seen that something was wrong.

"Rose?" He questions, unsure of my lie.

"James just do it ok..." Before I can finish my sentence, the doorbell rings. The hair on my skin stands and my blood runs cold. I very slowly put my phone back to my ear, as my hands shake.

"James, I have to go." I say and before he can protest, I hang up. I get up and peek out the window and see a black Ferrari Spider parked out front. What the fuck? Whose is that? I think to myself. I walk slowly to the door terrified that Pierce has found me. I peek out the glass part and see a familiar figure. I very cautiously and slowly open my door and standing by the entrance way with his green eyes staring back at me, is Leo Lloyd. A car drives by, their headlights flashing, illuminating Leo, and for a moment he looks like an angel. Maybe that's who he's supposed to be. My guardian angel. That could explain our insane connection. I stand there not knowing what to say. How had he found me? Who else knows I'm here? I ponder, as a million questions swirl around in my mind, when the only thing I can say is, "Leo?"

He gives me a small smile and walks closer stopping at the frame of the door. The rain continues to hit the ground around him.

"Finding you love was a task not made for the weak." He confesses.

"How did you find me?" I question, thoroughly confused on how he knew where I was. However, when he flashes me that infectious smile and those striking eyes, I can't even think straight. Instead, I focus on how happy I am that he's here.

"How I found you is not really important. What is important is that you're safe. Rose, I haven't felt this much panic in a long time. When Adeline showed up at my door looking for you, I could sense something was wrong. And looking at you love; I can tell I wasn't wrong to come find you." He frowns and puts his hand out to touch my face. He was cold and his skin was wet from the rain, yet I still melted into his touch.

"Come in." I whisper defeated, I'm tired of keeping all of this to myself. I need to just tell someone. And for whatever reason, everything inside of me is screaming that I can trust him.

Leo walks inside. I wait until he is fully in and check the surroundings of the house before closing the door behind us. He stands in the middle of the living room looking at everything, probably curious as to why I am staying here. I explain to him that this is my father's house and that it is the only place I feel the safest in. This brings on the question he wanted to ask me the moment he saw me open the door.

"What has you so rattled Rose? Tell me. I can protect you." He proclaims. If only he knew what he was going up against. I sigh and motion for us to sit. He follows behind sitting across from me in the living room. He stares at me anticipating what I am going to say next. I try to organize my thoughts and think things through before I say anything.

"Before I tell you, I just want to make it clear that I am a new person, a better person. What I'm about to tell you happened to a different girl. That girl died a long time ago. This is the first time I have ever told anyone what I am about to tell you." I ramble trying to make him understand. I had never told anyone the whole truth, but I figure if this man has gone through all this trouble just to find me, he deserves to know. Some part of me feels that he will understand and not judge me. I hope so anyway. I know that what I'm going to share is going to cast a dark shadow over me in his eyes, but I need him to know. I just need someone to finally know.

Leo sits silently, not interrupting the point I am trying to make. Finally, when I am ready enough to bare my soul to the man sitting in front of me, I begin.

"Three years ago, I met a guy in college. Pierce Adami. He was everything my mother had dreamed of for me in a man. He was wealthy and came from a good family. His parents had status and pull in the city. Pierce was Mr. Perfect in everyone's eyes. I on the other hand was a wreck back then, I was drinking and doing drugs- getting high any chance I got. I was going through a lot. So, when I met Pierce, I thought maybe this could be a good thing. He would fit the part, allowing me to still look good while continuing my usual behavior. You see, Mr. Perfect wasn't always so perfect. His poison was heroin. He had been the one to introduce me to it. Before him, I stuck mostly to pot and coke. Heroin was different though- and I knew after a few tries that I had to stop, because if

I didn't, I wouldn't be able to pull myself back." I could feel myself shaking when I felt Leo gently place his hand on my knee. His expression remained neutral, composed, as he silently offered me the confidence to continue. I knew at that moment that I could trust him. That he was genuinely listening and not judging me. I took in a deep breath before continuing.

"My involvement with Pierce became more serious and a year into our relationship he took me on a trip to Italy for the summer. We had been having problems in the past, but it only got worse with that trip. It started with petty fights and screaming. Then one day he pushed me, and I fell, spraining my wrist from the fall. He apologized and promised me it wouldn't happen again. I believed him. It was naive and even stupid on my part, since he had made that promise a couple of times before. Anyway, after that incident we drank and I did coke, while he shot himself up- erasing momentarily what had just happened; and things were fine again until they weren't. He went from pushing to hitting and hair pulling and then finally..." I couldn't even finish the sentence. I literally felt sick. I have never shared this with anyone. I don't even like admitting it to myself. Leo's eyes soften, as his body stiffens. I bite my lip gently, finding it hard to reveal the next part of the story as the memories resurface. I could feel myself breaking as I unbury the past.

"He raped me." I admit, as I look away.

"I wish I could say I left after that, but I didn't. He threatened that he would kill me if I did, and he tried- God did he try. The rape wasn't the worst thing to even happen." I let out a soft chuckle as I wipe away a single tear now falling down my cheek.

"The worst part was when I reached my breaking point, and I began praying he would just end me. Because I knew at the time, it would be the only way to get away from him." I confess, as I bring my hands up to my face covering my shame. I cried so hard that my body shook. I couldn't hold it in anymore. Keeping this secret all to myself had been slowly killing me. Leo looks at me, his eyes softening before me. As I continued to sob, I couldn't help but feel relief- it felt cathartic to confess this and to have someone hear it.

"Rose." He whispers, somehow heartbroken from witnessing my pain.

"The other night you told me you were a monster but trust me Leo you're not. Pierce is the monster. The last night Pierce and I were together, we had a horrible argument. Somehow, I mustered the strength to get the confidence I needed to call the cops and try and get help. However, Pierce was too cunning, the moment he heard me on the phone he put an end to it. I knew that he had finally snapped and that all those promises, all those threats of killing me were about to happen. He had shattered my wrist against the counter forcing the phone from my hand, then he beat me- relentlessly, before throwing me on the floor and wrapping his hands around my neck. I couldn't breathe as I struggled for him to release me. Desperately, I moved my hands around looking for something to defend myself with- there had been broken pieces of glass from dishes he had broken from a previous fight and a knife that had fallen from the counter. By some miracle I managed to grab hold of the knife even though it was nowhere near me at the time." I pause as I allow the memory to resurface.

"I always thought it was my father trying to help me survive."

"I grabbed the knife, and I stabbed him in the stomach. He cried out in pain and rolled off me from the shock. At that moment I was so high from the adrenaline that I didn't even know what I was doing, when suddenly the knife was back in my hand, and I stabbed him again and again. His blood covered my skin, there was so much blood. After realizing what I had done, I ran.

Leaving him to his own demise. I managed to get somewhere safe, and I called a friend, who flew me back home. The moment I got to New York, I made plans to leave. And when I was finally able to make my way to L.A. I started taking the necessary steps to recovery. I've been sober for almost two years now...He's supposed to be dead Leo. I killed him."

I confess the tears falling harder and faster than before.

"And he's back?" Leo asks, his expression becoming angry yet when he looks into my eyes, his features soften. He gets up and slowly moves toward me. He kneels in front of me very slowly, grabbing my hands and bringing them up to his lips where he kisses them, gently.

"I will kill him before he even touches you, Rose. This I swear, no one will ever hurt you again. I swear on my life." He promises. I look down at his beautiful face and try to smile. His words are moving, and I wanted to believe him, but I knew nothing, and no one could take him down. Pierce will be my downfall; it was only a matter of time.

"I can't go back there, Leo. He will find me, and you won't be able to protect me. I can't even tell anyone any of this because there's so much more to the story, that if anyone ever found out everything would change." I ramble. I don't tell Leo about the baby; I never want anyone to know about it. It is my pain to carry. I keep that secret locked up inside. It haunts my dreams at night.

"I swear to you Rose; I will protect you." He states. He is confident in his answer. And for a moment I let myself believe him.

"Come back with me, you don't even have to tell anyone. We can figure this out together." He offers. I think about it for a moment but decide against it. I can't ask that of him. Even though we both share this crazy connection we are still, practically strangers.

"I couldn't impose on you like that, Leo. This isn't your problem."

"Rose, anything that has to do with you, affects me now. I promised you that I would never hurt you and that includes protecting you from anyone that would. I swore to you I would kill any monster that tries to harm you. I intend on keeping that promise" He states firmly, holding my hands before getting up gently pulling me up along with him to my feet.

I know that involving him is wrong and selfish, but I can tell he isn't going to take no for an answer. So, I agree. He kisses my lips softly and promises me that everything will be ok. I pray hoping that it will be. I feel the safest when I'm with him, so maybe staying at his place wouldn't be the worst thing.

***

That night he helps me clean up the house as I pack my bags. I threw on Leo's shirt from the other night with a pair of jeans.

"My clothes look way better on you love, than me." He smiles. I can't help but blush as I continue on making sure everything in the house is in place. We plan on leaving tonight so we can get this whole thing over with. And by this, I mean explaining to everyone that Leo came to upstate New York to pick me up from my friend's cabin. The excuse would be that I wasn't feeling well, explaining why I wasn't answering anyone's calls. After getting the house more or less in shape, I grab my stuff and head out the door. Leo never leaves my side as I lock the door behind us.

He walks me to my side of the car, opening the door for me. I thank him then strap myself in as he goes around and gets inside. He is ready to go. However, I on the other hand, continue to fight the urge to stay in place and not go back. I can't help thinking that this will not end well for anyone.

During the drive back to the city we talk about this new arrangement. I will stay at his apartment tonight and go to my apartment with him and pick up some clothes in the morning. He tells me that he will be my very own personal bodyguard until the situation with Pierce is handled. I laugh at his attempt to be serious when he proposes this option. He is absolutely insane; I mean he has a billion-dollar enterprise to run and more important things to tend to than my drama. He of course pushes that assessment aside and tells me he will stick by me no matter what. I have to admit it feels nice having someone fully in my corner.

Returning to the city has my anxiety on edge. As we drive over the George Washington bridge, Leo must feel my fear as well, because he places his hand on my thigh and gives it a gentle squeeze.

"You're going to be fine. I'm not going to let anything happen to you." He assures me. I nod my head and stay silent until we get back to his place.

***

As we ride the elevator up, we stand side by side letting the silence consume us. When the doors open Adeline is waiting, her features tight probably from all the worrying. She practically charges at me and wraps her arms around me.

"Rose, don't you know how to use a cell phone? You had me worried sick!" She cries. I drop my bags on the floor and wrap my arms around her. I hate that I worried her. However, I knew I could never tell her the real reason as to why I had to leave. It would break me to show her all the horror I had endured. I rather she think of me as stone cold and jaded instead of some weak pathetic girl who got hit too many times by her drug addicted boyfriend who knocked her up only to lose the baby.

Adeline holds me close as I hold back my tears. Her familiarity is comforting.

"I'm sorry."

We both stand there letting the comfort of one another embrace us. Leo and now Elliot who walks in from the kitchen, stand in place watching us. Adeline pulls back and looks at me.

"What happened, because I don't believe that little story James has been feeding people. I know you Rose, and you wouldn't just take off like that without a word to me at least. I mean I understand not telling your mother but me, we always tell each other everything." She rambles trying to understand.

I couldn't tell her. It would literally shatter whatever pieces I have left. As is, lying to her kills me. She truly does deserve a better friend.

"I'm sorry it was a really stupid and last-minute thing; my phone didn't have reception, and I saw James before I left so I figured he'd tell you guys." I state, hoping she buys my poker face. She gives me a questioning look but decides to drop it, since there are other ears listening in. Elliot walks up and gives me a hug.

"It's nice to have you back from your little *vacation,* Rose. I will say though you scared the hell out of this man here." He says looking over at Leo. I let out a nervous laugh and frown looking at Leo feeling bad for scaring him. It wasn't my intent to scare anyone, but I needed to clear my head, running has always given me the opportunity to do so.

"Rose, you've had a long drive back, you should probably get some rest." Leo interjects. He wants to give me a chance to breathe because he can see the way Adeline is looking at me. We both know that she isn't going to let this go. I look over at her and nod in agreement with Leo.

"Yeah, I'm really tired. Adi I'll come by tomorrow and I'll tell you all about my little escape, ok?" I ask hoping she'll take the bait and leave. Adeline shakes her head, and Elliot takes it upon himself to walk her out. Leaving Leo and I alone.

"James?" He asks, probably catching the part where I told Adeline that I saw him last.

"You caught that?" I say almost in a whisper, nervous that he would be angry.

He nods his head and stays silent waiting for me to explain. His calmness is refreshing. I take a breath then walk further into the apartment, as Leo follows close behind and takes a seat.

"James and I used to date in high school. It was great until it wasn't. We both eventually figured out that we were better off as friends than boyfriend and girlfriend. Besides like I confessed to you the other night, I never felt whole in these relationships-they never felt right. So, when him and I broke up he took it harder than I did. Anyway, that day in Italy he was the one to come and get me. He's the only other person that knows Pierce is not a good man. He doesn't know what happened. I think he was too scared to ask, seeing the state I was in." I explain. Leo is still holding my gaze but remains quiet, allowing me to go on.

I continue, "So when Pierce showed up the other night, I was in a terrible place. My anxiety kicked in and I needed to go somewhere that understood and that was familiar, so I went to James' house, and we talked, and he stayed with me as I rode out my attack."

"He sounds like a good friend." Leo states.

"He is." I smile.

I then go on to explain how he was the one that wanted me to go to the police about Pierce. I explain how I couldn't. Leo, unlike James, understands my reasoning for not involving the police. He walks over and picks me up, placing me on his lap pulling me in closer.

"I'm so sorry, Rose." He whispers, breathing me in.

"It's ok Leo. I'm just happy I found someone as good as you." I smile, pulling away to kiss him.

He kisses me back gently at first, then as I wrap my arms around his neck, the kiss turns more passionate. His hands move to my hair giving me mobility to move to a position where I am straddling his lap. I can feel his want for me growing more and more as I lightly grind on him. He picks me up, never disconnecting from my lips and walks us up the stairs. My hands rummage through his hair, and I moan into the kiss as his hands squeeze my ass. His tongue explores my mouth, dominating the kiss. When we get to his bedroom, he places me on the bed and begins kissing my neck, gently exploring my shoulders before his lips trail down my arm. He grabs my wrist gently then grabs the other, noticing the matching marks.

"Rose." He whispers looking from the scar lines to my eyes. I can't fight the feeling of being overwhelmed. I slowly remove my hands from his grip. Leo is patient as he stays very still, watching me.

"Rose, look at me, please." He whispers.

"You don't have to tell me, but you can if you want to." He adds, his voice soft and coaxing. I swallow the lump in my throat that holds back my voice and decide to just tell him. He already knows everything else- well almost everything. What's one more thing?

"When Pierce first raped me." I begin then look down, too ashamed to look at his face.

"He shattered whatever pieces of myself still stood. He had been violent with me in the past but never like that. Him doing that was different: he took pieces of myself away from me and shattered the rest. I was so desperate to leave but I couldn't because he had too much control back then. So, I did the only thing that I could do." I state referring to my suicide attempt, before lifting my eyes to meet his.

"My Rose, my beautiful Rose." He states his eyes fill with sadness from my truth. He places both of his hands on my face as he holds me ever so gently.

"I was dead by the time the doctors got to me. However, by some miracle they were able to revive me. They said it was a miracle I survived...I guess some people are gifted a couple of miracles in their lifetime." I explain, thinking back to that horrible day in the hospital.

"I will make him pay Rose; I swear to you." He states earnestly. I don't want him to do anything that is going to get him into trouble. All I want from Leo Lloyd at this moment is for him to be with me.

"Can you hold me?" I ask timidly. I needed to feel him. He gives me a slight smile and moves me over, pulling me closer to his chest. As I feel my body adjust to his. I knew that from this day forward, Leo, and I would always be connected. He knew and understood parts of me that no one else knew or cared about, and he accepted me for who I am. A shattered girl fighting to keep the remaining pieces left within her, in place.

Chapter 17

ROSE

Since my return back to the city, I have made sure to steer clear of the outside world and everybody in it. Everyone now knew that Pierce had returned since he had been flaunting his existence all around New York.

James has been my outside informant since I got back. He continued to press me to go to the police, but I knew that I couldn't. So instead, I chose to hide and blind myself from the danger lurking outside Leo's luxurious penthouse.

I have managed to confine myself to the four walls of Leo's bedroom these past few days. I spend my days and nights reading from his very vast and intricate library and any little time in between I usually spend talking to either Leo or Elliot. I can tell they're both worried. Especially Leo but he masks it well. He never leaves my side these days- which I'm not too upset over, since I love every second, he's with me.

Today was a beautiful sunny day and I have chosen to spend it laying on my stomach, on Leo's very comfortable bed. I carefully look through my first edition Pride and Prejudice book, making sure I'm extra cautious as I turn the pages. I'm so focused on being careful that I don't even lift my head when Leo enters the room.

"Hello my love." I greet as I keep my eyes fixated on the words staring back at me for the millionth time this week.

Leo stays silent as he walks up to me and grabs the book straight from my hands. I physically cringe, as I watch him grip the book as if it wasn't nothing more than an ordinary book.

"Hey, I was reading that. And be careful, it was a gift from a really great guy I'm seeing." I whine, as I get up from my very comfortable position and try to reach for the book but fail miserably since he places it above his head.

"That must be some guy you're seeing, to give you this old thing." He teases, bringing the book back down in front of him as he scans it.

"Can I please have it back?" I beg, giving him the biggest pout I can muster. He gives me a small grin, and hands it back to me but doesn't release his grip on the book as he says, "Rose, you have been locked up in this room for far too long, you need to get out and get some fresh air."

"Leo, I don't need fresh air, I have air in here, besides I'm fine." I explain, slowly starting to believe the lie myself, as I grab the book fully from his grasp.

"No, you and I are going to that lunch event today. We are not staying in this apartment another minute longer. I understand that you're scared of that waste of a human, but I swear to you Rose nothing bad is going to happen." Leo states, not leaving much room to argue.

I want to believe him and share in the certainty that I would be safe, but every time I allow myself even two seconds of that fantasy my mind brings me back to the nightmare that is Pierce.

"I don't know Leo."

"Love, I swear to you I will not let anyone ever hurt you again. I will kill anyone who even dares to look at you the wrong way." He grins, knowing he wouldn't even hesitate. I wasn't sure if that part of Leo intrigued me or scared me.

Letting his words sink in, and trying not to disappoint him, I put the book down.

"Ok." I reply simply, as I begin to get off the bed.

"Very good, I had a dress delivered already and shoes as well, along with some other things. They're waiting in the guest suite. I'm going to start getting ready, I'll meet you downstairs when you're finished." He instructs, as he gives me a quick kiss on the forehead before helping me off the bed. As I turn around to leave, he gives me a quick smack on my ass, which excites me more than expected.

"Leo!" I scold, as I turn around to face him. He sees right through my false annoyance, as he gives me the most devious smirk. Sometimes, I have to focus on my breathing when I'm around him, because he truly does take my breath away.

"Sorry, love. I just find everything about you hard to resist." He admits, innocently. I quirk my brow but then turn around without another word and leave, using my hands to cover my behind. Leo lets out a low chuckle as I close the door behind me.

I make my way to the guest room next to his, where a beautiful black lace cocktail dress lays on the bed, next to an open shoe box revealing a beautiful pair of black Manolo Blahnik heels. I walk over to them and admire their beauty. They are absolutely gorgeous. A black, satin Alexander Wang clutch lays next to the dress. Leo really has great taste. As I walk over to the bathroom to shower, I see a box laying on the counter, with a note on top.

I grab the perfectly folded piece of paper and read it.

To my Rose,
I hope you like them as much as I like the thought of you in them ;)
Yours truly,
Leo

I can't help but giggle at his note before opening the box. Once I open it, I see the most beautiful lingerie set from La Perla, I had ever seen. He truly has exquisite taste. I smile deviously as I pull the set out of the box and look at the red lace thong with the matching lace bra. Tiny pearls hang from the fabric to add more detail.

I quickly make my way into the shower and lose myself with the thoughts of Leo stripping me out of the new lingerie set. I long to feel his touch as he explores every inch of me. And I want nothing more than to kiss and touch every part of him. I want to experience what it's like to fully be with him and have him claim me as fully his.

But with Pierce being so close I couldn't completely let go. I needed to figure out how to deal with him and soon because the longer I held out when it came to having sex with Leo, the more my body craved him.

Now that I have fully managed to depress myself even further, I get myself out of the shower and wrap a towel around my body as I look into the mirror. The girl who stares back at me, looks foreign in my eyes. However, after a few moments of deep breathing and a few attempts of psyching myself up I place my metaphorical mask on and relish in the face looking back at me. This was the Rose I needed to become. She was the woman who had literally left the devil and survived.

I blow dry my hair, so that my curls are nice and bouncy, deciding on wearing my hair natural. I then quickly finished up my look by adding some light makeup with the few things that I had brought over from my mother's house. After feeling some amount of satisfaction from how I look, I make my way back into the guest room. I decided against the new lingerie set, deciding it would be better to save that for later on, when I would feel ready for Leo to take them off of me. So, I put on just a plain black bra and panty and slip into my new dress. I admire how tight and flattering it fits me. Finishing up the look I slip into my new favorite heels. Not quite the stilettos I was used to but beautiful, nonetheless. Covered in black lace the three-inch heels completed the whole look. They were gorgeous.

I go back into the bathroom and take another look at myself in the big vanity mirror. I looked and felt ready to face the outside world. I can't help but feel a glimmer of hope that I could get past some of the trauma and go back to who I was. Feeling satisfied, I leave the bathroom and grab my clutch and head downstairs.

As I descend the stairs both Elliot and Leo are in their best suits waiting for me. Over the last couple of days Elliot and I had grown quite close. I really hoped things would work out between him and Adeline.

I wasn't sure if anything had happened between them as she hadn't stopped by these past couple of days which could only mean that Colin had somehow weaseled his way back into her life.

"Wow." Elliot blurts, pulling me away from my thoughts. I let a small laugh escape my lips from his overly dramatic reaction. When Leo's green eyes catch mine.

"You truly are the most beautiful woman I have ever laid my eyes upon." He states, as he continues to stare into my eyes from a distance.

"You look rather dashing yourself...You both do." I smile, as I break away from Leo's stare and look over to Elliot. Although, like a woman obsessed, my eyes automatically move back towards Leo.

I can't help but admire how handsome he looks in his black-on-black suit. His presence is absolutely devastating in the most devilish way possible.

"Well let's get this over with." Elliot shouts with fake enthusiasm clapping his hands loudly, breaking the trance between Leo and me. He extends his arm out for me to take along with Leo. I link my arms with both of theirs and we make our way towards the elevator. I wish I could say that I wasn't absolutely terrified to throw myself into the lion's den, but I trust that Leo would never let anything happen to me.

***

We arrive at the St. Regis Hotel in Midtown, where a company looking for investors is hosting a luncheon. It's all very business focused and extremely boring. However, Leo and Elliot had been hand selected and invited with other high society figures, making our appearance a welcomed surprise. They both held on to me tightly as we made our way inside, it felt as if they were both my own personal bodyguards.

My heart was truly touched by both Leo's and Elliot's over protectiveness of me. Elliot didn't know the exact details of what had transpired when it came to me, but he knew enough that he wasn't going to let go of my arm unless he was sure I wasn't in any danger.

As we walked further into the large venue, I looked around and thankfully saw no sign of Pierce, I didn't even see his parents. However, as my eyes continue to scan the room, my eyes happen to catch golden locks of hair sitting at a table in the back by herself. Thank God, Adeline was here. She seems to spot me too, by the way she practically jumps from her seat and rushes over towards me.

"Rose, I didn't know you were coming." She beams, as I loosen my arms from my security team and embrace Adeline in a hug. I've missed her, I needed to ask her why she's been so distant. But I knew that would be difficult as neither one of them would probably give us a moment alone at this event.

"It was a last-minute decision." I explain.

"Well, if you guys would like there's plenty of room at my table in the back, I came with my parents, but they seem to have gotten busy discussing all that exciting business talk they're so fond of." Adeline quips, as she looks at all of us, although she seemingly avoids looking at Elliot for too long.

"That would be great." Leo states. We follow close behind Adeline as we make our way to the table. I manage to walk next to Adeline and create a little distance from the guys.

"What's going on between you and Elliot?" I whisper.

"Nothing. I've just been busy; it's not like we're dating or anything." Adeline explains, a bit defensively. She's hiding something, she only gets defensive and nervous when she's lying. When we reach our table, I decide to drop the topic for now, trying not to cause any awkwardness.

We all sit, and order drinks. I can't help but notice the empty chair next to Adeline.

"So, Miss Adeline, did you bring a date?" Elliot asks, inquisitively.

"Umm, I actually did. I'm here with Collin." She smiles, sipping her drink.

"Adeline, no." I frown, holding back the want to plead with her to stop going back to someone who doesn't deserve her.

"Collin and I worked things out." She says, like it's the most casual thing in the world.

"Well, I think that's my cue. I'm going over to the bar to say hi to an old friend." Elliot states.

"I need to use the lady's room, Adeline can you come with me?" I ask hoping to talk to her privately and ask her if she has totally lost her mind. Leo squeezes my hand under the table making sure I was ok. However, I haven't seen any sign of Pierce, and I doubt he'll try anything in public. He would never risk tarnishing his golden boy reputation.

"Sure." Adeline says hesitantly, knowing my reason for asking her to come with me. We both get up and make our way to the restroom which is just outside the banquet room.

As soon as the door closes, and I see that the restroom is empty I immediately turn all of my attention to her.

"Adeline, you're the smart one in this duo, so please explain to me why you allowed Collin back into your life?" I ask, genuinely looking to understand. I mean doesn't she know she is worth way more than what Collin could ever offer her. Adeline lets out a sigh of defeat.

"I love him, I mean I've known him since we were five Rose. He was my first kiss, my first boyfriend, my first everything and despite all the bad things he's done I love him." She explains. My heart sinks from listening to her words. Not because I'm disappointed by her response but because for the first time in my life I get it. Love can do that to a person, completely blind them as they allow themselves to enter into a whirlwind of insanity.

"I just hope you know what you're doing because cheaters don't usually change. I'm sorry but you know it's true. He's done it before." I point out. I didn't want to pop her bubble; I just wanted her to understand that he would most likely never change.

"I do, I'd be lying if I said we fell back into place- because we haven't. I just want to see if there is anything left to salvage. We were together for over eight years, not counting grade school." She explains, a bit exasperated.

Before I can get another word out, someone knocks on the door. We both turn to see when Pierce walks in. My heart stops. Adeline looks confused by my sudden paleness and expression of shock; however, she doesn't question it.

"This is the ladies room." She points out.

"I know but I needed to speak to Rosie." He states, as he walks further in towards us, closing the door behind him. I cringe as I grab onto Adeline's arm.

"Well, I'm sure you can talk to her later, Rose and I, were just leaving." Adeline tries to reason as she grabs my wrist and pulls me towards the exit, however Pierce slams his hand on the wooden door to prevent us from opening it.

"I said I need to talk to Rosie."

"Adeline, why don't you go back to the table." I manage to say nervously, trying to keep my composure. The last thing I needed was for Adeline to get hurt, especially by him.

"No, we should get going...together." Adeline, argues. I try to signal for her to listen, but she completely dismisses my suggestive eye movements.

"Adeline, I'll be fine, please go." I practically beg, although I keep my voice steady. I can tell she wants to argue back; however, she nods her head and waits for Pierce to open the door and allow her to exit. As soon as she leaves, I feel a slight weight lifted off of my chest knowing she would be safe and not in the middle of this ugliness that is about to unfold.

"Finally, Rosie, I've missed you." He smiles as he walks towards me. Instinctively I back away from him in an attempt to get as much distance from him as possible. However, my back soon hits the wall. He extends both arms, caging me. I can feel my anxiety kick in. I feel like I'm back in the lion's den.

"What do you want?" I ask, silently praying. Pierce lets out a low cynical laugh and moves a strand of hair away from my face.

"You." He states simply. He then proceeds to wrap his hand around my throat. My whole body goes rigid with absolute terror. My breathing becomes more shallow as I struggle against his hold

"All I have ever fucking wanted is you!" He yells. My eyes burn from the fear circulating within me. However, before Pierce can go any further Leo barges in.

"Get your hands off of her!" Leo roars, as he runs towards Pierce and rips him off of me, throwing him on the floor. Adeline runs up behind Leo and grabs me.

"Oh my god, Rose are you ok?" Adeline asks as she steadies me, noticing what I'm sure is a forming bruise on my neck.

"I'm fine." I whisper, as my voice cracks. Leo stands over Pierce as Pierce lets out the most villainous laugh I've ever heard.

"Rosie, it seems you finally found someone who sees you for more than just your ass, good for you."

Leo kicks him on his side, surely breaking a few of his ribs. However, Pierce doesn't react.

"Is that all you've got? I don't even know why you're protecting this whore?" Pierce spits out getting up faster than he should've been able to.

"I am going to fucking kill you." Leo seethes as he grabs ahold of Pierce and slams him into the mirror decorating the wall. Adeline and I both look away shielding ourselves from the debris of glass falling all around us.

Pierce lays on the floor bleeding as Leo begins to swing at his face. He does this a couple of times before I yell.

"Leo, please.... stop! Let's just go, please!" I beg, trying to literally stop him from killing Pierce. I couldn't live with myself if he had blood on his hands because of me.

"Leo please!" I insist. Leo's hands drip blood as he drops Pierce from his grip and walks towards Adeline and I. Adeline stays quiet as I run over to Leo, making sure he is okay.

"Let's get out of here." Leo says as I nod in agreement.

"Adeline come on." I say as I turn to look at a very stunned and confused Adeline.

"Yes, sure, let's get out of here. Should we call someone?" She asks not really knowing how else to respond. Both Leo and I shake our heads no. Without another word she nods her head and walks out with us. I can see Leo's hands are covered in blood as he places them in his pockets, trying to conceal the evidence of what had just taken place.

We walked back to the table to gather our belongings. Elliot is sitting alone nursing his drink as he sees us approach.

"It's time to go." Leo informs him.

"What's going on?" Elliot asks now, fully alert as he stands stepping closer to me.

"Rose, what happened to your neck?"

Before anyone could answer, Collin approaches the table with a drink in hand.

"Adeline what's going on? Where are you going?" He questions, as he stands there watching Adeline grabbing her bag.

"Adeline and I are going back to her place; the guys were just walking us out." I say, trying to avoid a jealous tantrum from Collin.

"Who are you?" Collin asks, directing his question at Elliot as he tries to puff out his chest attempting to appear bigger than what he actually is and failing miserably. Elliot forms a smile flattered by Collin's lame attempt to size him up.

"Elliot Lancer, I'm a friend of Adeline and Rose." He explains, as he moves his hand out for Collin to shake. Collin being the asshole that he is, ignores Elliot's polite gesture. I can see Adeline turning red from embarrassment.

"Collin, I'll call you later." Adeline snaps.

"Yeah, sure, whatever. Call me later." He replies, taking a seat at the empty table continuing to drink from his glass.

Leo, becoming impatient, walks past him, shoving his chair slightly as he grabs my hand and walks me through the door and down the lobby until we reach the exit. Elliot and Adeline follow closely behind us.

We immediately go to Leo's car and pile in quickly.

"Rose, what was that back there? Has Pierce lost his mind? I mean, I know he's been gone all this time but my God he's changed!" Adeline rambles, as soon as I slide into the back seat next to her and close the door. I let a breath of pure defeat leave my lips knowing I can no longer harbor this secret from her. I had to come clean.

"Pierce was the reason I left New York."

Adeline blinks a couple of times trying to analyze my words.

"What? I thought you left for that writing program?"

"When I was in Italy, Pierce became another person, he hurt me..." I choke out, trying to hold my composure. Adeline's eyes turn glassy as she realizes what I'm telling her.

"Why didn't you ever say anything?" She asks gently, as she grabs my hand in an effort to comfort me.

"I didn't want you or anyone else to see me at that point in my life. James is the only one that knows a portion of the story." I explain, trying to hold back the tears that so desperately want to fall.

"Rose, you could have told me, I wouldn't have judged you."

"I was ashamed, Adeline. I needed to get as far away from everything and everyone, because being here and having to carry all that darkness was suffocating." I finally confess.

"I was drowning in the darkness that was consuming me from the inside. There are so many secrets Adeline that I have had to carry that have weighed me down all these years. I never wanted to put distance between us or anyone else that I cared about but I also knew that you or anyone else couldn't handle my truth. Especially since I still cannot handle everything that I have been through." I ramble, as my tears fall freely. It felt both freeing and terrifying to open up to her, but I couldn't hold it in anymore. I was cracking and sooner or later I was going to break and either myself or those closest to me were going to get cut from the shattered pieces left behind.

Chapter 18

ELLIOT

Guilt chips away at me having to leave Leo back at the apartment with Rose and Adeline after what had transpired earlier with Pierce, but I needed to find some answers. This Pierce fellow was becoming more of a pest as the days went by and he needed to be fucking exterminated. Not to mention, I needed answers in regard to this whole Cain, Rose, soul tie business, therefore I called the only person that I knew wouldn't resist the urge to come.

Michael.

And I knew if I told Leo who I was about to meet up with, he would want to come and probably kill him for placing Rose on Pierce's radar. I can't lie, from what I've pieced together and from the small bits Leo has told me I feel the urge to stake Michael myself for his cruelty in all of this. It's one thing to be a pawn and try to save Marie's life, it's another to give the gift of mortality to a boy that was already a monster.

I unlock the doors to Centuries, my sanctuary and walk over to my office. Immediately, I can feel a presence. And in one quick flash, Michael is right in front of me.

"How lovely of you to call me." Michael smiles, but before I can say anything else, I notice the presence of someone else in the room. A woman with a complexion that could be compared to snow and eyes that were the most piercing blue I had ever come across. It was Tristan, one of my many lovers from the past. My heart nearly stops.

"Tristan." I whisper, in complete disbelief. It's been centuries since we had last seen one another. And the last time we had, she had decided to leave me for some vampire she had spontaneously fallen in love with. Not that I cared or anything. I was never one to become too attached to anyone, although I will say, seeing Adeline with that asshole ex-boyfriend of hers did manage to thoroughly piss me off. I mean honestly, what the fuck does she see in him, especially when she can have me instead.

"Elliot, you're looking good as always." She smirks as she walks up to me, swaying her hips like the seductress I knew her to be.

"You don't look that bad yourself, love." I replied.

"You called me here for a reason." Michael interrupts, his tone bored as he watches Tristan's and my interaction. He never did like anyone touching his possessions.

"Yes." I refocus, "I need more information on the blade of Cain." I state flatly. Michael displays a wicked smile.

"I am afraid I can't help you there, it is before my time." Michael states.

"Then how do I speak to him? Maybe there is a way to amend the deal that was made." I try to reason, although based on the scoff that erupted from his lips it was probably close to impossible.

"I have been waiting centuries to get Marie back. Do you think I would fuck that up, so that Leo can have his little plaything?" Michael retorts, thinking my suggestion is the most ludicrous thing he has ever heard.

"Michael, you upset the balance once when you turned Marie, you can make it right now! Rose and Leo are soul tied. Ripping them apart will only cause more havoc." I try to reason, knowing this argument is futile. Rose doesn't deserve to spend an eternity in hell. She wouldn't survive. Michael looks at me then at Tristan.

"Tell me again, why did you two break things off?" He asks, deflecting my argument.

"I needed something new." Tristan smirks as she looks over at me. She truly did look just as exquisite as she did when I first laid my eyes on her. Her long black hair still falls beyond her small waist, and her cherry red lips were still alluring even after all these centuries. She was absolutely beautiful. However, she doesn't seem like herself, she's changed, I'm assuming it's from being with him.

"Michael, please just think about it." I plead one last time. Carefully holding my ground and wondering why he had brought Tristan with him to meet with me.

"No! I have waited long enough to be reunited with my true love, and I am not going to allow anyone to get in the way of that, not even you. Do not think for a second, I won't kill you, we might have been friends all those years ago, but you're the one that severed that friendship, remember?" Michael spits as he walks closer and closer towards me.

"How could I not, you upset the balance of our people Michael! Changing that gypsy girl ruined everything! She was his prophecy, and you took it. Now look at everything that has unfolded because of it! Leo and Rose will be the ones who suffer the consequences!" I boom, balling my hands into fists from the anger.

"You're the one that made that deal Elliot. Besides, Rose isn't Leo's true soul tie, not when Cain's soul is attached to her as well. She belongs to him too." Michael argues before continuing, "I'm sorry old friend but I will stop at nothing until Marie is beside me. Now, if you will excuse me, I have some actual business to conduct." He informs me, but before he can disappear, I halt him.

"If you won't do the right thing with Cain, then at least put down your rogue fucking soldier. That Pierce fellow needs to be staked!"

Michael laughs at my statement before turning his attention to the door and using his vampire speed to leave. I drag my hands down my face as I try and think of another way to help Rose and Leo. I'm so lost in my own thoughts; I didn't even realize Tristan was still here. She lays her hand on my shoulder in an attempt to comfort me.

"Elliot, there is nothing you can do, Michael will get what he wants, he always does." She explains, trying to reason with my tortured mind. However, there is nothing she can say that will make me feel any less horrible for what I have set into motion.

I lift my head from my hands and look at her, her blue eyes still holding a sense of the girl I once fell madly in love with- once upon a time when we were young witches growing up and trying to find our way in the world.

"How did you end up being on his side?" I ask, wondering how she had allowed herself to be associated with such an idiot.

"Power. I was blinded by the power that came with being with him. He's a man in love, making him one of the most dangerous creatures to ever exist. There is great power, when it comes to those who love as deeply as he does. There is nothing they won't say or do to make sure that they unite with the one who holds their heart." Tristan explains as she moves her hand to my face and rubs her thumb along my skin. Her touch ignites the memories of how she once felt pressed against me. How our desire and love for one another was the only thing we ever needed.

"Stay." I plead grabbing her hand and looking up at her. I needed her familiarity. I missed this feeling.

She stays silent then leans down and kisses me. I grab her as she wraps her legs around my torso. I walk us to my desk and with one swift motion I manage to push all the papers and everything else residing on my desk to the floor, before laying her on her back.

"I've missed you."

"I've missed you too." She replies, as she leans up and begins to rip my shirt.

"You always were impatient." I smirk, then move my way back to her lips as I begin removing her jeans. Her hand rummages through my hair as I deepen the kiss.

"You feel so good!" She breathes when my lips disconnect with hers in order to take her shirt off. Her body looks absolutely perfect. My pants tighten just from looking at her. However, I can't stop the fleeting thought of how divine Adeline's body is. I quickly shut the thought down remembering that she had chosen someone else.

Tristan takes my pause as an opportunity to free me from my suffering and undo my pants. She lowers them down and I move her black lace panties to the side.

She lays back down and looks up at me as I stand at the side of my desk lining myself up with her entrance. Then without any hesitation I lose myself within her. She gasps as I thrust into her. The sensation is euphoric.

"Are you this wet just for me? Or is it because of Michael?" I ask as I continue to thrust in and out of her. Her moans of absolute pleasure and the sound of our skin slapping together consumes the room.

"It's because of the power that ripples from the both of you!" She gasps in between thrusts. I continue to work her until I feel her constrict around me hard. She's so close and so was I.

"Fuck, you feel so good!" I groan out as I chase my release. After a couple more thrusts we both come undone. I pull out and empty myself onto her stomach. We both stay silent as we try to regulate our breathing.

"Good to know you haven't lost your touch Elliot." She smiles as she sits up, I pass her a few tissues to wipe herself off. I pick up my pants and button them.

"You haven't lost yours either." I smile.

We both get dressed silently, until she stops halfway.

"The only way to get Rose out of this, is if you can turn her and break the soul tie Elliot. Both ties will be broken, and Cain will come for you and the others. He will kill you. You need to let this go and allow the deal to happen. Once Cain gets what he wants, then you and Michael will be free. Don't think he hasn't been watching you all these years." She informs me as she finishes tying up her ripped shirt to at least cover her breasts.

"I'm aware, he's been watching me."

"Just remember what I told you. Nothing will stop Cain. None of them will stop to get what they want. Don't get involved because the last thing they will be thinking about or considering, is you, not even Leo." She states, before giving me a tender kiss on my cheek and leaving. I sit back down on my office chair and soak in her advice.

Reasonable as it seemed, I could never allow Leo to suffer this alone. I have to do everything in my power to make this right, and if I die trying, then so be it. Maybe that's the punishment that fits the crime after my role in everything that's happened.

***

I stayed at the club for a bit longer until I decided it was time to get back to the apartment. Once home I find Leo sitting on the sofa reading.

"Where are the girls?" I ask making my way to the new bar cart to pour myself a drink.

"Adeline went home, and Rose fell asleep. Where did you go?" He asks, eyeing my ripped shirt and disheveled appearance.

"Out." I state, as I down my drink in one gulp.

"You know the other day you never said what that birthmark on Roses shoulder was, although now knowing what I know I'm going to assume it has to do with Cain?" Leo questions. I pour myself another drink, taking a sip of it before looking back at him.

"It's the mark of Cain, he's literally branded her in order to have a connection with her, I have no clue how deep that connection goes, but it's there." I explain, pausing to down the rest of my drink. Leo looks at me then back at his book as he mulls over what I had just said.

"Michael is going to drag her to Cain himself, Leo. We need to prepare." I advise, trying not to sugar coat the situation. I didn't want to give him false hope. I wasn't sure how or if I could make any of this go away.

"I know and I will be ready." Leo declares. I grab a glass and fill it with scotch and pass it to him. I then serve myself another, before I take the seat across from him.

"To hell and back." I toast. Leo smirks at my words and clinks his glass.

"To hell and back and defeating the devil himself," Leo grins, somehow hopeful.

Chapter 19

ROSE

After the altercation with Pierce, I had pretty much become a recluse in Leo's apartment once again. I haven't left the comfort of his home in almost a week. I ignored numerous phone calls and texts, not having it in me to reply. The only person I couldn't ignore was Adeline. She has made it her personal mission to speak to me at least three times a day, which is excessive and borderline bothersome, but I understand. I know if roles were reversed, I'd be doing the same. Therefore, I find myself always making sure to answer her phone calls and meet with her whenever she drops by. She never brings up the elephant in the room, since I think a part of her is scared to know the answers to the questions she can't seem to ask. So instead, I talk to her about my writing, or about my relationship with Leo or anything else to fill in the time. In return, she keeps me up to date on everyone else, since I've been avoiding them. I feel guilty about not being able to say goodbye to my sister when she traveled back to Georgia or catching up with Jason, but I needed to figure out my life. Everything felt too out of place around me. I needed to steady myself and make sure things were clear before anybody else that I cared about got dragged into this mess.

As is, I felt bad dragging Leo into my chaos. He was now placed in the middle of my drama. I can also tell Leo feels guilty about what happened over at the banquet. In my mind, he should have zero remorse, he had still managed to save the day and come to my rescue when I needed him most.

As I sit in Leo's bed staring at my laptop, I flip through the typed pages of my book that I will probably never allow anyone to ever read. I needed to reflect on my past- emotions. I focus on some of the harder parts of my writings.

Numb is what I like to feel, not happy, not sad, just the feeling of nothing. Since, when I lack any sort of feeling I am safe. I'm safe from the feeling of disappointment and pain. As is, it seems I am completely numbed to the feeling of love at least that's what Pierce told me the night that we fought. So why is it that I can go without the feeling of love, but the feeling of pain seems to consume me fully, not even the drugs and alcohol that circulate within me are strong enough to fight the feeling off. Maybe, it should be taken as a sign of my own strength, that I am able to fight the effects of narcotics, but I know that's not it, it's because I'm weak and unable. I will never be strong enough to fight off this feeling, that's why I know I will never be strong enough to leave him, even after everything he puts me through.

I can't help the frown that takes over my face as I read a passage from the earlier stages of my relationship with Pierce. I truly believed that there was something wrong with me, even when I was with James, because no matter how hard I tried I felt nothing. There was no blissful warm feeling in my chest that coated my heart. All these past relationships made me feel inadequate and wrong, when in reality I just wasn't with the right person. I can't help but let out a small breathy laugh, as I come to the conclusion that I was never numb to the feeling of love. I just hadn't been with

Leo. I feel sorry for that younger, unknowing girl who had thought that she would never experience it.

I continue reading when I feel someone enter into the bedroom. It's Leo- all six foot five of him standing in front of me. I look up from my computer to see him staring at me with a wicked smile plastered to his gorgeous face.

"What's going on in that mischievous brain of yours?" I ask casually.

"I was wondering if you would like to go out, I mean you've been held in here for a week. I feel like you're my prisoner again. I know the last time that we went out wasn't the best experience but this time it will just be the two of us." He explains, hoping I say yes. I put my laptop down and close it so he can't see the screen and look up at him with a small smile. I want to be excited at the idea of going out with him, but I feel like I can't.

"I don't know. I mean I'm ok just lounging around here." I tell him. I don't want him to think I'm scared even though he knows I am. He lets out a small sigh then walks closer to me; I gently move my laptop away from me, so that he can sit.

"I know the idea of Pierce being out there terrifies you especially with what happened last week, but you shouldn't be. Trust me when I tell you Rose, I will protect you." He swears. As much as I want to say no, I know I can't. I don't want him to think that I feel he can't defend me. And I'd be lying if I said I didn't want to spend time with him outside of these four walls. I mean it's not like much is happening inside the apartment. Leo has been super respectful of me while I've been staying here, which I've greatly appreciated.

"Deal." I smile. He returns a devilish grin and gets off the bed.

"Ok, well I have some last-minute paperwork I have to do but after that, you're all mine."

I can't help but smile and even blush like a schoolgirl at his comment. I liked the idea of being all his. He was definitely all mine in my heart at least.

We eventually end up going over to my mother's house to grab clothes for our date. Leo is taking me somewhere fancy for a night of wining and dining. The apartment is empty as we make our way inside, since my mother and Charles were out to dinner with the Carey family. They were developers from England that have been going back and forth with Charles and Jason with regards to some business deal. Not looking to waste any time, Leo and I make our way up to my bedroom. I immediately head to my closet as Leo takes a moment to look around but stops short when he grabs the book on my nightstand that I had been reading when I was last here. My cheeks instantly burn when I realize what he's holding.

"I didn't realize literary classics started printing covers with half naked men." He smirks as he flips through the pages.

"Oh my god, give me that!" I say, rushing towards him as I try and grab the book from his grasp.

"Not a chance, love. I want to see what you read behind closed doors." He laughs as he dodges my attempt at snatching the book and takes a seat on my bed.

"Go and get dressed, I'll be here." He smiles smugly, as he continues to scan the pages. Trying not to be late to dinner, I give him a long-lasting glare, before heading to my closet and grabbing the red dress I have in mind for tonight's outing. It's a cocktail dress that is tight fitting in all the right places and has an open back. It's elegant yet sexy. And to pair it off I match it with a pair of red strappy heels. I grab my clothes and go into the bathroom turning on the water to my shower and jump in. I wash my body and my hair making sure every inch of myself is perfect for tonight.

Hopping out of the shower I wrap my white fluffy towel around me and brush my teeth. I opt to blow dry my hair and curl it. For my makeup I do a glam look, with a bold red lip and black shadow on my eyes. Creating the perfect smokey eye effect. I look good and most importantly I feel good. I look down at my wrists and decide to not wear my usual Cartier bangles, feeling secure enough with Leo. I no longer felt the need to hide.

An hour later I walk out of my bathroom fully dressed and ready to go. I walk over to the giant man lying in my bed fully invested in my smutty romance novel. However, the moment I step in front of him he looks up and places the book beside him.

"You look stunning, love."

I blush from the compliment as I walk over to where he is now sitting up and give him a gentle peck on his cheek.

"Are you ready to go, or do you want to finish that chapter?" I ask playfully, as I pull away from him to grab my purse for the night.

"As tempting as it sounds to continue reading this filthy little book of yours, I much rather see how many of those scenes we can recreate after dinner." He teases, getting off the bed and drawing me closer to him, wrapping his arms around me. I loved being in his arms. It felt peaceful.

"Well Mr. Lloyd you might just get lucky after all." I whisper before pulling away and begin heading for my door, Leo follows close behind thinking about the prospect. I walk down the stairs grabbing onto the railing the last few steps as we are met by Pierce. His stone-cold eyes meet mine causing me to stop.

"Well don't you look nice, *Rosie*." He smiles sadistically, getting off on my fear. Leo immediately pushes me aside as he stands in front of me. However, choosing not to let him fight my battles any longer I pushed past him down the stairs.

"Get out of my house!" I snap, as I allow the anger that is coursing through me to take the lead. Leo takes a step towards me but allows me the space I need to confront my demon.

"Well, aren't you the brave one, now that you have your own personal bodyguard. But tell me this Rose, do you think he would be there, if he knew what a pathetic little slut you are?" He spits, as he stays perfectly still, continuing to watch me. His eyes are full of hatred. Leo, however, moves past me and in a flash has Pierce pinned against the wall in my living room. The dry wall practically shattering from impact.

"I'm going to enjoy every second of killing you." He seethes.

"You're a stupid son of a bitch for allowing yourself to love such a frigid whore. She is incapable of love. She's only good at taking what she wants!" He states, before being silenced by Leo's grip around his throat, pushing him further into the wall.

"She is capable of love; she just wasn't capable of loving a disgusting human like you."

"Well, I guess now that you and I are the same, maybe I should see how she reacts to me now." Pierce states, as he looks from Leo to me. However, the face that stares at me no longer looks like the face that has haunted me all these years. No, this face was worse. It was the face of a demon. His eyes were more sunk in, creating a dark shadowing around his pale skin. Dark red veins protrude from his skin under his now glowing red eyes as fangs emerge from his mouth. The scream that rips from my throat must catch Leo off guard because Pierce is able to break free from his hold and comes barreling towards me.

He immediately grabs me by my neck and pulls me closer. I struggle trying to breathe. I tried prying his hands off me, but he wouldn't budge, his strength seemed extreme. As I continue to struggle, Pierce seems to grow tired of my weak attempts and throws me to the floor. I cry out in pain as my head hits the floor. I place my hand on the back of my head and feel the wetness of blood coat my skin.

I couldn't understand what had just happened. How he had been able to just throw me so carelessly and effortlessly. It felt inhuman. However, before I can question it further Leo tackled Pierce to the floor. He briefly looks back at me. I realize his facial features have changed. His once angelic face had morphed. It looked like the same demonic face that covers Pierce's; shadows and veins surround his eyes and the red eyes match those of Pierces' although Leo's fangs seem larger. As much as I wanted to scream, I didn't.

I don't fear him.

I knew right then and there that I didn't care that Leo was obviously *different*. I finally had someone in my corner who was willing to fight for me and I wasn't going to let a silly little thing like fangs get in my way.

They fight each other with an extraordinary strength that I can't explain. It was as if they had absorbed the strength of a thousand men. Not to mention, they displayed a speed that would literally go against every law in physics. Leo fought harder, stronger. He matched every hit and kick with an even more powerful punch. Leo throws Pierce into my mother's bar cart, fueling Pierce further. He races towards Leo, tackling him into the staircase, his head bouncing off the bottom step. I cry out as I take in the scene before me. Pierce takes Leo's moment of weakness as an advantage, as he rushes towards me.

"I always did want the honor of being the last thing you see Rosie before those pretty little eyes of yours grow dim." He laughs. I can feel the tears begin to stream down my face. I can see his demonic face perfectly. He continues to smile as he moves his hands to my hair. He grips it hard and lifts me up. I cry out in pain. He then grabs my body holding me against him and inhales the scent of my neck. I'd choose death itself if I could, over being touched by this monster.

Right as he is about to bite me, Leo comes up behind him. However, Pierce moves faster, throwing me back on the floor, before Leo can stop him. My head ends up hitting the table and the vase comes crashing down. Shards of glass slice through my arm and my cheek.

"No!" Leo yells although it sounds more muffled since both my hearing and vision seem to be going in and out. I feel like I am slowly losing consciousness. It's becoming harder and harder to keep my eyes open as my head pounds viciously.

Pierce shoves Leo, knocking him into the wall. Leo shakes it off. His anger was almost palpable as it rippled off of him in waves.

"You're going to have to try a lot harder than that to take me down." Leo taunts running at the speed of light taking Pierce down again. The floor shakes from the weight of both men crashing into it.

"You think she's so innocent and perfect, why don't you ask her why I spared her life in Italy? Why don't you ask her where my baby is?" Pierce asks. How dare he say *my* baby.

Leo fumes from Pierce's words and within a split of a second slams Pierce into the wall in front of me, where a half a million-dollar painting from some famous French artist my mother loved, hung. The canvas was fine, but a piece of the frame had broken off. Leo took the piece of sharp wood and managed to stake Pierce in the chest. I could see Pierce's body go limp. He was dead. Within seconds, Leo kneels beside me as he tries to lift me up but falters when he feels my blood coating his hand.

"Love, you're hurt." Leo says as he tries to soothe me, gently caressing my cheek. Tears continue to stream down my face as I try to wrap my head around everything that had just happened. When out of nowhere, Pierce grabs Leo and in one swift motion snaps his neck.

"Leo!" I scream in horror as I watch his body go limp. I swear on everything holy, that something within me awakened. Something cold and powerful. I manage to lift myself up into a sitting position as I stare at Leo's lifeless body. Pierce approaches me slowly. Stalking his prey before striking. Enjoying every moment of it.

"What did you do!" I scream. Tears sting my eyes from anger. Pierce looks down at Leo.

"Now Rosie, where were we?" He asks.

I try to move but just end up cutting my leg with a shard of broken glass.

I want to get up and fight, with everything in me. I want to be the one who kills him once and for all.

"There is no one left to protect you, Rosie. It's just you and me." He taunts as he wraps his fingers around my hair.

"I'll kill you." I spit, meaning every word. This time I wouldn't fail.

"How? You are nothing but a pathetic human. Nothing more than a shell of a broken little girl, who lashes out. So many daddy issues. You could never get the love of a man, because every man that you want only wants one thing from you." He roars, pulling my hair tighter.

"All they wanted was your body, nothing else. And you gave in every time. I'm sure Leo here is no different. I think after I'm done with you, I'll kill him. It wasn't part of the arrangement I made but I don't really care." He rambles. His eyes were full of darkness.

Instinct makes me reach out my hand in the hopes of forcing him to release his hold of my hair. When he unexpectedly lets out a yell, removing his hold instantly and taking a few steps back away from me. I had burned him with my touch. I could still feel the heat radiating from my fingers. I could feel the skin around my birthmark begin to sting as I picked myself up.

"What the hell?" He booms, completely taken back. I have no idea what had just happened, but I needed to use it to my advantage.

He rushes towards me again but this time something stronger rips through me as my anger takes over and in a flash of pure unadulterated power, I send him flying across the room without even touching him. He falls to the floor unconscious.

In complete shock, I contemplated what the hell had just happened. However, the sight of Leo lying unconscious on the floor shifts my attention.

I manage to walk over to him, dropping to my knees, trying not to focus on the pain coursing through me and instead grab a hold of his body.

"Leo." I whisper, placing my hand against his ice-cold skin. He has no breath and no heartbeat.

"Please wake up." I cry. He couldn't be dead. This couldn't be happening. This was not the way he was going to go. Pierce wasn't going to take anyone else away from me.

"Leo!" I scream. My head is pounding from the pain. I want to pass out, but I fight it. I could still feel a surge of power coursing through me. I shake his body as hard as I can praying, he wakes up. Then in a quick motion his eyes pop open.

"Rose." He calls out. I move back to where I was previously and look into his beautiful green eyes as they stare up at me. I let out a breath of relief.

"Don't you ever do that again." I scold. He lets out a painful chuckle then sits up taking a look at my bruised face. He frowns at what I'm sure is a horrid appearance.

Then without any warning Pierce rushes towards us once again, grabbing me in one swift motion and throwing me once again to the floor. He crouches next to me wrapping his hand around my throat. I can feel my life desperately slip away from me but before it does, Leo is quick to his feet as he rips Pierce off of me throwing him across the room. I try to catch my breath as Leo, practically beats the demonic life out of Pierce.

I scream out in absolute anger, allowing my rage to explode from within me. Suddenly, I see Pierce fall to his knees as he cradles his ears and head in pain. Blood begins to spill from his mouth and ears. Leo, still gripping his shirt, looks shocked, unsure of what is happening. I can feel my own strength amplified. Every inch of me is pulsing. My rage is completely fixated on him.

"You don't get to be the one who kills me! You don't get to be the one I see last, and you sure as hell don't get to haunt me anymore. I'm sending you exactly where you fucking belong, and somewhere you will never be able to meet *my* child. Burn in hell you sadistic bastard!" I scream, as I get up and walk over to where Pierce is kneeling. I push past Leo and in a moment of strength I reach down, and grab hold of his neck the way he had done to me so many times before and snap it. I watched as his body hit the floor. I feel nothing. Absolutely nothing. When suddenly without much thought, I plunge my hand through his chest and rip out his heart tossing it next to where his lifeless corpse laid. I collapsed soon after. Whatever had possessed me and given me the power to slay my own demon had left me and I felt the absence in my soul.

Leo grabs a hold of my body. I could feel the pain from my injuries amplify as I struggled to move but all I could see were flashes of those all too familiar violet eyes.

"Rose." He yells with concern, as he kneels next to me and grabs my face looking for the damage that is clearly evident. His bloody fingers soaking my skin.

I no longer have any strength within me, but it didn't matter, I had been the one to slay the beast. He was never going to hurt me again.

"I don't feel so good." I whisper, struggling to keep my eyes opened. Leo panics and lifts me into his arms.

"Rose stay with me." He pleads as he moves me to the kitchen counter, laying me out. I feel myself struggling.

"I'm going to do something Rose, but you're going to have to trust me." He explains quickly, trying not to waste time, when I feel something drip on me. I try to focus my blurring vision and after a few seconds I manage to see what it is, it's blood, Leo's blood. He grabs my head and lifts it up as he positions his bleeding wrist closer to my mouth.

"Drink." I could hear him say.

"Rose, you have to, please." He begs. I decide to trust him and take a leap of faith. I drink from his wrist and before I know it, I can't seem to stop. I want all of it. The more I drink the better I feel, which only urges me further. Leo tries pulling away, but I won't let him. Finally, he pulls me back.

"I'm sorry." I whisper looking down, embarrassed. He sighs in relief, as he lifts my chin, forcing me to look into his beautiful eyes. His mouth was still stained with his own blood from tearing open his own flesh to save me.

"You just found out I'm a vampire and you're the one that's sorry?" He asks.

"Yeah." I explain then see the gash on his shirt he must have cut himself when he got pushed to the floor. I place my hand over it, and he winces.

"I thought vampires were supposed to heal?" I ask. Leo lifts his brow confused as to how I know that. Obviously, he hasn't kept up with the amount of vampire shows and books today's world was now into.

"I haven't been feeding lately. Healing will take a bit longer." He explains. I can tell he had been weakened. Then without even thinking, I grab a piece of glass off the floor and cut into my arm.

"What are you doing?" he asks, panicking as he watches the blood drip from my arm.

"Drink. You're hurt." I state. He looks confused and hesitant.

"It's okay. I want you to." I reassure him, as I move closer towards where he stands. He looks at me curiously before grabbing onto my forearm and sinks his fangs into the already ripped wound. I cringe a bit before allowing his venom to overtake me. A feeling of pure ecstasy consumes me. The feeling unlike any other high I had ever experienced.

I feel myself becoming weaker the more he drinks. But before I have the chance to say anything Leo pulls himself away. As we both take a moment to breathe, we stand there in silence both covered in blood. After a moment he offers me more blood to heal, the gash that now covers my arm. Once I release, I focus on our surroundings and a feeling of panic washes over me, "my mother!"

Leo looks at me confused before finally catching on. They will be back soon and will without a doubt lose their minds once they see what is left of their beloved home. Not to mention there is a dead demon in their living room.

"I'll call Elliot," is all he replies, before I can question him any further. Leo walks away to discuss the details with Elliot. I walk over to where Pierce's dead body lays as I look down at him. It's poetic justice in my mind. He ripped out parts of me for his own satisfaction. It's only fair I ripped out his heart for my own.

Leo gets off the phone and looks in my direction, "let's go upstairs and get cleaned up, Elliot is on his way. He will fix this whole situation." He assures me. I'm confused, is Elliot a vampire as well? Leo grabs my hand and walks me upstairs to my bedroom. I open my door and walk straight into my bathroom. Leo looks around my room inspecting all of my things that make my room mine. I can tell he's trying to calm his nerves by focusing on the small details of my room. I begin to wash my hands, slowly removing the blood that covered them. In an almost trance-like state, I watch the pink water swirl down the drain.

"Interesting room." He calls out. I can't help but let a weak smile play on my lips as I walk back into my room. I then place my hair into a high ponytail feeling the dried blood stuck to it- I definitely need to shower. I feel hot and slightly overwhelmed.

I can see Leo studying my bookshelf.

"Nice assortment." He compliments as he continues to scan them, taking his time to really look at my collection unlike he did earlier. It is nothing like his, but it still holds a special place in my heart.

"Thank you." I say then walk over to him and give him his clothes that I have in my drawer.

"You still have these?" He smiles, trying to lighten the mood. I nod displaying a small smile. I had just killed a man. I had been possessed by something I couldn't even explain. It had given me the strength of the Gods themselves to do what I needed to do. Yet, the only thing I wanted to do was talk to him about my pregnancy. I needed him to know the truth.

"Look, I just want to clarify something before we go any further." I state, addressing what Pierce had said. Leo looks at me, already knowing where the conversation was about to go.

"I... I was pregnant once." I state feeling my eyes well up. I've never said that out loud to anyone. I have kept this to myself for the past two years.

"I lost the baby." I continue.

"Rose, I'm so sorry." He says, placing his hand lovingly on my cheek.

"I never told anyone. Pierce didn't even believe me. But that baby was the strength that I needed to leave." I explain, becoming more emotional. Leo wraps his arms around me.

"You would've been the most amazing mom." He smiles. His tone is soft as he gently caresses my back. I appreciated his words.

"Rose, since we're confessing things, we should probably discuss..." He begins still holding me. I move away from his arms and look up at him, "the vampire thing?" I interrupt.

"Aren't you a bit scared?" He asks.

I look down and touch his face, there are still blood stains on his skin from when he fed. His features, even covered in blood, are a pure mix of human and angel.

"Can I see your face?" I ask, curious to see all of him, even the part of him I can tell he doesn't like showing- at least not to me.

He takes a minute debating his options then moves his face to the side and then looks back at me, displaying his true nature. I move my hand lightly and trace the veins that run under his now sunken eyes. He looks uncomfortable, it makes me frown that he feels ashamed.

"You're beautiful. I still feel the same butterflies I did from when I first met you." I reply- to me he is still the gorgeous Leo Lloyd I met all those weeks ago. He looks at me confused.

"Rose, this face is not beautiful, it is the face of a demon. I am a soldier of Lucifer. The devil himself picked this face." He explains, almost insulted that I would dare compliment this side of him.

"Just because the devil himself picked the face doesn't mean he picked the soul." I explain. To me, he was beautiful inside and out. I could care less about his appearance. Leo lets out a dark laugh then looks at me, his eyes still red and his fangs still poking out.

"I don't have a soul." He explains, then goes on to ask, "now do you fear me?"

I take a moment and inspect his face once more and decide that he might not have a soul, but he must have something that allows him to feel because I know he loves me and cares about me.

"No, you saved me Leo, why would I fear you? I told you before you're not a monster. You're my guardian angel." I explain, meaning every word. He gives me a small smile then morphs his face back to human.

"I think you saved me. When are we going to talk about what went on back there? That wasn't human Rose." He explains gently, trying not to freak me out. Not that he really could, at this point.

"I don't know. All I know is that I want to wash this blood off of me." I answer. I didn't want to get into all of that. Talking about that means acknowledging everything that had just happened downstairs, and I didn't have the mental strength to do that right now. It was too much.

We stay silent for a moment, before I decide to move and walk into the bathroom, he follows me in.

"What if I'm not the guardian angel you think I am?" He asks. I frown at his accusation. I look up at him and pull him closer and kiss him. It was soft and gentle. I could still taste the faintness of metal on my tongue.

"I was wrong calling you, my guardian angel." I state pulling away from the kiss. Leo looks at me confused by my words. His eyes begin to shift downwards, feeling hurt from my statement. I grab his face, making his eyes meet mine.

"You're my avenging angel; you were willing to send the devil himself back to hell."

He holds me closer.

"I love you Rose." He confesses. My heart begins to beat faster. I don't know if it's the fear of hearing those three little words or actually feeling like I can say them back and mean them for the first time. Or maybe it's the fear of being in love with a man that is basically dead, and the future is completely and utterly unknown to us. But what I do know is that I have never felt so connected to someone in my life.

"I love you, Leo." I whisper.

After the words leave my lips, he kisses me. Gently at first but then passion takes over.

He locks the door behind us, but before things get too heated, Leo's phone dings. It was a text from Elliot letting him know he was in the middle of handling everything. Apparently, Elliot was a very old and powerful witch, with the ability to make everything appear back to how it was and disappear whatever didn't belong.

Feeling a lot less stressed we decide to take the opportunity to seize the moment and not think. The mess we left behind was being handled and we were both left in the aftermath. His eyes are glued to me as I undress in front of him. He then does the same. His broad body looks absolutely magnificent in the shallow lighting as he slowly strips his pants off.

After slipping off my dress and shoes I am left in my red lingerie, and he is left in his boxers and t-shirt. Both of us are still covered in blood. I look him up and down taking in those incredibly sexy tattoos that cover his arms. I want him right now. My body craves him.

"I knew that set would look beautiful on you." He grins, before taking his t-shirt off cautiously. I watch the expression on his face, become more uneasy. I'm a bit confused by his sudden change in demeanor, until I notice his chest. I let out a small gasp seeing the scar lines going diagonally down his chest to his stomach. I walk closer to him and place my hand on his skin, the ink surrounding it trying to camouflage the very large marks left behind from God knows what. I slowly move my hand to trace it. He stays still and stiff.

"What happened?" I ask looking up at him.

"My father." Is all he says. My heart literally breaks for him. How can a parent be so cruel? Although I guess I would know. Words can be just as painful, even leaving invisible scars just as deep as any whip.

"Leo..." Before I can finish, he turns around, displaying his back. It seems his chest was just child's play compared to the cruelty displayed on his back. Scars scattered all over the place. It looked as if he had been beaten for years. These must have happened while he was still human. I gently trace the marks with my fingertips, careful not to trigger him before kissing him gently on the shoulder where a mark appeared. I feel his body relax under my lips in what I can only assume is relief. Without a word he turns around and grabs on to me before kissing me.

"I guess we both have scars." He states his thick English accent soaking through.

"I guess we do." I reply solemnly, before meeting his mouth again. I could feel all my pain drift away.

Chapter 20

ROSE

We both fell asleep that night in each other's arms in my child-hood bedroom. My mother and Charles would be back tomorrow, so Leo and I didn't have to rush back to his place. I felt safe and secure in my room with Leo by my side. Even with the events from the night before plaguing my mind with reruns. Part of me knows I should wake up, but I can't seem to do so. Something or someone is somehow keeping me in a hazy slumber. Violet eyes stare into my own, it's the man from the dream that I had when I had first returned home.

"You are strong Rose, strong enough to be a Goddess. Remember what I told you the last time we met. You need to come find me. For I will unleash the darkness that resides within you, and we will become one when you die, you and I are soul tied."

After hearing those familiar words rattle around in my brain, I force myself to wake up. I felt frazzled yet somehow aroused by the stranger and his words. Something inside of me felt drawn to him. When I notice Leo still fast asleep next to me. I stare at him for a moment realizing just how much I truly loved him.

I took a long breath and decided that now would be a good time to go for a run. I needed to think and clear my mind. I slowly make my way out from under the comforter and change into a pair of spandex shorts and a black hoodie. I grab my sneakers in the corner of the room and place them on my feet. I grab my cell phone and headphones as I quietly make my way down the stairs noticing how neat and tidy the room looks. It's as if last night's nightmare never occurred. Trying not to think about it, I walk over to the elevator.

I make my way out of the building and place my headphones in my ears blasting whatever upbeat song that pops up on my playlist first and begin to run. Everything becomes a blur as the morning crisp air wakes me up. I focus on my pace rather than everything that happened last night. I didn't want to think about whatever magic coursed through me or rather possessed me last night, or discovering that the man I love is a vampire, which means he is technically dead and that probably others exist, or the fact that I had murdered my abusive ex-boyfriend- and to top it all off, didn't feel an ounce of remorse for doing it. I'd be lying if I said I wasn't happy that he was dead, relieved even.

As I continue to run, I find myself in front of St. Patrick's Cathedral. I walk up the steps staring at the grandness of the building in front of me. I couldn't help but think that there was a chance that I would burst into flames just from walking in. Deciding to put that thought in the back of my mind, I step forward and open the door. The scent of incense brings back flashes of memories from my childhood- when my father would hold my hand and walk us to our seats to meet my mother and my two other siblings. I step further in, noticing the church is empty with only a few people spread in between the pews praying. I walk in a bit more and slide into an empty pew in the back and stare up at the crucifix. I look down feeling unsure if coming here had been the right thing to do. The darkness I felt within me would eventually surface. I could feel it. Maybe there would be nothing to redeem, I wondered.

"I can release all of that darkness Rose, if you would only come find me." An all too familiar voice whispers inside my head. His words echo as I sit perfectly still.

"I don't want to release it; I don't want it at all." I explain silently, hoping the voice can hear me.

"No, my Rose you can't deny such a gift, you have to let it consume you so that you can control it." He practically purrs, as his voice fades away. I could feel an emptiness in me that wasn't there before.

As I sit thinking about everything, our Sunday service priest approaches me.

"Rose." He smiles as he looks at me, probably reminiscing of the little girl he had once known.

"Father John." I greet, with a polite smile.

"May I?" He asks, nodding towards the empty seat next to me.

I nod my head in acceptance and move over to give him more room. He sits down and stays quiet for a moment then turns to look at me. He was an elderly man, who had warm brown eyes and white graying hair.

"It's been a while since I've seen you here, my child. What has led you back to us?" He asks, his voice kind and gentle. I don't even know how to begin to answer this seemingly simple question. How do you explain to a priest that you had slept next to a soldier of Lucifer himself and killed another?

"Darkness." Is all I can reply, not offering any more details. It isn't a complete lie per say, but instead a gloss over of the truth. Darkness is what led me here.

"You know Rose, darkness can only consume those who don't allow light in. If you choose to stay there, then it will take hold of you but if you choose to fight and let the light shine through then the darkness has no choice but to leave." He explains. What he says makes sense, but it also seems easier said than done. How am I supposed to allow something that I don't even know truly exists? It has been so long since I have felt light in my life.

"Father, do you think redemption is for everyone?" I ask quietly, scared to hear his reply. He looks at me, his eyes saddened by my question, probably wondering what prompted it.

"Yes." Is all he says trying not to pry. A bit of relief flows through me as I look from him back to the crucifix that lays ahead of me at the front of the church.

"Belief isn't for everyone, but faith is something everyone craves." He explains as he begins to get up. I take in his words as they hit me in the gut like a ton of bricks. He was right. You don't have to believe in something to have faith. A life without faith is a dark road. That's what I needed...Faith. Faith in myself that I would get through the darkness that lies ahead.

Father John gets up from the pew offering me a small grin before walking back down the aisle. Before he gets too far, I call out, "Thank you." He turns around once again offering me a kind smile as he continues forward. I stayed there for a couple more minutes contemplating life before deciding to leave.

I don't run back to my apartment, instead I walk, mulling things over in my head, trying hard to put things into perspective. By the time I get back to the apartment Leo is up. He seems nervous.

"You're back." He says making his way over to me from the living room, where he had been standing looking out over the city.

"I'm sorry for leaving this morning but I couldn't sleep." I admit as I take my hoodie off leaving me in my black sports bra. I walk over to the kitchen and grab a bottle of water out of the fridge. Leo follows behind me.

"I tried calling you, I was worried." He explains. I feel bad that I ignored his calls. I didn't even hear my phone ring. I take it out from my pocket and look at it and see I had indeed missed two of his calls. I realize my phone has been on silent.

"I'm sorry Leo. If I'm being honest, I needed time to think." I explain. He looks at me curiously, intrigued by my confession. He takes a seat on the bar stool that faces towards the opening in my kitchen and waits for me to continue.

"I decided to go on a run and ended up at the doorstep of St. Patrick's Cathedral. So, I stepped inside and ended up having an interesting, short conversation with Father John. He reminded me that you can still have faith even if your belief is shaken. And it made me realize that I shouldn't be afraid anymore. I need to have faith that this is all going to end well." I explain. I feel a sense of relief explaining this to him.

"I have faith in you, Rose." Is all he says as he gets off from the barstool and walks over to me and engulfs me in a hug.

"I have faith that you and I will be ok." He reassures me. I lean my head further into his chest and let out a sigh of relief. He is my safe haven, a force field that not even the devil himself could get through.

"I have faith too." I whisper, enjoying his hold on me. He squeezed me tighter letting me know that everything would be ok. That I would be ok.

Chapter 21

ROSE

Too many secrets have been revealed and there were still so many others that laid hidden in the shadows, waiting to be uncovered. A few days have gone by since everything had happened, and still Leo and I haven't been able to figure out how I had managed to conduct any sort of power the night Pierce was killed. A big part of this is because I can't seem to bring myself to talk about it. And Leo being who he is, doesn't push the topic either. I think he's scared that if he pushes too hard, I might break.

The better part is that in my mind it has nothing to do with my role in Pierce's death, but instead the events of everything leading up to it. My brain was still having a hard time wrapping itself around everything that had happened. I just needed more time.

Pierce is once again being considered a missing person; his parents are doing everything they can to locate him. I have to admit, I do feel some degree of sympathy for them, since they probably never knew what a monster their son was.

The only good thing to come about from all of this, was Leo's transparency about the past, revealing just how broken he was. I think it bonded us even more. We've become completely inseparable since then. However, we still haven't had sex as crazy as it may sound. Yes, we sleep in the same bed, and we kiss like crazy, but we haven't taken that next step. I think we're both a little scared, although Leo seems to be more on edge than I am when it comes to becoming more physically involved. He has kept no secrets from me, since I discovered what he truly is, a *soldier of Lucifer*.

He doesn't like to talk about it much, but I can't help myself and ask questions every chance I get. For one thing I learned that holy water is not friendly to vampires. Garlic is apparently good enough to eat; Leo absolutely loves it. Sunlight is considered manageable with Elliot's spells to protect him. Crucifixes are a myth, when it comes to harming them. Leo actually told me he used to wear one up until a few years ago. And driving a silver or wooden stake through the heart is lethal. He also shared that a vampire does possess the power to compel a human. Although, he swore to me that he had never tried to compel me.

Another fact that was surprising to learn is that Leo apparently doesn't have a heartbeat or a soul. I think out of everything he had confessed to me; those two revelations haunt my mind the most. The one I had the most trouble believing was the one about him missing his soul. I couldn't believe it was true. I can feel the stitching of both of our souls with every glance and every touch.

I have continued staying in his apartment where I've learned more about Elliot's warlock powers and just how old he really is-although he won't tell me his true age. He says that it is one of the many secrets he possesses that he'll take to the grave. Although, I think he's just too vain to reveal just how old he really is.

We've actually grown quite close since I've been here. He seems like a really good guy. I'm glad Leo has him in his life, he needs him. He's been helping me figure out where the power I wielded the night of Pierce's death came from. Always gentle when breaching the subject and never pressing too hard for unimportant details. Elliot only harps on the facts regarding the power, not the events that occurred. I've been honest with him with just about everything, except for the small detail of the man with the violet eyes. I don't know why, but I just can't seem to tell either one of them about him, it's as if my mind wants to keep him locked away for only my own thoughts to possess.

***

I arrive at Centuries and grab a booth. Elliot comes over to sit with me while I wait for Leo to pick me up. He had a meeting he needed to go to today, which I had to force him to attend. He promised he would come and get me as soon as he was done. The club is relatively quiet, as workers move about getting everything ready for opening.

"How are you doing darling?" Elliot asks, sitting across from me, with a concerned look on his face. He's been asking me this question for days, and every day I have the same response

"I'm good, Elliot. How about you?"

He gives me a tight lip smile and nods. Him and Leo are both getting fed up with my replies. I know they want me to tell them exactly what I'm thinking, but I just can't. I'm not ready to acknowledge any of it yet- not fully anyway. I can accept a lot of the supernatural craziness like Leo being a vampire, and Pierce being one too. However, human realizations seem to be a harder pill to swallow. I had to accept the fact that the villain in my story was truly dead, it's a lot for me to process and even believe. I had been running for so long and harboring all of this fear that I just needed some time. Not to mention we still didn't know who had turned Pierce and why. I'm assuming he turned a while ago and the night he snuck up on me, he was able to get into the apartment because my mother had stupidly invited him in, the first night he came to see me.

Elliot takes a sip from his scotch then looks over at me with a lazy smile and replies, "just fine, love."

We sit for a moment in complete silence just enjoying our drinks when Elliot's once relaxed body stiffens. He gets off the bench on his side of the booth and stands in front of where I'm sitting and shields me from whatever has him so unnerved. Then out of thin air I see the man from the elevator all those weeks ago. He peeks over Elliot's shoulder and flashes a wicked grin at me.

"Elliot, it's so nice to see you." He smiles; however, Elliot quickly sticks his arm out and with a gust of magic, throws the man back.

"No." Elliot speaks with a slight laugh in his response. Everyone in the club seems oblivious to the encounter, as they all stay busy, getting the club ready for the night.

The mystery man gets up and walks back over to us, ignoring Elliot's obvious want for him to leave. He takes the seat across from me that Elliot had been sitting on. Elliot then gently moves me over and sits next to me. I stay quiet and still, a bit fearful to move, as I watch the man now sitting in front of me. I can tell that whoever he is, his intentions are not good.

"Rose." He smirks, his eyes full of what I can only describe as chaos.

"Do I know you?" I ask politely. He slowly looks at Elliot and smiles wickedly. This only enrages Elliot. I can feel the anger rolling off of him as he sits there, waiting for this man to give him a reason to jump on him.

Turning back to me, with that sickening wicked grin he leans closer placing his hands on the table then says, "more than you know."

I stay quiet as I try to mull over his cryptic response while Elliot continues to stay silent. I could tell he was nervous.

"My name is Michael, and I have been searching for you for quite a long time." He smirks, his eyes studying my every feature, as I try and think of what to say next. However, my response is cut short when Elliot mutters something under his breath and Michael begins to cry out in pain as he grabs onto his head. Elliot then takes the opportunity to get up from his seat and grab Michael by the arm dragging him off the bench.

Michael continues to moan in pain, when all of a sudden Leo walks into the club. As soon as his eyes meet mine, he uses his vampire speed to run towards us, grabbing Michael out of Elliot's grasp and pinning him to the wall.

"What are you doing here?" Leo, questions him through gritted teeth, his true face coming to the surface. Elliot makes his way back over to where I am and stands in front of me, once again trying to shield me.

"I just wanted to get to know your new girlfriend, Leo." He smiles. Then without hesitation Leo swings at Michael's face, causing Michael to spit out blood from the impact.

"Oh, come on Leo, I won't sleep with this one too." He says snidely. My eyes go wide as I take in what he said, who the hell is this guy? However, before I can ponder the thought longer, Leo throws Michael to the floor. They very quickly become a blur as they beat each other with what can only be described as superhuman rage.

"Leo!" I scream, as I try to get past Elliot to stop him. However, Elliot won't let me through.

"Get her out of here!" Leo booms. Elliot immediately turns and grabs my arm. I look over at Leo as Elliot drags me away from the fight. I try to push against Elliot, trying to turn back, but as I struggle to loosen his grip, I see Michael punch Leo causing him to move his head and spit blood out from his mouth. His now red eyes flash with anger, as his eyes find me, "Get out of here!"

I quickly run up the stairs to the third floor of Elliot's club where the private rooms are. I go into one of the offices and close the door behind me, leaving Elliot outside as I begin to pace waiting for Leo to come.

As I pace up and down the dark room, I can hear yelling and items breaking. Glass shattering and bangs of what I can only assume is broken furniture being thrown around below me. Finally, after what feels like forever Leo walks through the door. His crisp white shirt now covered in blood, his once perfectly styled hair now disheveled and his eyes that looked so bright and sweet this morning turned dark and cold. He walks further into the room, closing the door behind him and stands in front of the window.

"What the hell was that about?" I demand.

"Nothing for you to worry about Rose. I apologize for screaming at you the way that I did. It was out of line. I just didn't want you to witness any of that." He explains, still looking out of the window not showing me his face. I sigh with disappointment, at his coldness. I don't understand why he still feels the need to hide things from me.

"Leo, look at me." I plead as I place my hand on his shoulder. He ignores my request then speaks, "Michael and I have known each other for over two hundred years. He is much older than I am and much stronger." Leo states then goes silent for a moment before he turns around to face me.

"Michael is evil incarnate. We have a long and complicated history and well let's just say that we both have a deep seeded hatred for one another."

"Why?" I question my curiosity taking over.

"Why do most men fight...a woman." Leo states. I can tell this is a painful topic for him to talk about. He looks ashamed and hurt. My heart nearly breaks in half just by seeing his reaction to his own words.

"Her name was Marie." He whispers. I look at him, trying to remember where I had heard that name before. Then it clicks, that day by the elevator when I first encountered Michael. Why would he think I look like her? That's a bit odd unless Leo has a very specific type. My mind races as my paranoia takes over. The twisted ugly feeling of jealousy takes over.

"Do I remind you of her?" I ask examining his reaction. He looks up at me and his expression looks horrified like he has just seen a ghost. However, he tries to mask it with confusion and deflect my question by asking his own, "Why would you ask me that?"

"Because Michael seems to think we look alike." I state looking to see if he'd bite. I could feel him holding back something, something big.

"You are nothing like her." He states almost trying to reassure himself.

"Leo, what the hell is going on? If you don't start explaining I'm walking out that door and leaving." I threaten. I want answers and I want them now. And I don't like the feeling of not being able to trust him. He's making me question too many things.

Leo looks up at me with a scowl on his face. He didn't like that I threatened him, but it is a necessary evil in this situation. I can see his brain turning, trying to gather the words he so desperately wants to keep to himself. Finally, he walks over to the bed in this very dark room. Which makes me realize, Elliot put me in one of his "private rooms." I have no intention of sitting on it, knowing the nefarious things that have happened on it. I guess Leo doesn't share the same disgust. He sits on the edge and motions for me to sit next to him. I hesitantly do as I'm instructed.

"Marie, was the first woman I ever fell in love with as a human." He begins. These words hit my chest like a bullet, I wasn't expecting his full transparency on the matter. I start thinking that maybe knowing this secret isn't such a good idea. I needed to know, even if what he tells me is painful to hear.

"I had just come back from war and had started working in the court of France. My father was basically the right-hand of the king during that time and he was trying to train me to take over when he died. I never had any interest in politics, so any chance permitted I would sneak away and walk the grounds. I loved the solitude of just being able to walk the gardens or halls alone until I saw her. She had just arrived in France and from the moment I saw her I was infatuated. It wasn't until later that I understood why. Everything about what I am...what she was is alluring. Our condition allows us to pull you in, enthrall you with our presence and crave us. And Marie knew exactly how to pull me in. I was *human*, everything I felt was more, desperate and severe. At the time she was the most beautiful and eloquent woman I had ever met. However, looks can be deceiving." He explains, looking at me as if telling me to keep this in mind.

"You see, I didn't know it at the time, but Marie had been involved in a very long relationship with Michael whom you just met. She was the very definition of deception. She would lie if it meant she would get her way- especially when it came to me and Michael. She had us all fooled. However, I must admit that when it came to finding this out, I was the last to know. The night she turned me; it was nothing more than a mere game between her and Michael. She cared nothing for me, and I ended up paying the price with my soul." He states coldly. I can tell he is trying to hide the pain and the betrayal hidden behind his forest green eyes. I remain quiet, careful not to interrupt his train of thought.

"It might have started off as a simple game, but I know, Marie was truly starting to fall in love with me. What I didn't know was that our connection would bring on her demise. Michael played the biggest role."

"What happened to her?" I ask.

"Our order came and took her." He explains.

"Your order?" I ask.

"There is a lot of politics that comes with being a vampire, let's just say Marie pissed off the wrong people." He explains vaguely and a bit rushed, as if he didn't want me to focus too hard on his explanation. I brushed it off, curious to know how he had survived.

"What happened to you?"

He shows a small smile as he reminisces, "Elliot found me."

I desperately want to press him for more answers, but I know I shouldn't. I know he's holding back. I can feel there is more to the story than what he is letting on. However, for now I will let it go. I can see the deception in his eyes. And I can't help but think that whatever he isn't sharing will somehow break us in the end.

Chapter 22

ROSE

Ever since I have stepped into the world of the supernatural, I have learned that it can be just as complicated as the normal world. It feels like everything around me has changed and I'm still trying to figure my way through it. Days have passed since Michael came barreling into our lives, causing a shift in me and Leo's once perfect bubble. Unfortunately, that bubble had been deflated. Leo has decided to keep me at arm's length since the discussion about Marie had occurred. I can't lie and say the shift in his demeanor wasn't painful, but I pushed past it and kept acting as if nothing was wrong. It was just easier to silently pray that this would eventually pass, as I hoped things would go back to normal. It was easier than to ask questions that I felt I wasn't ready to know the answers to. Besides, I know for a fact that Leo finds the past difficult to discuss with me. I could understand his need for more time, since I could also use a little extra time to process things as well.

This new understanding and revelation prompted me to go back home and stay at my mother's apartment until things settled and we had both worked through our thoughts. Going home would also give me the opportunity to work through some of my own issues as well. I've always worked out my problems alone. I just functioned better that way. I guess it was a defense mechanism since the thought of exposing any of my issues to anyone around me seemed more severe than the issues at hand.

I feel a bit guilty leaving without giving him any warning, but I know that if I tell him, he will persuade me to stay. He gets this look in his eyes when he wants something and I'm too self-aware enough to know that I'm not strong enough to deny, especially when it comes to him.

However, my guilt seems to fizzle out a bit when I remember his cold goodbye this morning, when he left for work and left me in bed without even so much as a kiss. And that is very un-Leo like of him. I mean sure we haven't taken the relationship to the next level in terms of sex, but Leo loves to kiss and hold me. These days however, he has kept his distance so much so, that I just can't stomach it anymore. His distance feels almost suffocating. So, when he is officially gone, I take a shower, to try and procrastinate what I know I need to do and then once that doesn't work, I get dressed, pack my things and leave.

When I arrive home the house is empty as expected. My mother had mentioned that she and Charles were going away for the week for their anniversary. I have no complaints, since it gives me the perfect environment to stew in my own thoughts and feelings. Although I will say that my home no longer looks the same. Now I just see flashes of demons, blood, and pain.

Just one more thing to stew over and hyper fixate on- especially since I've been trying to exorcise those memories from my mind.

After taking a couple of deep breaths and grasping onto whatever strength I still had left inside of me, I walk into my apartment and make my way over to my bedroom. Without even hesitating, I close my door and drop my bags to the floor. Then immediately kick off my heels and throw myself onto my bed - which I've missed more than anything. The feeling of just lying in the room that has given me so much comfort over the years is soothing. I shift on my bed so that I'm looking up at my white ceiling as I allow my mind to finally digest everything that had happened. But the only thing I can think of is, what the hell am I doing?

After I begin to break everything down, the only conclusion that I'm left with is that I'm insane. I mean for the love of God; I'm in a relationship with a vampire! A vampire who is holding some kind of dark secret that could probably get me killed. Yet, I've allowed myself to love him, literally giving him my bleeding, beating heart. I've gifted him my trust in the hopes that it won't backfire. And as if that wasn't enough, I murdered my ex-boyfriend to not just save myself but to save him too. I had played God, or rather some entity had allowed me to play God, and I had managed to defeat the monster. The fear had somehow subsided, but I could still feel the sting of the pain of everything that had happened. Sometimes I think it'll never go away- scars don't go away so easily.

As my thoughts become heavier, my mind begins to quiet as my eyes slowly start to close and sleep takes over. My body and mind finally gave in to the fact that I was drained.

The space around me is black, which makes it hard for me to see, until I notice the glow of fire that appears. It came from a torch cemented onto the wall. It illuminated the dark space around me. As my eyes try to adjust, allowing me to see where I am. It looks like I'm in a cave of some sort, but there's no entrance or exit, just darkness. As my eyes continue to scan the space around me, my body stiffens, and my breathing quickens. I was not alone. Someone or rather something was here with me.

"Rose, my beautiful doll." A deep, familiar voice echoes through the empty space. The voice is all too familiar and alluring. I spin around, trying to see his face, but the more I look, the faster the glow from the fire dies out.

"Who are you?" I ask, deciding to stop moving and allow him to come to me. I couldn't explain it, but I could feel I wasn't in danger. There was an unsettling energy that surrounded us, but not a dangerous one.

He didn't reply, which made me want to say something else, but just as the words are about to leave my lips, the fire goes out completely and a gust of wind hits my back. I scream when I feel a cold hand on my shoulder. Every single nerve in me is telling me not to turn around, but I can't help it. I turn around as my eyes open, I can see the mystery man, his violet eyes hold me captive.

"I miss you doll. Come find me, for I will unleash the darkness that resides within you, and we will become one when you die, you and I are soul tied."

"I don't understand. Please, who are you?" I ask.

"Your God." He states, then pulls me closer in towards him. It felt as if he was getting ready to kiss me but before he could, my eyes shot open and I'm back in my room.

My heart is practically beating outside of my chest as I look around frantically, trying to gain a grasp on my reality. The mark on my shoulder burns but quickly dissipates as I take a couple of deep breaths trying to calm myself down.

As I try to settle myself my phone rings. I quickly grab it out of my back pocket in case it was Leo and internally cringing at the thought. However, I take in a breath of relief when I notice it's Adeline.

"Hey." I answer, although my voice comes out shakier than I would have wanted it too.

"Hey, I was just calling to see how you were doing, we haven't spoken in a bit. Are you ok Rose?" She asks, her concern evident through the phone.

"Yeah, I'm fine. Just had a weird dream, that's all." I explain as I sit up and cross my legs as I try to get more comfortable.

"Oh ok, I was wondering if you wanted to meet up and maybe grab dinner tonight, like old times. I miss you."

"I miss you too, but I just got back home from Leos and I'm trying to lay low. Some things came up and I just need to deal with them tonight. But, if you want, maybe we can have dinner this coming Friday?" I suggest, feeling guilty for not accepting her invite, but knowing that I was in no shape to interact with anyone tonight, not even Adeline. She's silent for a moment on the other end as if analyzing my words.

"What happened?" She asks.

"Nothing major, just some small drama that came up." I try to reason, even though I know she isn't going to drop it.

"Rose, come on, you can tell me anything...did Leo do something?" She asks, her tone now more concerned and borderline anxious.

"No, well not exactly. It's just that Leo has been pushing me away these past couple of days and I don't know why. I feel like I'm in this weird place with him and I don't know if I'm really what he wants or a placeholder for someone else." I say speaking the words I had been struggling with the last couple of days, unable to accept that it could be a real possibility.

I can hear Adeline take in a breath on the other end of the phone as she thinks through what I revealed to her. And in true Adeline fashion, before I even hear her voice, I can feel the optimism though the screen of my phone.

"Rose, that can't be true. Leo loves you; I mean just the way he looks at you, you can tell. It's borderline creepy at times, it's like he wants to devour you."

I can't help but let out a small laugh from her choice of words. He probably does want to devour me, what he doesn't know is he already has. He has devoured my soul and my heart; they are fully his. He's always telling me that he doesn't have a heartbeat. However, I know it's not true because my heart beats enough for the both of us.

"I don't know Adeline. I mean I want to believe that he does but after everything that's happened in the past with guys, I just have so many trust issues with them- including Leo. I mean when I'm with him I try and bury them and it's easy because I'm so blinded by my want for him that it's manageable. However, once the blindness disappears it is replaced with doubt because now, he's hiding something, and I can't help but feel all these trust issues and insecurities rush to the surface." I try to explain.

"Rose, why don't you talk to him? Don't do the thing you always do when things take a turn for the worst, which is to run or hide from your problems. I can only assume that what you went through with Pierce was awful and very traumatic, but Rose, Leo is not Pierce, and you know that. Don't let that be an excuse for you to run from something that can be amazing. Don't let Pierce take this happiness away."

I understand what she is trying to say. I do have a tendency to run and hide from most of my problems. I mean that's the reason I got into drinking, sex, drugs, partying and when all of that failed me- suicide. I never dealt with any of my issues, hence the need to run and hide. But not this time, I've decided that I should march back over to his apartment and fight for what I want, which in this case is us.

I stand up from where I'm sitting and begin to put my heels on, "You're right, I'm going to go over to Leo's apartment and talk to him. I'm not going to run this time, because for the first time in my life I actually feel something for this person, I feel real love." I state as I grab my bags and keys to leave.

"That's what I like to hear. Now Rose, I expect details at our next girl's night." She demands, which only causes me to smile.

"I promise, you'll get every juicy detail. I'll call you tomorrow." I explain, as I make my way out of my room and down the stairs. We finally say our goodbyes and I get into the elevator. As I ride the elevator down, I notice I have six missed calls on my phone from Leo. I decide not to call him back since the last thing I want is to lose my newfound confidence by hearing his voice on the phone.

****

When I arrive at Leo's, I ride the elevator up nervously. As the elevator doors open Leo appears practically out of thin air and corners me. He's wearing gray slacks and a white dress shirt. The top three buttons are unbuttoned, and the sleeves are rolled up. He looks a bit disheveled, if I'm being honest. He is still wearing his suspenders which I find oddly adorable and sexy. It's a rare thing to see a man wear those these days. Leo's wardrobe could sometimes be a bit old fashioned yet sexy as hell.

"What the bloody hell Rose!" He barks harshly, walking closer towards me. He's angry that I had disappeared.

"We need to talk." I state flatly, ignoring the intensity of anger in his eyes. I don't want to lose my confidence, so I push past him and walk into the living room. Leo follows close behind, his arms crossed, as he narrows his gaze on me.

"I'm not happy. You're pushing me away and I want to know why... No scratch that I demand to know why, because I think after everything, we've been through I deserve an answer." I say firmly holding eye contact with those bright green eyes. He takes a breath then shakes his head trying to word his next statement carefully, as he uncrosses his arms and runs a stressed hand through his hair.

"Look, I'm sorry, I just think that *this*, what we're doing is wrong, Rose." He confesses. I feel a sharp pain hit my chest. He's going to break up with me. I can't help the anger that is unleashed as I see the uncertainty in his eyes. If I can't run neither, can he.

"Why? Is this about Marie? Are you still in love with her?" I question, as I try to remain calm, although my anger can't help but seep through as I practically spit the accusation at him.

"No. I just think this is wrong. I mean for fuck's sake Rose I don't even have a heartbeat. I kill humans with no remorse. I am a demon and then here you come along and make me feel something... for a *human*." He explains his anger pooling in his eyes, as he tries to push me away. He makes a bold choice by putting emphasis on the word human as if it's blasphemy to love me.

"No, you don't get to throw these facts in my face. We've been through this. I don't care. And maybe that makes me a bad person, but I don't care. I love you, Leo. I don't care what you did in the past. I don't care what you do now, all I care about is you and that you love me. And ok, you don't have a heartbeat. Who cares my heart beats enough for the both of us because I'm in love with you." I ramble, not able to control the words as they fly out of my mouth.

"You don't even know the things I've done. My heinous acts of self-pleasure. My love for the kill, my excitement at the sight of seeing the life drain from the lives I've taken." He confesses, his voice steady, although his eyes are wild. I'll admit his candor knocks me off balance a bit, but I'd be lying if I said I cared at this moment.

He looks down and sighs, "I'm not worthy of your love Rose. Not after every sin I've committed."

I can see the pain flash in his eyes from confessing all of his inner thoughts to me, but I ignore it. Red flags are probably flashing all around me but when it comes to Leo, I can't see clearly. I only see him.

"Leo, do you love me?" I ask, in a desperate attempt to try and prove my point.

"Yes."

"Then what's the problem? The way I see it, is that I love you and you love me. If you wish to bring in the point of either one of us deserving the other, then maybe we are both doomed. Because I haven't been a saint either, but when I'm with you all of that pain and darkness goes away. So why can't that be enough! Why can't we be enough?" I ask.

"Rose there's so much more, so much you don't know." He tries to clarify but I cut him off.

"I understand that. I don't know all the facts Leo but why can't we just relinquish the past if only just for tonight? I'm in love with the man that you are now. Let's just leave the past in the past and focus on the present."

He looks at me contemplatively, like he's dying to give in but won't allow himself to let go, so I make the first move and kiss him. At this moment the only thing I cared about was him. I wanted him, all of him.

His lips press hard against mine as I run my fingers through his hair. Soft moans escape my lips, as his hands explore my burning skin. Every inch of me is on fire from just his touch. I eagerly move my hands down to his pants, so that I can begin to remove the barrier that separated us, but he detaches himself from my lips. I can't help but whimper from the loss of contact, his eyes look into mine as his true face appears. I try catching my breath. Leo slides down to the floor, anger and defeat plaguing him.

"We can't." He states. I walk over to him and place my hand on his cheek. His vampire face fully displayed. I kneel to the floor in front of him so that he can see how unaffected I am.

"I don't care, Leo."

He looks away ashamed and my heart breaks from his lack of confidence in my ability to see what he truly is, which is beautiful, because at the end of the day it's his soul that shines through. I place my hand on his chin and position his face towards me and kiss it.

"I can't control myself when it comes to you." He explains. I want to give him anything and everything that he desires. I press my lips to his cheek then to the veins that trickle out from under his more sunken eyes. Then finally to his lips, he kisses back slowly and cautiously.

"I trust you." I state moving myself back as I trace his lips with my finger. He looks down at me then reconnects our lips. Our kiss becomes heated and passionate. I move myself onto his lap as he holds me with his big hands firmly planted on me, palming my ass through my jeans.

I moan into his mouth from the pulsating feeling coming from between my thighs, placed there from just his touch. He manages to get up from the floor with ease as he still maintains contact with my lips. My heels slip off as we make our way upstairs trying not to have sex in the living room where Elliot can walk in on us at any moment.

Once upstairs, Leo kicks the door in with his foot and walks further inside his bedroom and throws me on his mattress. His growing bulge shows me he wants me just as much as I want him. I can't help but lick my lips at the sight. I want him more than anything. I want to feel his hands ravage me. I want his lips to mark me as his. And lastly, I want to feel him inside me knowing it's the closest we'll ever be. I want him to completely devour me.

He looks at me as I lay on my back. I lean up using my elbows to see his eyes fill with lust and hunger. He looks angelic even with his vampire face. He walks closer, never losing eye contact. Then with one swift motion he rips my jeans off. He leans over me as I lay flat on the bed, breathing me in. He takes off his suspenders that now hang low on his waist. It was incredibly sexy to see. I move my hands towards his zipper and finish what I had started and begin moving his pants down.

"Your beautiful Rose. Your light is bewitching." He whispers taking in my appearance. I can feel my cheeks heat up with embarrassment and my toes curl with excitement. He helps me take my shirt off then tosses it somewhere in the room. When he looks back to me, his eyes connect with mine, as he moves his hand to my hair and touches it.

"Beautiful." He whispers, then begins trailing warm kisses down my neck.

"Leo." I moan. I pull him closer by tugging slightly on his hair.

He keeps moving down grasping my covered breasts with his large hands and massages them. His white shirt is still on. He continues to suck and kiss my neck, feverishly. I move my hands to unbutton his shirt as he focuses on me. He must have grown impatient from my struggle with the never-ending number of buttons, because in one swift motion he rips it open and throws it across the room. I take in the large scars that cover his skin along with the mirage of tattoos that try to cover them. I gently trace a few as Leo stays perfectly still.

As I lower my finger further down his stomach, he gently grabs my hand and places a loving kiss. No words had to be exchanged because we both knew that we no longer had to hide from one another.

Now that we were both basically bare now. Exposed to one another. Leo wastes no time as he rips my bra and thong off in a desperate attempt to remove the last materials between us.

"You're absolutely stunning, my love. I want to worship you." He pants. He trails his kisses down the valley of my breasts.

"Leo," I breathe, as I run my fingers through his hair, tugging ever so gently. He only smirks and continues to kiss my flesh working his way down my body until his lips meet my sex. He places a soft kiss to my skin and glances up at me through those gorgeous lashes of his, then continues to use his lips and tongue to serve me. I moan and writhe beneath him. He holds me down in place with his large hands as he continues his movements. He's merciless and greedy with his hunger for me, I'm a moaning mess and can't stop screaming his name as he explores further and further. He laps his tongue on my bundle of nerves before lightly nipping at the sensitive skin. Then like the demon he says he is before I come undone, he stops and continues trailing kisses on my inner thigh. His hands run up and down my bare skin teasing me with the promise of more.

"Please." I beg. He looks up from his new position, between my legs and smirks. That sight alone was almost enough to send me over the edge he had me on.

"Your wish is my command, love." Then without any warning he pushes two of his large fingers inside me and pumps them in and out mercilessly, using my already wet entrance as his invitation to continue. I can barely see from the amount of pleasure.

"Did I make you this wet, Rose?" He questions, after he removes his fingers and licks the evidence of my desire for him. My eyes go wide as I nod my head vigorously, unable to reply verbally.

Unsatisfied with just my gesture, he pushes back inside me and quickens his pace, then moves his head down back to my sex and licks my entrance before biting down a bit more harshly on my clit.

"Leo." I scream. He looks up at me with such hunger, that I can't help but moan just from the sight, as I throw my head back and allow myself to revel in the feeling of his fingers.

"That wasn't an answer, love." He growls, as he lowers his head back down and devours me. The pleasure is blinding.

"Yes Leo, yes." I chant as I allow the intense pleasure to roll through me. God, if his fangs are deadly then his tongue is absolutely lethal.

"I'm the only man that can make you feel this good." He practically growls as he teasingly toys with my clit. "Isn't that right my love?"

"Yes, Leo." I pant, growing more and more impatient.

Feeling satisfied from my ego boost, he moves his tongue up my thigh and licks my skin. He playfully bites me, causing a surge of excitement to run through my system. My curiosity of what his fangs must feel like surprises me.

He looks up from the opening of my thighs and gives me a devious smile as he curls his fingers one last time causing me to release. As I try to catch my breath, Leo gets off the bed and takes off the last article of clothing, his black Tom Ford Boxers. My eyes go a bit wide when I see all of Leo's fully grown erection. It is quite the sight. His shaft is large and perfect. The tip of his perfectly thick head is glistening with precum, practically begging my tongue to have a taste. He is fully ready, and so am I.

It has been a very long time since I have let a man touch me in such an intimate manner. In all actuality I don't think I have ever actually slept with someone who has made the experience feel this intimate.

I readjust myself on the bed as I try and catch my breath as he crawls on top of me. Holding his large frame up on his forearms, his muscles and tattoos glistening from a light coat of sweat. He places his hands in mine and kisses my cheek sweetly, he then kisses my neck and for a moment I think he might bite me but, no.

"I love you Rose. Never in my life have I fallen so deeply in love with another." He confesses then kisses my jaw and then my cheek, before he moves down and kisses the corner of my mouth until finally, he reaches my lips. His kiss is soft yet greedy. His tongue inserts itself as it dances with my own. He reluctantly pulls away from me. Making me realize that I just wanted to feel his lips pressed against mine- forever.

"Rose, are you sure you're ready?" He asks, his eyes staring at me attempting to read my expression, to make sure I'm truly ready to take this next step with him.

"Yes, Leo, I'm ready. I'm fully ready to give myself to you. I love you Mr. Lloyd." I confess. He lets a sweet smile appear on his beautiful angelic face before he lets his smile turn to a smirk.

He slowly rubs my cheek with his hand, as he slowly makes his way inside of me. I gasp from the feeling of him entering me, his large size stretching me to fit him perfectly. His eyes never leave mine wanting to see my reaction to every thrust. Our bodies move in perfect synchronicity. He peppers kisses down my neck, then when he finally gets to my shoulder he pulls away and looks at me,

"I'm going to try something." He states although it sounds more like a question than an actual statement. I nod my head, a part of me curious and a part of me nervous to see what he does next. After a second of him debating what it is he wants to do, he thrusts inside of me and bites down on my shoulder both feelings practically sending me over the edge. I scream once again a mixture of pure pleasure and ecstasy. He sucks on my flesh draining me but fueling my want for him. I wrap my arms around his neck as I hold him in place, relishing the feeling. I feel my blood drip down my skin as he continues to drink and thrust into me. My fingers run down his neck, until finally he detaches himself, trying not to drain me completely. Then he kisses me, I can taste my own blood in his mouth as he pours all of his love and need for me into this beautiful kiss.

"You're everything to me." He whispers, my blood staining his once perfect skin.

He thrusts into me a couple more times, before we both climax together. My fingers run down his back as I hold onto him. He keeps his lips pressed to mine as we let our bodies truly become one.

"You're my happily ever after." I whisper, once he removes his lips, allowing me to catch my breath. He moves his forehead, so it leans against mine as he takes me in.

"If I have it my way, you'll be my happily forever...no after." He whispers. I smile at his sentiment, then kiss him gently. I never knew the beauty there was behind loving someone this deeply.

He soon rolls over and lays on his back, giving me a moment to compose myself.

"I love you." I say in between breaths as I try to regulate it. He looks over at me and traces the marks he left on my shoulder.

"I love you." He reciprocates and moves closer, wrapping his large frame around me.

"I'm sorry if I hurt you, I just thought you might want to know what it's really like being with me... as a vampire." He explains. I smile at him knowing he is finally realizing I take him for all that he is.

"It was amazing. I can't even explain the feeling, it was euphoric." I ramble, still riding the high of pleasure he had just given me. I can sense the smirk on his lips as he holds me closer.

"I'm sorry for pushing you away, it wasn't my intent, it's just that I got nervous." He confesses.

"It's ok, just please don't do that again. All you need to do is talk to me." I turn over in his grip and place a kiss on his chest as his arms tighten around me. I'm in heaven. I should have never doubted his intentions when it comes to us. However, there is still a part of me that knows my heart could still end up hurt if the relationship went south, but he was worth the risk.

The moon shines perfectly on us as we lay here basking in one another's company. For the first time in my life, I feel undoubtedly loved. I see a small smile spread on Leo's face as I lightly trace the marks that cover his chest. I frown thinking that someone could do such a thing to such a beautiful man.

"If you're a vampire, why do you still have scars?" I ask as I gently trace the white lines that run from his chest to his stomach.

"Holy water." He states with no emotion evident in his voice. He avoids eye contact with me as he speaks. I'd be lying if I said I wasn't confused by his response. He must have understood since he then begins to explain, "He used to dip the flog in holy water. Therefore, since these marks were made with it, not even vampire healing will make them go away."

I feel a throbbing pain in my chest as I hear him explain. It must be horrible having to walk around for eternity with marks reminding you of such a terrible time in your life, never being able to rid your mind of those memories.

"I'm sorry Leo." I begin but am cut short when he gently grabs my hand and says, "let's switch the topic."

I understand, so I go to the most obvious thing that we can speak about, his tattoos. I find them fascinating as I inspect them further to see all the small intricate details that surround them. Leo lets out a low chuckle.

"Why do you have all these tattoos?" I ask mindlessly as I move my finger from the large white lines to the ink that covers parts of his body. He takes a breath then looks at me with a lifted brow. Maybe I should have picked a different topic I think to myself.

"You know when you live as long as I do, sooner or later you just stop feeling. Your human emotions dissipate, and you succumb to the demon especially when your emotions mostly consist of anger and grief. After a while I stopped feeling...the tattoos make me feel human. I like the pain that comes with it." He explains, then gently lifts my chin so my eyes can meet his.

"Until I met you. You have made me feel things I haven't felt in a really long time. You've made me feel human again."

I smile listening to his words. I love that I am able to make him feel something other than sorrow. As his eyes stay locked onto mine, I feel my heart pound against my chest. Leo takes this moment as an opportunity to place his large cold hand right over my heart, and closes his eyes, as if focusing.

I can't help but feel a bit of fear in the back of my mind. Not because of his words, not because he is a vampire but because of how he makes me feel. I'm terrified that one day this feeling will be ripped away from me. I can't imagine my life without him anymore. After a few long seconds he notices my silence and looks over at me. His face, perfectly lit by the moonlight. I know he can feel my anxiety rising.

"Rose, are you alright?" He asks, his face riddled with concern. I stay silent. I'm not sure how to express to him what is troubling me. I don't want to sound stupid and insecure.

"Nothing's wrong, I'm just nervous." I confess. I'm nervous that the faster I fall for him, the harder it will be to outrun these feelings of fear.

"What makes you nervous? Is it because of what we just did?" He asks, looking guilty like he had done something wrong. The last thing I wanted was for him to feel or think that I regretted my decision to give myself to him because I don't.

"No not at all, however, it does make me nervous to know just how much I liked you biting me." I laugh lightly. I mean, it felt wrong to like it. It wasn't a human thing to do, yet it felt so amazing. Leo lets out a small chuckle and looks at me.

"Darling, what happens in this bed is between you and I. So, if that's what you like, then it will be my pleasure to serve you." He smirks, allowing his fangs to emerge.

I giggle and nuzzle my head in his chest from slight embarrassment. I can feel the laughter erupt from his chest as he wraps his arms around me.

"Love is a funny thing." I mutter into his chest as he lets another laugh escape his beautiful lips.

"Why is that?" He asks, still holding on to me, although now he is perfectly still as he waits for me to further explain. I slightly pull myself away from his embrace so that I can look at him while I explain.

"Because I was on the run from an actual monster and then you, who claims to be a monster, is the person I'm running to." I state barely above a whisper. He lets a small smile show, breaking away from the super serious look he was sporting before. I can't help but laugh internally at the thought of him always being so serious.

I then continue on by saying, "I'm nervous that what we have is going to be ripped away from me." I whisper.

"Promise me this is forever...Your forever." I say, internally begging for him to commit to this. I know making him promise isn't some magical contract that makes this relationship invincible, but it would make me feel better. Leo is a man of his word. It will mean something to him.

He looks over at me and smiles, as he moves closer then gently places his hand on my cheek, caressing my skin. I wonder if it feels weird to him to feel the warmth coursing through my body.

As his eyes lock with mine, he takes a moment to take in my features before kissing my forehead. I close my eyes and let myself relish in the feeling of this sweet moment. He pulls away too soon and places his pinky out gesturing a pinky promise. I can't help but let out a small laugh as I look from his pinky to him. A big smile takes hold of my face as I wrap my pinky around his and let him speak.

"I promise you, my love. This is forever, you will be *my forever*."

Chapter 23

MANDEE

The smell of burning sage attacks my nose, as I sit across from my favorite aunt, Mariana- Mari for short. Her big brown eyes look even larger with the thick black rimmed glasses she wears as she looks over at me. She goes on and on about everything that she has been up to these past couple of weeks. I feel slightly guilty as I realize how much time has passed since I had been able to come up here and visit her. She always makes the most amazing tea and dishes the most salacious pieces of gossip. Sadly, I haven't been able to see her in a while, since my parents have been driving me crazy about getting an internship at the district attorney's office, hoping it will somehow convince me that law school is indeed for me. I absolutely adore my parents and respect them both, immensely. However, just because my father is a senator and I am his only child, does not mean that I want to follow directly in his footsteps. I have dreams of my own, and passions that I would like to pursue that don't involve verdicts and motions, and whatever else the job entails. That's why I love coming over here to Auntie Mari's house. She is the only one that understands my love of art, since she herself shares the same interest for it. It's our own little secret.

As my aunt continues to tell me all about her gardening and the art class that she teaches at her own local studio, I can't help but notice how different she looks- weaker and more fragile than usual. I decide not to say anything and just sit and smile, listening as she gushes about her life. I always admired her for being content with the little things she holds so dear. She and my mother are sisters but are complete opposites. My aunt Mari is more of a free spirit, laid back and carefree unlike my mother who is a complete control freak and is way too up tight.

My aunt has remained unmarried and pretty much a wild child her entire life. She is a local artist here in Connecticut and has used her earnings to travel the world. She has never stayed in one place for too long until recently. In terms of being tied down, she has dated many men throughout the years but swears that men will age you and therefore discards them when she feels the wrinkles coming on. She likes to say life is too short to be stressed by someone who is only good for one thing and one thing only. Not to mention the idea of someone being tied to you for life is suffocating. And as much as she swears up and down that those are the exact reasons for her lack of a husband, I simply think that she's just never been lucky enough to fall in love.

"Mandee, I need to tell you something." She states abruptly. I look directly at her as she snaps me out of my thoughts. Her face that holds so much youth even though she is well into her fifties is serious. And her usual warm inviting eyes hold a look of uneasiness, which makes me even more nervous.

"Look I know your mother doesn't like you visiting me, but I had to see you and as much as I enjoy our catching up, I have something rather important to discuss with you. You see I'm dying." She explains, her voice unwavering as she states the last part. I gasp. Surely, I misheard her, there was no way that she was dying.

"What? What's wrong?" I ask, panicked, as I look to her for answers. She leaned back on her floral fabric couch that seemed older than her Victorian home and let out what sounds like a defeated sigh.

"I have cancer, but I need you to listen. There's something you need to know, something your mother will never tell you because she refuses to acknowledge it herself, but something is coming Amanda, and you need to be ready." She states, determination fills her eyes. I can't help the look of pure confusion that takes over my face. I mean what do I have to be ready for besides law school applications and LSAT's. Maybe it is the medication she is taking for the cancer? As much as I want to voice my question, I remain silent, so she knows that I am listening.

"Our family, Mandee, descends from a long line of gypsies. Our blood, however, belongs to a very special clan that permits us to carry magic within our veins."

It is probably wrong to laugh while a dying woman is telling you something she believes to be true. However, the idea that my mother is a gypsy and possesses magic is too much. There is no way she could be a gypsy, let alone a magical one. Besides, even if we did descend from a lineage of gypsies, what makes our 'clan' so special that we get to carry magic in our veins?

"Laugh now but it's not a joke Amanda." She states sternly using my full name.

"Auntie, gypsies seriously?" I question.

"Yes, our ancestors date back to the first clan of Romani Gypsies; however, a small sector broke away from them and traded in their mundane lives for great power. We became the most powerful of any clan. Our sector became one of the three leaders to a very large and influential group of powerful gypsies. Our sole purpose was to become the watchers of the children of the night. That included the soldiers of Lucifer and all the creatures that were part of Lucifer's mission." She explains. What the hell does that even mean?

"Vampires and witches, supernatural entities." She clarifies, reading the confusion on my face from her absurd explanation. She can't honestly expect me to believe anything she is saying. I mean, she's including not only supernatural creatures but the devil. This definitely has to be the medication talking. There is no such thing as magic or vampires. Those types of things belong strictly in fiction, like romance novels or scary thriller movies. And the last time I checked we were Roman Catholic; we did not worship or serve the devil. As is, when she mentions Lucifer again, I fight the urge to make the sign of the cross.

"I know it sounds weird Amanda but listen to me, something is coming and the power that our ancestors cultivated through the years resides in you. It has been with you since you were a little girl. You are the only one who can stop the darkness from coming. You have the gift of Hellfire in your blood." She says then breaks out into a fit of coughing. I'm quick to my feet as I rush to the kitchen and grab her a glass of water, my hands shaking as I bring it over to her.

"Auntie this can't be true I mean these things simply just do not exist. I'm just a girl from the Upper East Side, who is trying to get an internship with the attorney general this spring and finally get my life together to make my parents proud. I don't have time to be taking on dark forces. Besides, what the hell is Hellfire?" I ramble.

"No, my dear you are more than that and you will have to make time Amanda. You will come to see that soon enough. One of our own is in great danger and they need you." She urges. I let the words sink in and try not to take it so seriously. This all has to be some side effect from whatever drug she is taking.

"And Hellfire is the gift you were given from our ancestors, only one in every generation gets the power to wield the fire." She further explains, only causing more confusion. We sit there for the rest of the day talking about the past. And as much as I want to say that this is all hocus pocus, a small part of me believes it to be true.

Before I leave, she goes into her bedroom and brings me a necklace with a stone attached to it, it's an Aventurine ruby. Which she explains is a stone that will keep my mind in check and encourage my powers. I smile and give her a hug before thanking her.

"When you awaken Amanda, you won't be able to fight it. Embrace your destiny and burn those who wish to take it from you." And with those parting words, that were borderline disturbing yet encouraging she embraces me in her arms and makes me promise not to tell my mother anything that has been spoken here today. I reassure her that I wouldn't, knowing that if I did, my mother would probably institutionalize me in a mental institution.

I make my way to my convertible and drive back to New York. The drive back feels different. I feel different, like I have this new sense of purpose in my life which doesn't make any sense. I can't fully understand it, and I plan not to think too much about it once I'm back home. After all, none of what she told me could be true. At best it's a family legend, but nothing more.

Once back to the craziness of New York City, I meet up with Jason at his apartment and instantly pull him in for a hug. I let his familiar embrace calm me.

"Are you ok, babe?" He asks, as he pulls back and looks at me with those big brown eyes of his. His brown hair was a bit messy, giving him that boyish charm I loved so much as he looked down at me from his six-foot position.

"I'm fine." I lie, as I once again pull him towards me before letting out a calming breath before deciding to go out to dinner.

I feel like I hardly ever get to see Jason these days since he's always working. I'd even go as far to say he's become obsessed. I try not to hold it against him but now that school is done, I thought I'd have a bit more time with him. However, it seems I'm still stuck sharing him with his other love...work.

As we drive over to the restaurant, he tells me how much he's missed me and how he is looking forward to having a nice night out. He promises to spend more time with me and less with work. I just go along with everything he says even though I know deep down that's a bullshit promise.

We end up going to this amazing little Italian restaurant in Greenwich Village and have a delicious authentic Italian dinner together. He tells me all about his day and how he is working hard with Charles, and I tell him about my aunt and the sad news of her sickness. We talk a little bit about basically everything and manage to have a nice time together. I try to keep my answers short and to the point dismissing the big elephant in the room. There is no way I was going to share with him all the gypsy stuff Aunt Mari had told me. I love Jason and trust him, but I didn't want to freak him out. I also wanted to find out a bit more about all of this before I go involving him. Involving him will only make things more complicated. I am not going to start spilling secrets that I can't even decipher myself.

After we finish up our dessert, Jason pays the bill, and we get into his car and drive back to my place. The drive back is filled with small chit chat much like dinner was. We have been together since college, and he still gives me butterflies when he looks at me. He stopped at a red light where he took the opportunity to grab my hand and bring it to his lips.

"I missed you."

I can't help but melt. I truly do love him; he still makes me feel the same way he did when we first met in our psych class. The light turns green and before I can respond everything goes black. I manage to fight and open my eyes and see glass everywhere. Broken glass covers my skin tearing open small wounds. As I try to get a hold of my reality, I realize we're on our sides now. The car had flipped to its side.

I look over at Jason who has blood running down his face. I move my hand to try and touch him. Fear fueling my movements. He has to be ok. I manage to move my hand to touch his arm and then I feel the weirdest feeling. A burst of power courses through my veins. It's like my whole body comes alive. However, that only lasts for a few moments before everything goes dark.

***

I wake up feeling fast movements as I lay in what I assume is a gurney. I am in a hospital. My eyes burn from the bright fluorescent lights. I struggle to remain conscious.

As they wheel me down a long corridor, my eyes fight to stay open, I begin to get flashes of memories. They quickly flood my mind, filling it with details and premonitions. I see monstrous faces and blood everywhere. People from different time periods. I see a flash of myself standing in a burnt field along with three other women all dressed in what looks like white linen nightgowns from what appears to be a medieval time period. A ring of fire surrounds all of us, however we don't look scared, if anything we look empowered. The images keep shifting and as I focus more on the images that try to drown my mind, I notice a familiar face. Rose, she is in a black dress laying on a monstrous man's lap while he drains her. Her lifeless body lays there drained of any life. I run towards her screaming. I need to protect her. However, I am stopped when the monstrous man looks up, smiling as the blood he had taken from Rose drips down his pale skin. His violet eyes meet mine and I am frozen in place unable to move.

"Rose!" I shout again, trying to fight this feeling. I need to save her. Everything in my body is screaming at me to save her.

"Rose... Rose...Rose!" I shout over and over again. I jerk and push against the restraints that the doctors and nurses have placed on me to keep me still. As I go to scream for her again, I feel something prick my arm and that's when everything fades to black.

Chapter 24

ROSE

I lay on Leo's bed still basking in the most amazing night of my life. My eyes are still closed not wanting to acknowledge the day and stay here with him, in this beautiful moment we have created. Needing to be closer to Leo I roll to my side and extend my arm to wrap it around his waist. His cool skin feels refreshing under the heat of the covers that shields us from the morning crisp air that came with mid-September. Just as I'm about to fully situate myself in my new position a bang on Leo's door jolts me awake.

"Rose!" I hear a familiar voice shout; Leo stirs awake and sits up, now fully awake and alert. I can't help but stare at his ripped muscles flexing as he sits on the bed. However, I'm pulled from the sight when I hear another knock. I immediately sit up as well, pulling the comforter to my bare chest, wondering who could be in his house banging on his door this early in the morning. Then the mystery person starts to shout once again, and I realize it's Adeline. I look over at the clock on the nightstand. It's seven in the morning and I feel the sudden need to strangle her for interfering with not only my blissful moment but my sleep. I mean seriously what the hell is she doing here? Then without warning she barges in.

"Adeline what the hell?" I practically screech.

Adeline looks from me to Leo realizing what is happening then quickly looks away from the scene in front of her, like this was the most pornographic thing she has ever seen.

"Your brother and Mandee are in the hospital. They had a horrible car accident last night. We all tried to get a hold of you, but no one could reach you." She explains.

"Is Jason, ok?" I ask, practically jumping from the bed.

"Yes, he's fine. Not even a scratch on him. They're saying he is a walking miracle. Mandee on the other hand is sedated. She's not doing too good." She explains. My chest tightens at the thought of not being there last night. I begin to move off the bed, when Adeline quickly adds,

"I'll go wait for you downstairs." She quickly shuts the door behind her.

As soon as she is out of sight, I jump out of bed gathering my clothes that are scattered across the room. Leo follows my lead by also getting out of bed and getting dressed. I grab my phone and head out of the room.

"Do you want me to come with you?" He asks.

"Yes, I don't want to go there by myself." I state. I know my mother will be furious with me for not answering her calls last night. I'm not going to lie; I am pretty angry at myself. Leo rushes towards me with his vampire speed and grabs me by my waist pulling me towards him.

"He's fine and I'm sure Mandee will be ok. Now let's just go." He assures me then grabs my hand and leads us down the stairs to where Adeline is waiting for us.

We all pile into the elevator and ride it all the way down to the lobby where we then make our way outside to where Adelines car is parked right in front. The ride is silent, none of us knowing what to say. My legs won't stop bouncing and I keep picking at my fingers from my nerves although when Leo places his hand over mine, my anxiety dissipates.

After what feels like the longest car ride of my life, we arrive at the hospital. We all rush through the hospital doors to the private area where my brother and Mandee are. Mandee's parents paid for the private room so that they could have privacy with their daughter.

Jason, my mother, Charles, James, and Collin all sit in the waiting room area as we walk in. Jason immediately runs over to me and extends his arms out to embrace me in a hug. I can tell he's nervous. I place my arms around him and hold him tightly. After thinking the worst possible scenario this morning, I needed to see him.

"Are you ok? How's Mandee?" I ask moving back and placing my hands on his face as I inspect him to make sure he really is ok.

"I'm fine Rose, it's Mandee that has everyone scared. Where were you last night?" He asks.

"I'm so sorry I didn't come; my phone was off. I was dealing with some things, which I know is not an excuse, but you have to believe me when I tell you I would have never not come if I would have known what happened last night. I'm so sorry Jay." I plead, silently hoping he will forgive me.

He looks at me, with a frown on his face, but he doesn't question my honesty. He knows me well enough to know I would never not come when he needs me, unless it is for a very good reason. My mother on the other hand thinks my answer is comical, based on her overdone villainous laugh. She stands up from her seat and walks towards me. We all look at her anticipating her next move.

"Rose come on, how many times do we have to go through this, your brother nearly died, and you couldn't bother to stop what you were doing with this new man in your life that will probably not even last until the end of this week. Rose, when the hell are you going to grow up and stop being so selfish!" She scolds as she walks over to where I'm standing then stops once she's fully face to face with me. My jaw drops from her accusation about Leo and me. And my heart sinks with guilt.

I can feel Leo's anger as my mother continues to stare me down, not even bothering to acknowledge that there are people around us. However, before I speak, I squeeze his hand silently signaling him to not say anything. This is not his battle.

"I'm sorry mother." I say quietly now that all eyes are on us.

"You're always sorry Rose; I mean Jesus Christ you're parading this new relationship around when your ex-Pierce has just come back from who knows where and is now missing again. How do you think that makes his parents feel, especially knowing that he came back for you. And I'm sure Mr. Lloyd here is a decent man but let's face it Rose you don't have the capability to hold down a relationship, you weren't even responsible enough to keep your phone on. What if your brother would have died, then what would you have done?" She asks. Tears begin to stream down my face. She has managed to hit every crack that is trying to mend itself in my chest and reopen all of my healing wounds.

"You have no idea what you're talking about!" Adeline snaps.

Me along with everyone else look towards her, shocked at her sudden outburst. Leo pulls me closer as if somehow trying to shield me from all of this.

"Adeline it's ok." I whisper, as I pull away from Leo and then look at Jason.

"I'm so glad you're ok Jay and I hope Mandee wakes up and is fine. I really do but right now I think it would be best if I go." I ex-plain. Jason nods his head knowingly, then gives me a hug. When I turn back around Leo is glaring at my mother, James as well, probably furious from her remarks about Pierce.

"Yes Rose, run like you always do, like you ran to California to get away from your horrible family. You are a spoiled girl, you know that. If your father was here, he'd be even more disappointed in you than I am right now." She spewed.

I take a moment to try and calm my bubbling anger from spilling over. I pity her at this moment. She thinks she knows everything, but she is the spoiled one, the poor girl who grew up with nothing and sold her soul in order to get everything- except her soul wasn't the one being collected by the devil...it was mine.

"The only thing dad would be disappointed about when it came to me is that I have allowed you to push me around way more than I should've. He would have thought of you as a monster and a gold-digging bitch. I feel bad for you. You slap on your mask every day to show everyone around you, you belong here, well you don't, and you never will." I say looking directly at her as my feelings for her spill out. A part of me feels like I should feel bad for saying all of these horrible things to my own mother, but how can I feel bad when what I'm saying is the truth.

Everyone stands silent as they keep their eyes on my mother waiting for her to respond. She walks up with no emotion on her face and strikes me straight across the face. My face whips to the side as I place my hand to my stinging cheek. Automatically I can feel Leo move closer out of instinct to intervene, I quickly push him back.

"She's not even worth it, let's just go." I tell him then look at my mother once more before walking to the door and leaving.

Leo and I take a cab back to his apartment. The drive is filled with awkward silence. I know he wants to comfort me and make everything better, but I don't want to deal with any of it. So, I move to the complete opposite end of the cab seat and stare out the window. When we get to his apartment, I walk inside not knowing what to do. I just want to be alone. I should have gone to a hotel or something. I really do need to get a place of my own.

"Rose, are you ok?" His eyes search mine, desperate for a true answer. I decide to fake it trying not to drag him into this neverending cycle of toxicity.

"I'm fine." I say then walk further into the apartment.

"I'm going to go take a shower." I tell him as I make my way upstairs. I know he senses something is off, but he gives me my space. As I walk up the stairs I can feel the anxiety course through my veins, my chest feels heavy, and my head is pounding. I can feel my breathing become heavier as I close and lock the door to the bathroom behind me. I don't even make it all the way into the bathroom before I fall to the floor and completely break down. I hate that she did this to me, that she made me feel weak and insecure. I hate that she makes me feel like I am the only problem in this whole equation. That everything bad that has ever happened is my fault. Ever since I was a little girl, she has always kept me at arm's length and has always thought the worst of me.

As I allow the overwhelming amount of emotions to pass, I can't help but slightly hit my head with the back of the door a few times feeling surges of anger. I needed to feel something, anything other than that burning feeling of pure rage.

In a flash Leo is at the door banging on it, worried that I'm somehow hurting myself, which I guess in a way I am.

"Rose let me in please." He pleads.

I stay silent trying to suck up my tears. I don't want him to see me like this.

"I'm okay." I say just above a whisper, my voice cracking. He jiggles the doorknob, desperately. I know he will keep trying until I either let him in or he breaks the door down himself, so I reach up and unlock the door and move up, so my back is no longer blocking the entrance. He comes in, his eyes sad as he looks at my face and looks deep into my red puffy eyes.

"Your mother was way out of line; you cannot listen to her." He tries to assure me, but I won't listen. I can still hear her words swirl around my head reminding me of my fuck ups.

"You know when I got together with Pierce it was the only time in my life, she was actually proud of me." I confess. His frown deepens.

"I disappointed her more when I left him than any other time before and that's saying something." I sniffle trying to regulate my speech.

"I was a different person back then and Pierce only made it worse. He let me indulge in everything and then made me pay the price."

I cry into Leo's chest as he holds me, rubbing my back in soothing patterns assuring me, he has me. And for the first time in a long time, I believe that someone does indeed have me. Leo would never let me fall. He would never break me.

After what feels like forever, I pull away feeling like I have to actually shower and just try and move past this horrible day. He steps back as I begin taking my top off and notice he is staring. I feel a bit shy, in such bright lighting. I feel too exposed. I halt my movement and look back at him.

"Do you mind?" I ask a small smile threatening to play on my lips as he eyes me from head to toe admiring my slender figure.

"No, not really on second thought, I think I'll join you." He answers then begins to strip out of his clothes before I can protest against it. His shoulders were so broad, and his skin was so tight around his corded muscles. He was just big in every aspect. My jaw drops from seeing him fully naked in front of me. I've seen him naked before but it's still a shock to the system every time I get a full view. His body is more than impressive; it's as if Michael-Angelo sculpted him himself. I couldn't look away which only caused a smirk to appear on Leo's smug face.

"Your turn." He grins, wanting to see me in the light. I, on the other hand, am a bit more hesitant. It's not that I am ashamed of my figure, especially since he has made it more than clear that he loves every inch of me, but I just feel so bare in this moment between us that it makes me hesitate.

"There is no need to hide your body from me, my love. I saw it last night and it was a sight to be worshiped." He says as he steps closer to me closing the space between us before he cages me between his arms against the wall. He nibbles at my ear then leaves a trail of warm kisses down my neck. I feel his hand very slowly move its way to the hem of my shirt and begin to lift it. His fingertips slowly brush over my skin.

I allow it. I want to be comfortable with him and allow him to see all of me like he is allowing me to see all of him. He moves my top up over my head then throws it across the floor. I stand there silent as his eyes look down at my body, still not completely exposed due to my bra. He takes this moment to kiss my lips then moves towards the marks left behind by his fangs and licks them. It sends a shiver down my spine.

"Mine." He growls. In the past, possessive behavior would have sent me running, but hearing these words from Leo only makes me want to run into his arms. I am his, completely and utterly his, for as long as he will have me.

He pulls me forward then turns me around, so the front of my body is facing the wall while my ass is pressing into his groin. I move around craving to tease him a bit. I can hear a low groan escape his lips. He unclasps my bra then slowly removes it. His touch is gentle and tender. He slowly moves his hand and runs his finger over the birth mark on my shoulder blade, as he places a small kiss next to it.

"Have you always had this mark?" He asks.

"Yes." I breathe trying to contain my arousal.

He presses himself against me since my pants are still on and moves my hair to the side kissing down my neck. It is the most erotic sensation I have ever felt. He nips and licks my flesh as he moves his way down. When he gets to my back, he snakes his hands around my waist and unbuttons my jeans to pull them down effortlessly, leaving me in my panties. I turn around and he pushes me once again into the wall now holding my hands above my head as he smiles wickedly at me admiring my breasts and my exposed body although my panties still serve as a barrier for what he truly wants. We both stay silent as he takes in my body. I squeeze my thighs together in anticipation as he begins kissing down my neck then my breasts, taking one nipple into his mouth.

"Leo." I moan. He stops what he is doing then trails back up and kisses me.

"I want to try something with you, I have never done this before but maybe this will help." He explains. I nod my head with want, starving for him to proceed. He looks down, releasing my hands then bites into his wrist and grabs my own and bites into it. I push my head back in ecstasy. He places his wrist in front of me and I know what he wants me to do. I remember how amazing his blood tasted from last time. It's addictive. I grab onto it and begin drinking as he does as well. We both stand there basking in one another. We both look into each other's eyes as we feast on each other's bodies. I never thought this would be a normal thing in my sex life, but I guess when you're dating a vampire a blood kink is bound to happen.

We both release at the same time, "you and I are now one, my beautiful Rose." He states then without warning he crashes his lips on mine. It's euphoric, transcendent, the most amazing kiss I have ever felt. Blood drips from both our mouths as our tongues fight for dominance. The sticky red liquid drips onto our bodies, painting us with each other. He moves his hands grabbing and squeezing my ass, signaling for me to jump so he can carry me into the shower. I do as instructed and wrap my legs around his waist. He walks us both into the shower stall. I turn the water on and as the hot water hits us both it only intensifies the moment further. His lips remain attached to mine, kissing me feverishly, tugging on my bottom lip hungrily. The way he tastes only makes me want more; it's like a drug the more I get the more I want. I run my hands through his wet hair rummaging through it and pulling ever so gently. He moves his hands to the very delicate and thin lace band of my panty and rips them off without any struggle. I shriek from the shock of him just tugging them right off then go back to kissing him. He then detaches his lips from mine and looks directly at me with his forest green eyes and smirks. He places his lips to my neck, roughly kissing me then pushes himself into me without any warning. His large throbbing member stretching me out, to fit him perfectly.

"Fuck!" I moan in pure bliss. His movements are rough and sloppy, and I love every second of it. He moves his lips back to my own as his tongue collides with mine. My moans send vibrations through his mouth as he continues to kiss me. My hands continue to run through his hair as his hands lay small smacks on my ass causing small yelps to escape. I can feel him smile through our kiss when a small whine leaves my lips from his large hands slapping my skin.

"Your ass. Your pussy. Your heart. And your soul all belong to me." He growls in my ear as he thrusts into me after every statement. I squeeze my eyes shut as I allow the pleasure to build inside me. The knot of what will soon be my orgasm tightens from every word he speaks.

"It's all yours Leo, I've only ever belonged to you."

He kisses me harshly and his thrusts grow more aggressive, as he hits the right spot over and over again. I can feel my orgasm cresting and after he pumps into me a few more times I'm thrown right over the edge of pure pleasure. I cry out in absolute bliss as he continues to thrust into me chasing his own climax. I can tell he is close to the edge, by the way his movements grow more rapid and desperate. He holds onto my ass, his fingers digging into my hips as bruises begin to form from the strength, he is using to hold on to me as if I am going to slip away. I scratch my nails down his back, sure to leave a mark, although I won't be able to see them since they will heal instantaneously.

"I love how you came all over my dick love, claiming me as your own. I belong solely to you, forever...my forever." He states, then kisses me feverishly. With a few more thrusts he cums inside of me and continues to power through until he feels fully satisfied. I nuzzle my head into the crook of his neck as I try to regulate my breathing.

After gaining some composure I move back to look at him, as his eyes find mine. He seems fascinated by the quick rising and falling of my chest. He places my back against the wall and uses one hand to hold me while he raises his other to my rising chest that is trying to catch up on its breaths.

"What are you doing?" I giggle as I look at him, concentrating on his bare hand placed on my beating heart.

"I want to feel your heartbeat." He states, smiling as he looks at his hand pressed to my skin.

"I have walked this earth for centuries and have heard the sounds of a thousand different noises, yet the sound and the rhythm of your heartbeat brings me more joy and fulfillment than any other sound." He smiles as he looks up at me through his beautiful wet lashes. The water hitting him perfectly. I move my arm to cup my hand to his soft cheek and slightly rub my thumb on his cold skin. I loved this man with all of me.

"You're my everything." I whisper as I look from his eyes to his lips.

"And you are mine." He responds then kisses my nose sweetly. He then proceeds to place me down and I can't help but sway from my legs being so weak. He holds onto me for balance and smirks knowing he is the reason for my unsteadiness.

"That was amazing." As I look at his porcelain like face, I notice the red that is smeared around his lips, then I realize mine are probably covered in blood as well. I look down on the bathroom floor, a little shocked to see the water had turned pink as it swirls down the drain from our blood being washed off of us.

"Yes, it was. That was mostly us, but the blood does intensify the sex." He grins. Blood or no blood his sex is intense.

"Is it bad that I actually like doing that? I don't mind you...you know, the biting..." I confess, feeling heat rush to my cheeks from the embarrassment of telling him that. The water is still beating down on us. I know I asked him that last night too, but I feel like I have to ask again, because I know deep down, that doing that with him had to be just about the dirtiest thing we could do sexually.

He pushes my wet hair away from my face, "no, it's not weird at all, it's supposed to feel good to humans." He explains then moves his hand down to my thigh.

"This spot here is my favorite. It's the most sensual place to bite a woman." He confesses moving his fingers ever so gently across my skin. I shudder at his touch. He has full control over my body, and he knows it.

I can't help but feel a little jealous that he had basically just confessed to doing this to other women. He must sense my jealousy, because he lifts my face to meet his and lets a small smile show, "I never swapped blood with anyone before." He tells me. It makes me feel a little better that we have done something together that was new for the both of us. I'm not blind, I know that there is probably not a lot of things that he hasn't done in the bedroom, especially since he's been having sex for centuries, but it still gives me butterflies knowing we had something no one else had.

"I'm sorry, it just bothers me the thought of you with another woman." I confess. He lets a small laugh out, probably because me being jealous of a century old vampire is ridiculous. I mean he has had lifetimes with women.

And he'll have more after me. My subconscious viciously reminds me.

"I never thought of you as the jealous type my Rose."

I give him an unamused glare, annoyed by his response.

"I have had many women, yes, but I haven't been in love with any of them. You, my beautiful angel, are the only woman I have ever truly been in love with." He smiles. I can't help but feel a thousand butterflies unleash themselves in my stomach. He always knows the right thing to say. It was stupid of me to even mention anything. I know what Leo and I have doesn't compare to anything else for either of us. We are the exception.

We both finish showering and climb out. I step out first then feel Leo stop. I look back to see his face with an expression of anger.

"What's wrong?" I ask not understanding what just occurred within the last couple of seconds. He presses his finger into what feels like a bruise on my back side. I gasp in pain from his action.

"Fuck, Rose I'm so sorry." He pleads. I hate that he feels like he has to apologize, what we just did was not apology worthy. It was consensual and amazing. He made me feel wanted and good and most importantly loved. I turn around and move his face to look at me.

"Don't ever apologize. I'm fine Leo, you didn't do anything but give me the best orgasm I have ever had in my life." I explain, smiling trying to be serious but also go about this light heartedly.

He gives me a small smile, even though I can still see the conflict he harbors in his eyes. I placed a small kiss on his lips to reassure him before I walked to the counter and grabbed a towel to dry myself off before going into his bedroom to change into a pair of his sweats and t-shirt. He comes out a moment later and admires me from the door frame. I know he loves seeing me in his clothing.

He changes into joggers and a t- shirt then lays out on the bed. I on the other hand grab the clothes from the bathroom and make my way to the washer and dryer in his apartment. I put my clothes to wash then realize how much time has passed since this morning. It is already the afternoon. As I am turning on the machine my phone rings. It's Jason. I immediately answer.

"What's wrong, are you ok?" I ask, worry taking over every nerve in my body.

"Yeah, I think I should be asking you that question." He states.

"I'm fine, Jay, you know how mom is." I explain. He lets out a sigh as if that wasn't what he was referring to.

"I mean how are you with the Pierce thing she brought up." He explains. My heart sinks from hearing that name.

"Who told you?" I ask, wondering how much he knows.

"James." He explains. I take a breath of relief because that means he got the kids version of the story. Before I can reply he speaks again, "look mom just left and I really want to talk to you, but Mandee seems to need you more. She finally woke up not too long ago and she has not stopped asking for you." He explains. I am a bit taken back by this given that Mandee and I could barely tolerate one another. Why the hell would she want to talk to me? Nevertheless, I tell him I will be right over and tell Leo that I am leaving. Before I made my way out the door, I quickly changed out of Leo's sweatpants and into a pair of jeans. As I was leaving, Leo asked if I wanted him to come with me, which I replied no. I figured since this morning was already a horror show I didn't want to subject him to another one.

Chapter 25

ROSE

I don't waste any time as I make my way straight to where Mandee's private room is, and I see Jason standing outside the door. He looks more relaxed than earlier. He gives me a hug and explains how Mandee's parents have gone home and all she's been asking for is me- which strikes me odd, but I don't question it, instead I follow behind him as we walk into her room. She's sitting up with her naturally curly hair tied up into a big messy bun and her normally golden olive skin looked a bit more pale. Not to mention her brown eyes were completely bloodshot. Cuts and bruises scarred her face as she looked at me with anticipation.

"Rose." She whispers her voice weak but purposeful. I look over at Jason silently asking him to leave us alone, which he does. Once alone I sit on the chair next to her bed and look at her. She looks weak and frail but also different. There's a buzzing energy about her that I can't help but feel in my veins. It's almost like a familiar feeling trying to find its counterpart.

"Rose, you need to go, he's coming for you!" She bursts, as if she has been holding in that message for too long of a time. I look at her confused, not quite understanding what the hell she's talking about, who is coming for me and more importantly how does Mandee know?

"Look we don't have the time for me to go into a full-blown explanation all you need to know is that the car accident changed something. I don't even fully understand it myself. All I know is that I'm supposed to warn you that he's coming." She explains.

"Who is *he*?" I ask, trying to understand her better.

"I don't really know, but whoever it is, he's coming, and he is the embodiment of pure evil." She explains as her information sends shivers down my spine.

"I don't understand, why me?"

"You are the promised lover, promised to *him*. When you turned twenty-two your soul tie was enacted, and he wants what belongs to *him*. You are a descendant of Marie. You are meant to take her place. By All Hallows Eve he will come to claim you." She explains.

My body goes numb as I take in what she had just said. What the hell does she mean by descendant or soul tie? Me and Marie are related? Is that why Leo is attracted to me? Am I some kind of replacement for her? Question after question suddenly swirls within my mind, to the point that I begin to feel lightheaded.

"Look Rose I know it's a lot to take in but I'm going to get more answers, my aunt will know more. You need to run and hide. It's not safe for you here." She begs. I feel like my world is spinning off its axis and I don't know how to stop it.

"How do you know all of this?" I ask her.

"It's a long story. And if I'm being honest, I don't even know the entirety of it. All I know is that when I woke up from the accident, I felt a surge of energy and heard whispers of what is to come. I felt I needed to help you. I'm supposed to help save your soul, whatever that means. But Rose, you need to leave whatever is coming for you is already on the move. You need to leave and when I check out of here, I'll come and find you. Trust no one." She warns. I nod my head and assure her that I will leave, but first I needed to pay Leo a visit and get to the bottom of all of this. Marie seems to be a recurring name in all of this craziness since the very start.

"And Rose." She speaks, shaking me from my thoughts.

"Beware of the man with violet eyes."

***

I practically storm out of the hospital assuring Mandee that I will do as told and call her so she will know where to find me once she is discharged in a couple days. I take a cab straight to Leo's house, hell bent on finding out once and for all what the hell is happening. I have absolutely no doubt in my mind that Leo and even Elliot knows more than what they are saying.

I take the elevator straight up and charge into the apartment.

"Leo!" I call out. I walk further in and find Elliot, a woman I don't know, and Leo in the living room. I march straight up to Leo feeling an overwhelming feeling of anger.

"You and I need to talk." I manage to say, as the tone of my own voice surprises me. It was so cold and harsh.

"What is going on Rose?" Leo asks, immediately getting up and grabbing my hand to walk me to his study so that we could talk in private. The moment the door closes I yank my hand away from his grasp. Leo frowns from my movement, as he takes in the realization that I'm really pissed.

"Am I related to Marie? Or oh yeah, am I promised to some mystery man in hell?" I scream, now feeling my anger fully surface.

"How did you...?" He begins to ask, but he quickly closes his mouth when I cut him off.

"I want to know about me somehow being related to Marie. Explain. Now." I demand.

His eyes hit the floor in shame, causing my heart to shatter at his reaction confirming that it's true, we are related. I take a step back, panic taking over.

"When we slept together did you think of me or her? Was I some sick way for you to be able to feel close to her again?" I ask, tears threatening to spill. He looks absolutely gutted by my accusation.

"Rose it's not like that I swear. I didn't find out about you being related until recently. And of course, I thought of you my love, you're the only woman I have ever truly loved, I swear on my life." He rambles, moving closer and reaching his hand out to grab my chin forcing me to look into his eyes. Sincerity floods them. I don't know what to believe anymore. I move my face away from his grasp.

"What about the soul tie? What the hell is a soul tie?" I demand, feeling my whole world crumbling before me.

He looks down and frowns. Then Elliot and the mystery woman walk in.

"Is everything ok in here?" Elliot asks, realizing his own answer as he sees the distraught looks, we have plastered on our faces.

"What do you know about this soul tie, Elliot?" I ask. I needed to know the truth. Elliot freezes in place as he looks from me to Leo, giving me the verification that he knew about this too. There has to be some explanation to all of this. I don't want to believe that Leo would intentionally hide this from me. I wait for one of them to speak when the mystery woman walks forward, causing both men to look at her.

"My name is Tristan." She greets me. I stay quiet not knowing how to respond.

"I can understand why you're not feeling pleasant, Rose." She states. How does she know my name? I am about to ask when she cuts me off.

"Your bloodline is connected to one of the most powerful and notorious gypsy families of Lucifer's clan. Meaning you had the incredibly rare opportunity to be bonded with one of his soldiers. Your soul is tethered to Leos, it's destiny's way of picking out your perfect match to oversee." She explains. My mind goes into overdrive as I think back on everything, so I guess the connection between us wasn't special at all, it was all due to some supernatural magic.

I look over at Elliot who nods then goes on to speak, "it's not as simple as that."

"You see your ancestor Marie was promised to Cain, one of our rulers, him and her were soul tied. However, she and Michael broke it. That very sacred tie needed to be amended for the balance of things to remain untouched, so a deal was made that the next soul tie would be given to Cain as compensation and since soul ties are rare it landed on you...centuries later." He explains.

"So, me and Cain...I'm assuming the same Cain from the bible are soul tied?" I question.

"Yes and no. Your soul tie is split in half, so to speak. You see Cain couldn't just claim you as his match he had to be added to you. Your true soul match, that was prophesied for you is Leo." Elliot further explains, gently. I can tell he's trying to give me all the information I need without setting me off.

"So, Leo and I have this deep connection because of some supernatural connection?" I ask, my eyes burning with tears. Elliot and Tristan both nod their heads.

I turn to look at Leo then ask the question I most desperately needed answered, "Was any of this even real?"

"Of course it is my Rose. You are my beloved and what I hold most dearly in all of my existence. With or without the soul tie you belong to me just like I belong to you." He explains hoping to reassure me. And even though his words soothe some of my hurt, I still can't fight the feeling that comes with being deceived.

"How could you say that? This whole relationship has been a lie! You have been lying to me this whole time. I feel this way for you because of some supernatural prophecy. Oh my god is that why I've never been able to fully fall in love?"

Leo nods his head then looks down, ashamed to keep looking at me.

Tristan then interjects, "It's almost like your body is immune to them. Since your soul has been looking for its other half all of these years, therefore anything less is undesirable to you. And even more so since you have two souls attached to you. You see a normal soul tied gypsy would be able to form bonds and have relationships outside of their tie, even though it would never feel right. They would always walk around feeling the ache of what they are missing. However, since you have been blessed with two ties to your soul there's no room besides those who your essence craves."

I can slightly hear Leo screaming at Tristan for telling me that. Suddenly, I feel like I can't breathe, I'm having a full-blown panic attack. It's all too much. I can feel Leo quickly approach me as he tries to hold me. Both my heart and soul feel like they are being ripped out of my chest.

"All these years I thought there was something wrong with me. I thought I had been cursed to never love another and be forced to live like that for the rest of my life. Always craving that feeling of need, to love someone and have them love me back." I explain as I pull myself away from Leo. I physically feel my heart break.

"I'm so sorry, my beautiful Rose. I am so sorry it took me so long to find you and I'm even more sorry I lied to you." He states, his voice thick with sorrow.

"You promised you'd never do anything to scare me, Leo. And lying fucking terrifies me and you did that over and over again." I exclaim as I push myself away from him, not acknowledging his apology. I was too angry to listen to him. Leo looks at me pained by my reaction not knowing what to say or do.

"You hurt me." I whisper as I look away from him and let the words echo around us. Leo and I stare at one another and the look of absolute devastation that takes over his face is enough to almost have me run into his arms- but I don't. Instead, I hold my ground.

"How do I break a soul tie?" I ask, turning to Elliot.

"You can't." Elliot states flatly not even throwing anything out to be considered.

"So, I'm stuck being given to Cain as his other half?" I question as I feel myself begin to shake from the idea of going to hell...like actual hell and being paired off with the original murderer.

"You can break a soul tie, however doing so is a suicide mission. Cain would kill you, Leo, and anyone else who helped you do it. If you decided to change, like Marie did, your beloved Leo's heart would be ripped from his chest and fed to you, the moment your skin turns pale and cold. Cain is not the forgiving type." Tristan explains. I stay silent as I let this new revelation replay in my head. I didn't want anyone to die or get hurt because of me, but I also didn't want to be shipped off to Cain.

"That birthmark on your shoulder, is the agreement that was made...by me." Elliot confesses. My heart nearly gives out when he says the last two words. He was the one who had done this. How could he? What gave him the right to give this burden to someone else.

"How could you?"

"Rose, it was a long time ago. Michael had been like a brother to me, and he needed my help. The moment I made that deal I knew I had messed up, but I swear to you I will make this right. That's why Tristan is here. She is working for Michael, but she wants to help us. She's going to help us evade Michael for as long as it takes to think of a solution." Elliot rambles desperately trying for me to understand and to not hate him. And as much as I wanted to, I didn't. He couldn't have possibly known that it was me who would be affected.

"Michael turned Pierce, didn't he?" I ask, as I think back to how Pierce kept mentioning an agreement of some kind. Elliot slowly nods his head, as if he was unsure of how I would react. I stay silent as I try to process everything, and I can't help but think about what he said about the birthmark. My mind concentrates on all the times it has burned.

"It was Cain." I mumble under my breath as I look down, remembering all the times it was him who helped me. He was the man with the violet eyes.

"What did you say?" Leo questions as he breaks me from my thoughts.

"Nothing. Look, I have to go." I ramble desperately needing to leave. However, before I could move, Leo grabbed my wrist and pulled me towards him.

"You said Cain, so what did you think of?" He asks sternly.

"Cain is the reason I killed Pierce."

Both Elliot and Leo look from one another taking in what I had said. It makes the most sense, why would he want someone to hurt his other half. I mean he couldn't have someone kill what he thought belonged to him.

"It's possible, he could have channeled just enough energy to her through their connection to help her in that moment of desperation. Bonds have been said to bring on power if their tie is strong enough." Elliot further explains.

"How can they even have a bond; she's never even seen him." Leo states trying to figure out what's happening. However, as his words leave his lips, I think back to the violet eyed man in my dreams. I decided at least for now, to keep that small fact to myself until I had more information. If it was him, a part of me knew that he wasn't going to hurt me.

"I think we need to take a break." I say, feeling my heart completely shatter. Leo immediately shakes his head as he moves to grab my hand. I quickly pull away. Elliot and Tristan take this moment to leave the room as they close the door behind them giving us the privacy that we need.

"Rose, please I'm sorry that I lied but I swear on everything that I hold sacred I will never do it again." He pleads.

"I know." I whisper. I then add, "It's not even about the lying Leo, because as much as you have hurt me, especially after I have laid everything bare to you, I can't be the cause of you getting hurt...or worse. If we're not together then no one has to die, I won't have you sacrifice yourself trying to save me, I know our bond is deeper than our soul tie, which is exactly why I can't have you making a plan to take Cain on. The idea of you putting yourself in harm's way because of me makes me want to die. Now maybe it's the soul tie, amplifying all of my feelings when it comes to you, but even though I am so angry I will always protect you, Leo. It's funny how you say you don't have a soul, yet I can feel our souls actually intertwined, I guess I know why." I say as I reach my hand out and gently wipe away a fallen tear off his beautiful face. He grabs my hand and pulls me closer. Now that I know Cain is watching me, I can't have Leo involved. He'll hurt him; I know he will. This tie creates such a feeling of emotion and attachment to your other person that I know Cain will do anything to make me fully his and I can't have Leo being a casualty.

"Rose, you know as well as I do, I can't be parted from you, and I will not stop until I know that you are safe. Even if I have to lay my life down and sacrifice everything to protect you. I told you before I'll burn it all. I don't care about the consequences that follow me, only that I will have you." He tries to reason, only making things harder.

I shake my head trying not to make this any more complicated or harder than it has to be. However, he isn't having any of it. He grabs me more firmly and forces me to look at him, "if we separate, you're still going to be tied to him."

"Yes, but he won't hurt you to get to me." I reason. Leo frowns at my candor. However, it is the truth. I would rather be the one to die than him.

"I told you I was set on the path of damnation. I just never thought you'd be part of it."

I walk to the elevator and try to make my exit as quick as possible, however, his vampire speed beats me to it. He grabs my wrist pulling me to the wall caging me between the wall and him. I'm forced to look into those green eyes of his. His face etched with determination, as his eyes fight the tears, I can see he is holding in.

"You have to let me go." I beg. Leo shakes his head.

"You know I can't do that Rose, please we can find another way. I know I messed up but please, we can make this right." He pleads, slamming his fist into the wall next to me, making me wince.

"Leo, we have to stop kidding ourselves that this was ever going to work, we are not some made up characters in someone else's story. We're real, which means I don't get the happy ending. I'm sorry but it's just how my world works. Everything I touch turns to ash. Now please, you have to let me go, I'm begging you." I sob. The words burn my throat as they exit my mouth. Hearing the realization of what my life is, kills something within me-my hope. He closes his eyes and lowers his arms in surrender to my pleas. I give him one last glance before making my way to the elevator. As the elevator door opens and I make my way inside, the sound of his voice halts me.

"You and I are not done, Rose. Remember what I told you, I am a man that gets what he wants and what I want is you."

Chapter 26

MICHAEL

I need to speak with Tristan. She has been disappearing too much for my liking lately. As I make my way to the front door to my apartment, she opens the door.

"Where the hell have you been?" I question, already knowing the answer from the smell of witch on her. I think it's funny that she thinks she can hide the fact that she's been fucking that witch from me.

"Setting the trap my love. Everything is going exactly how you want it." She purrs as she moves closer to me then wraps her arms around my neck.

"Someone's been naughty?" I chuckle as I look down at her and place my hand on her chin firmly and pull her into a rough kiss. She will never compare to the woman that is Marie, but she certainly does have a way of keeping me entertained until I am reunited with my lover. She deepens the kiss by licking my lips asking for entrance which is graciously granted to her. She has done good, breaking those two up. I needed Leo out of the way so that I could get to Rose easier. Nothing and no one is going to stand in the way of getting what I have wanted for over two hundred years.

"You fucking that witch was not part of our agreement." I growl as I kiss her neck, then wrap my hand around it, feeling her pulse beneath my hand, she's nervous.

"I don't like sharing my toys with others, darling." I hiss. She nods her head understanding my command. I give her a large grin, to show her my gratitude for her comprehension of my needs.

"You've been such a good girl with all of this, that I have a surprise for you." I smile deviously knowing how much she is going to like my sinister surprise. She looks up giving me her full attention, as I find myself staring at her perfectly swollen lips.

"It's in your bed chambers." I smile deviously knowing how much she is going to enjoy the spell books I had found in my old boxes. They are full of the darkest magic that exists in all the realms. They should be enough to help figure out a way to get Rose to hell. Cain never did explain that part of the deal. All I know is that her time has come, therefore she needs to go.

Tristan drops her hands from my neck as she lets a big grin take hold of her face and races to her room. I follow behind her and lean against the door frame as I watch her gasp with excitement when she sees the old grimoires on her bed.

"Michael, they're lovely!" She beams, as she grabs each one and flips through them, taking in the power they radiate.

"Only the best for you my devious pet."

Tristan turns around with a mischievous smirk and places the books down before she makes her way over to me.

"We are going to send that little bitch to hell." She smiles, before pulling me close and kissing me. My one hand immediately moves to her waist as my other wraps around her neck.

"Yes, we are." I grin, before giving her one last kiss and pulling away. I didn't want to further distract her from the plan, so I left her room and poured myself a martini. I sit looking out my window and taking in the city views. Even with all the craziness that I can see from here, I can't help but think back to that night when I saw them knife Marie with that blade. The blade that would be rather handy right now to send Rose to hell. The blade of Cain. The look on her face as they dug that horrid weapon into her still haunts my mind. The heart crushing moment replays, haunting me every second of everyday until I fulfill my promise and get her back.

As I continue to get lost in thought, I decide to go for a walk. I needed to clear my mind. The crisp cool air feels nice on my already cold skin. I see couples walk hand in hand and regular humans buzz around as they try and do meaningless tasks. I never liked the idea of humanity. I mean what's the point. You're going to die in the end. I'll never forget how grateful I was when my father found me. He truly was the only father I ever knew. How he took me into his estate in Transylvania and waited for me to turn into the man he wanted me to be to gift me with the most amazing gift anyone could give somebody. He didn't only give me life that day he gave me a purpose. Much like Marie did when I found her in that field. As I continue to walk, I see the small Romanian restaurant where I like to dine now and then and walk in. It brought me back to my days spent in Romania, my home.

The owners greet me kindly as usual, and I sit in my own personal section. I came here more often than I'd ever like to admit. Their food was delectable, and it was nice being able to speak to them in my native tongue. When Marie and I are once and for all fully reunited, I fully intend on going back there. I've had enough of seeing and living in all these other countries. It has been too long since I've been home. I hadn't even been able to see my father in all these years.

As I look through the menu to eat, I can't help but feel this pulling feeling in my chest like I'm being pulled into another thought. Then I hear it, my heart almost gives out when I hear that voice I hadn't heard in centuries.

"Marie?" I say out loud. No one seems to notice as they all go about their business.

"My lover, you need to listen. Cain is allowing me to channel you to give you this message. On All Hallows Eve that is when you need to send Rose to him, he will descend onto earth and collect what is rightfully his." She explains. Her voice feels so good to hear. My heart that I didn't even know still existed feels like it actually might begin to race.

"I'll do it, I swear to you, my love." I promise her.

Then the connection is gone, and I am left alone once more. I place the menu down and look around trying to think of what to do next. All Hallows Eve was only a couple weeks away. I needed to speed things along. I will collect what's mine, when that night comes.

Chapter 27

ROSE

Words cannot describe the absolute pain I feel deep inside my chest. For someone who studied writing, I find it almost comical that I don't even have the words to describe the anguish that burns within me. The past couple of days have been difficult as I hide out in Adeline's apartment. Although today I have decided it is time to go home. I needed the familiarity of my space and the comfort of my own bed. Adeline of course is protesting my leaving, knowing that being around my mother right now is probably not the smartest idea. Especially since we have not spoken since the hospital incident. However, I needed to be alone right now and going home was just about the loneliest place I could go to. It would give me the space I needed to process everything and grieve. After going back and forth with Adeline, she finally concedes to letting me go back to my house.

I waste no time packing the few items I have here and express how grateful I am to her for letting me stay at her place. As soon as I make my way out of her apartment, I hail down the first cab I see and get in. It takes everything in me to walk through the front door of my building. I exhaled once the elevator doors opened to my apartment.

I drag myself up the steps and walk into my room, closing the door behind me. As I see my nice warm bed, I decide to take a shower, somehow thinking that it would cleanse me of all the bad things that have happened these last couple of days. As I get undressed, I can't help but place my fingers over the bruises on my hips and the bare piece of skin that was once marked by Leo's fangs. The reminder of what I had is enough to knock me over. We were never going to be able to reclaim that connection again, it had been tarnished by his lies and Cain's claim on me.

I try not to think about it as I jump into the shower. The water feels warm as it runs down my tired and pained body. I hadn't slept during my stay at Adelines. I couldn't allow myself to stay still. If I did, I knew that everything would come crashing down on me.

I finish showering, wrapping myself in a white fluffy towel, before making my way to the bedroom to get dressed. As I walk by my bed to get to my closet, I see a piece of paper and what looks like a dead rose lying on it. I hadn't noticed it before. My whole body goes rigid, Michael had been here. I don't know how I knew, but I did. I felt the certainty of my thoughts deep within my bones. I slowly make my way to the note clutching my towel tight to my chest as I pick up the piece of paper and open it.

Rose,
Can't wait to see you soon.
Xoxo – M

I drop the note from my hands back onto my bed as I try to calm myself. How did he get into my house? Vampires need to be invited in. It must have been my mother or Charles. Just the thought of that vile man anywhere near my family makes me want to vomit. Although, as much as the fear he inflicted tried to worm its way through me, I also couldn't help but feel angry. I was seriously pissed off.

How dare he come into my home.

How dare he try and rip me away from the only happiness that I have had in so long.

And how fucking dare he, try to take me down.

He has crossed a line, and I will make sure he doesn't get a second chance to do it again. So, I very quickly grab my phone and call Leo. He'll know what to do. Just because we can't be together doesn't mean we can't kill Michael together. Besides, who else can I call, he's all I have.

Hearing his voice when he picks up the phone feels like a bullet straight to my heart. However, I quickly recover once I look at the dead rose lying on my bed- mocking me.

"I'm in my house and Michael has been here." I state trying not to waste time with details. However, I didn't have to say much more than that, because Leo assured me, he and Elliot would be right over. And they were. I was just about finished putting on my black turtleneck when they barged into my room. Leo rushed over to me, looking me up and down to see if I was ok. However, he still kept his distance from me as much as he could.

"What happened?" He asks as he looks from me to the dead flower and note.

"I don't know I was showering and when I came out that was waiting for me." I explain looking at the piece of paper that was now in Leo's hand. He reads the note before crumpling it.

"I'll kill him."

"He's coming for me Leo; time's running out. Mandee said so herself. By Halloween my time will come to an end." I explain.

What Mandee had told me that day at the hospital still rattles inside my mind, she was being discharged tomorrow, and I still haven't been able to run anywhere and hide like she had told me to.

"Who is Mandee?" Elliot questions, looking up after examining the dead flower.

"My brothers' girlfriend. Apparently, I am not the only gypsy in New York." I state. Elliot seems intrigued by this newfound information.

"A true gypsy, I haven't run into one of those in a very long time, very intriguing," he mumbles to himself. Leo looks at him annoyed, probably thinking we have bigger things to think about.

"She told me that I needed to leave and hide and that she would come find me." I explain hoping they can make more light of it than I can.

"Then we'll leave." Leo states. Elliot and I both look at him a little shocked that he isn't more concerned with fighting.

"Think about it, we have the upper hand by knowing the deadline. Michael thinks he'll hit us with the element of surprise, so if we leave and strategize it will only put us ahead." Leo explains. It makes sense. Us leaving would give us time to think things through, without feeling the pressure of Michaels presence. I can tell Elliot agrees.

"Ok, we leave in two days, it gives us enough time to get our affairs in order. We'll take the jet and go to our chateau in Paris." Elliot states.

"Paris?" I ask. I thought they'd say we'll hide out in New Jersey or Connecticut, not Europe. I haven't been there in a while. Not since Pierce.

"That works." Leo states, then looks over at me making sure I agreed.

"Let's go to Paris."

***

The very next day, Elliot and I walk into the cold hospital room where Mandee is sitting up signing discharge papers. My brother has already gone to work, and her parents had to attend this press junket for his campaign.

"Rose? What happened, what's wrong?" She asks as both Elliot and I enter her room. She wearily looks over at Elliot not knowing exactly who he is or if he can be trusted. It's like I can sense her hesitation. I wonder if that's a gypsy thing.

I look over at Elliot then to Mandee and walk over to her bed, Elliot follows behind me.

"This is Elliot, he is a witch and he's going to help us." I explain. Mandee carefully places the pen down and looks at Elliot not really knowing if she should trust me or not.

"Give me your hand." She states, looking at Elliot. Before I can ask why, Elliot happily obliges and places his hand in Mandee's. She then closes her eyes and after a few silent seconds she opens her eyes and smiles with relief.

"I can tell your intentions are pure."

"How did you do that?" I ask.

"I've had a lot of free time on my hands." Mandee half-heartedly jokes.

"I only wish to help you two young gypsies. However, it seems that you are the one who is going to be the most helpful." He explains as he looks at her intrigued. I on the other hand am completely baffled by her ability to read him like that. I mean I thought she just found out she is 'special' so to say. I also can't help but wonder if I can do the same.

"Look, Elliot, Leo, and I are leaving for Paris tomorrow, and we want you to come with us. We need you." I inform her, hoping that she agrees. Every bone in my body is telling me that she is the key to helping us.

"Why Paris?" She asks, looking between Elliot and me.

Elliot then goes on to explain how Leo and him have a chateau there that no one knows about, and how we should all be safe until we come up with a plan.

"Mandee, I just want to warn you that what we are all getting involved in is so much bigger than what you think, I just want to make sure you understand this before you sign up." I explain. Mandee stays quiet as she thinks about my warning.

"I understand that Rose, but I have to be involved, I can't avoid this feeling that is telling me to help."

I take in her words and nod my head understanding her pull towards all of this.

"Let me finish signing these papers to give to the nurses so we can get the hell out of here." She winces slightly as she goes to move. Elliot grabs the vile that he brought with us from his pocket and hands it to Mandee.

"Here take this, it will help with your pain. It'll heal you more quickly."

Mandee takes the vile from his hand and looks at it weirdly, probably wondering what it is. Then without a second guess she opens it up and swallows it. Her face scrunches in pure disgust.

"That's disgusting." She complains.

"Yes, vampire blood when not from the vein does tend to taste foul." Elliot explains, causing Mandee to practically gag.

"I'm sorry, did you just say vampire blood? Did I just ingest blood? Whose blood did I just drink? Oh my God, is that sanitary?" She rambles, as her mind begins to spiral. I'd be lying if I said I wasn't slightly relieved. Her showing the slightest bit of uncertainty assured me that I wasn't the only one scared. Elliot quickly assures her, and her uneasiness seems to calm down when she goes to move again and realizes she's fine.

Soon after, she is done filling out the paperwork a nurse comes into the room to collect them.

When we finally get to the car, we call Jason to let him know that I had picked up Mandee from the hospital.

"What do you mean you picked her up; I was supposed to get her after work?" He questions over the phone.

"Babe, it's ok your sister offered to get me out of there earlier. I didn't want to be there longer than I had to." Mandee reasons. Jason stays silent for a moment as we all look at Elliot's car screen where the phone was hooked up so that it was on speaker.

"Ok, well I'll see you after I get off from work then." He tells her, sounding skeptical.

We all give each other weary glances knowing we had to be packing for our flight for the next day.

"No, it's ok, Rose is going to help me settle in and then tomorrow her and I are going on a small girl's trip together." Mandee explains bracing herself for what Jason would inevitably say, knowing that it was absolutely bizarre that his girlfriend who had never gotten along with his sister would say that.

"Ok, what the hell is going on? Rose, I know you're there on speaker, what's happening? Mandee, you just got out of the hospital, so I don't understand how you and Rose are going anywhere?" Jason asks, growing more and more agitated by the silence that now fills the call.

"Look Mandee and I have been getting along recently and with her being out of the hospital I told her about this little retreat that one of my friends from Connecticut told me about. She thought it would be a good idea to come along especially after everything she's been through recently." I explain. Mandee looks over at me from the front seat giving me an approving smile for my lie.

"Are you even up for that Mandee? I mean you just got out of the hospital, and just yesterday you were complaining about being in so much pain." Jason reminds her.

"Babe I'm fine, we'll only be gone a couple of days I promise." Mandee reassures him then looks at me hoping that we are able to sell this lie.

Jason lets a sigh of defeat escape his lips and we all know we have him.

We go back and forth giving him false details about our retreat in Connecticut until finally, he feels ok enough with our story that he stops questioning us. And eventually he allows us to get off the phone.

"He really loves you." Elliot states as soon as the call disconnects.

"He does. He's the best boyfriend a girl could possibly ask for, I'm more than lucky to have him in my life." Mandee says as her eyes get wider from talking about Jason.

"Ok enough boyfriend talk. What I want to know is who told you about your...gift?" I ask.

"My aunt. She seems to think my family descends from gypsies. Although based on yesterday and today I want to say she's not wrong in thinking so."

"From your mom's side or dad?" I ask curiously.

"Mom's." Mandee replies. I can't help but let a small laugh escape from the disbelief that Mandee's perfect mother, the trophy wife of all trophy wives, is part of a supernatural gypsy clan.

"Your mom, the head of basically every social circle in this city is a descendent of an ancient gypsy clan that is tied to Lucifer?" I ask, as my disbelief takes over.

"Yes, although my aunt says she doesn't accept it."

Interesting, very interesting is all I can think. Nothing is as it seems in this city. Before I can ask any further questions, I remember the reason why we are all in here in the first place, to get answers.

"Can we go and see your aunt?" I ask. Elliot gives me a questioning glance through the rearview mirror as Mandee contemplates the idea.

"Yeah, let's go, that's actually not a bad idea."

Chapter 28

ROSE

The drive to Mandee's aunt's house was a good two hours but it seemed shorter than that due to all of us discussing what the next few steps would be once we arrived in Paris tomorrow.

"I hope she is able to help." Mandee says as we pull up to her aunt's very charming house in Connecticut. It's a beautiful Victorian style home with green vines and moss clinging to it. Her trees display different color leaves as the crisp fall air gently blows them around the ground. We all get out of the car and walk up to her door. Mandee knocks and waits for her aunt to come and greet us. After several seconds there is a petite woman who looks to be in her fifties in front of us. She looks a lot like Mandee, although she appears more tired and ill.

"Welcome, please come in. My name is Mari" She smiles as she moves to the side to welcome us into her beautiful home. It's colorful and warm. Her walls are lined with books and stones. Family pictures hang on her walls as well. And a very strong smell, of some kind of herb wafts through the air.

"It's very nice to meet you." I greet as I walk inside as she closes the door behind me.

"Likewise. So, you guys are Mandee's friends, you're all so young and beautiful." She smiles.

"Auntie, I'm sorry to intrude but we need to talk to you." Mandee explains. Her aunt's face now grows more serious as she looks at her niece then to me.

"What did you say your name was?" She asks walking closer to me then placing her hands on mine.

"Rose Autry." I tell her. She hums in response then as if a power surges through us her eyes open wide as if she is seeing something within me, and she begins talking.

"You my child are very special, to our kind, you share our gifts. Yet there seems to be something blocking your abilities...a mark. You are bonded to a supernatural that walks this earth yet also bonded to a much more powerful entity that hides behind darkness...but you already know that. You're bonded to a man, a soldier of Lucifer. He binds you to him. However, I sense something more although this can't be...No this can't be right." She mutters as she grips my hand tighter. How does she know all of this?

I wonder what she is sensing. And as if she can read my mind too, she speaks, "Soul tied. My dear girl, you and your soldiers are soul tied, and you will have to make the ultimate choice, sacrifice yourself for the one you love or sacrifice the one you love for yourself."

Then as if the connection is lost, she releases my hand and steps back, a bit out of breath. And I am left standing in the wake of the destruction her words left behind. Mandee immediately moves to her side and grabs her as Elliot gently places his hand on my shoulder as if sensing I needed to be steadied. After a few silent seconds we all walk over to the living room and take a seat.

"What exactly is a soldier of Lucifer?" Mandee asks as we all sit down. I look over to Mandee's aunt and decide it would be better for me to answer her question since she seems a bit out of it.

"Soldiers of Lucifer are vampires. They were created to guard him all those years ago." I explain. Mandee's eyes widen as she stays silent taking in the information.

"I have to say, Leo Lloyd being a vampire is not that much of a shock." Mandee states. We all let out a small laugh, even her aunt, at Mandee's truthful statement.

"What exactly can you tell us about this soul tie business?" I ask, hoping she can shed some new light on the topic.

"I don't know much but there are legends in our history of vampires and gypsies. If I'm being honest, I don't really know them that well, what I do know is being soul tied to a vampire as a gypsy is incredibly rare. It's the most connected bond one person can have with another. You and Leo's souls are intertwined, however there seems to be another that has claim to your soul as well, which bears a heavy consequence." She explains. I let her words sync in as Mandee talks to her aunt about her own questions. The room seems to disappear as my thoughts take over.

"What did you mean when you said a mark is blocking my abilities?" I ask.

The room goes silent, as both Elliot and Mari look at each other.

"The mark on your shoulder was put there, as a seal to Cains and I's agreement. However, it seems as time has progressed he has been able to solidify the connection between the two of you and channel his power through that mark. And by doing so, he has gained the ability to suppress your gifts." Elliot explains.

I sit quietly as I take in what he had said. I can't help but wonder, why I had been the descendent chosen for this, I mean honestly, why me?

"You, I sense you're something more than human?" Mari states breaking me out of my thoughts as all of the attention goes towards Elliot.

"You'd be right, love." He smirks.

"Witch." She says, a small smile spreading on her lips.

Elliot shakes his head; Mari then goes on a bit of a ramble as she asks question after question about him. Mandee and I look at one another and I motion for her to follow me as I excuse myself from the room. I needed to tell her about the dreams. Especially because I know that she had seen the man with the violet eyes when she had that awakening. Elliot is so focused on talking with Mari that he is completely distracted to notice Mandee and I leave the room.

We walk to the bathroom down the hall, and I lock the door behind us.

"I need to tell you something. I trust the others full heartedly but not even they know this." I begin to explain. Mandee silently nods her head as she waits for me to go further into detail.

"My other soul tie that your aunt sensed is Cain as you know..." I pause, needing to organize my thoughts.

"He is the one who holds claim over the other half of my soul, and Mandee, he has been visiting me." I state, not even fully realizing how bad that sounded until the words left my lips.

"Visiting you, like he's here in New York and he's following you?" She questions, looking for more clarification than what I had given her.

"No, he comes to me in my dreams, and he always says the same thing. 'Come find me, for I will unleash the darkness that resides within you, and we will become one when you die, you and I are soul tied.'" I recite. She takes a second to process what I had told her. I then add, "He is the man with the violet eyes. It is the only part of him that he has allowed me to see."

And as if the biggest realization hits her, her eyes go wide, "I saw him, he was draining you, and I tried to stop him, but he stopped me in my tracks." She rambles.

"He was in my awakening." She states. We stay silent for a moment letting the realization set in before we both get shaken out of our thoughts by Elliot calling for us.

"Let's just keep this between us." I mention quickly before she unlocks the door. She nods in agreement, and we make our way back to the living room.

"Everything ok?" Elliot asks as Mandee, and I take our seats.

"Everything is just fine." I assure him.

We all converse a bit more before Elliot decides that we should all get going since we have an early flight to catch the next day. By the time Mari walks us to the door she is hugging Elliot goodbye, absolutely captured by his charm.

***

The drive back into the city is quiet as we all try to process everything that is happening and everything that is about to come our way. Finally, after dropping Mandee off at her apartment Elliot drives me to my own place. However, before I make it out of the car, he stops me.

"He should have told you everything, but Rose, he wanted to figure things out first. In all the years I have known Leo he has never acted the way he acts when he is around you. And I know you broke things off to protect him from Cain. I applaud you for that, but please don't be angry with him for his lie. It was done with the purest of intentions to keep you safe. And the soul tie, what you feel for one another is real. The soul tie might connect you, but it doesn't control you." He explains. I take in all of his words, and I completely agree with him. I know Leo held out information from me because he thought it best and I know the feelings that we share are real. Although I guess at the end of the day it really doesn't matter since I'm going to be stuck with Cain in hell for all of eternity. But even though I can logically understand his reasoning, for his lies it still doesn't fix the fact that feelings don't follow logic. And my feelings were hurt from his omission of the truth.

"I know Elliot, and I'm not angry, I promise. I'm just hurt, I'll get over it eventually" I assure him, even though I don't believe my own statement a hundred percent. Without saying anything else I give him a tight smile and open the car door before making my way to the entrance of my building.

I make my way to the elevator and try to focus on the tasks ahead of me, like packing and taking a nice hot shower, to distract myself from everything else going on around me. I feel almost excited at the thought of cleansing myself of the day, and having the ability to clear my head, with the escape of a relaxing shower.

The doors of the elevator finally ding open, and I walk into my apartment and immediately go to my bathroom. The moment I step into my shower and the water hits my skin, I feel my muscles instantly relax. The sound of the water drowns my thoughts as I let it consume me. For the briefest of moments, I didn't have a worry in the world. Right now, I'm more than grateful for Elliot casting some sort of incantation that blocks Michael from entering my home, along with any other supernatural being...including Leo. No one can come in or out, unless invited in.

Once the water starts to turn cold, I turn off the water and step out onto my bathmat. If it were up to me, I would stay in the water forever letting it drown out all the chaos surrounding me. However, it was now time to face reality.

After I dry myself off and change into a pair of my own black sweats, I contemplate throwing one of Leo's t-shirts on. They let me sleep more peacefully. However, I opt against it and go with one of my own.

Now that I'm fully dressed, I blow dry my hair and place it into two sleek Dutch braids and do my skin care routine feeling somewhat in control. After I look at myself in my bathroom mirror, I walk into my bedroom and begin to pack. I grab a little bit of everything. I'm not really sure what we're going to be doing over there and for how long we'll be staying. As I finish packing my last black pair of leggings into my suitcase, I push my elbow against the top of it to get it to close and zip it shut. By the time I finish it's already well into the next morning, I'd be leaving for the airport in only a couple of hours.

By some miracle, I somehow manage to pass out on my mattress and drift off to sleep. Sometimes I wonder if death would be this peaceful. I wondered if this would be the feeling that consumes you when you turn into a vampire? I've been thinking about that a lot lately, the transition from human to vampire. Would I accept it if Leo gave me the option? Would I exchange my supposed halo for horns? Leo holds me in such a bright light and angelic view, I wonder if I changed, would he still hold me in the same light?

***

The next morning came faster than expected and I practically had to use all of my strength to reach for my phone which had been buzzing for the past few minutes. The sunlight burns my eyes as it peers through the windows. After the full realization that it is in fact morning and I have an early flight to catch, I lunge out of bed. It's eight am and our flight leaves at ten. Mandee had been the culprit of my phone screaming at me to wake up. I redial her number and she picks up after the first ring.

"I woke you up, didn't I?" Mandee answers, a bit judgmental. Between her and Adeline I wasn't sure who was more annoying when it came to time management.

"No." I lie as I try to conceal a yawn. As I place my phone on speaker and scramble around my room getting ready.

"Good! Then you should be ready in the next ten minutes when I come by to pick you up to meet the guys at the airport." She explains. I place my phone on the bed, slightly panicked as I start to get dressed.

"I'll stop and grab us some coffee, so see you in a few." she informs me.

"I'll be ready." I assure her as I continue to get dressed.

"Good, because I'll be there soon. Bye Rose." Before I can respond she hangs up the phone. I manage to throw on a t-shirt and a pair of comfy sweatpants. I rummage through my sock drawer for thick white socks and put on a pair of chunky white designer sneakers. I go into the bathroom and rush through my morning ritual before brushing my teeth then immediately grab my bag and luggage, along with a black sweatshirt in case I got cold on the plane and make my way downstairs. I go over to the kitchen and grab a banana muffin off the rack and wait for Mandee's text which comes as soon as I am about to place the muffin to my lips. I text her that I'm on my way before making my way down to her.

When I get to her car, I'm not surprised by the view in front of me. Mandee looks absolutely perfect. Her hair and makeup are perfectly done, and she is dressed in snug fitting blue jeans with a lavender ruffle top, with white sneakers. She walks over to me, and hands me a cup of coffee.

"You look...comfy." She states, as we put my suitcase and my carry-on into her trunk.

I grab a pair of black sunglasses from my bag and put them on while taking a sip of my coffee.

"Thanks for the coffee." I say dryly, feeling tired, exhausted and nervous before walking to the front door of her car.

"Chipper as always." She mutters as she gets into the driver's seat.

"Well then, let's go to Paris!" I say trying to muster up as much enthusiasm as possible even though I'm running on about three hours of sleep.

"There's the spirit." She teases as we drive off.

Chapter 29

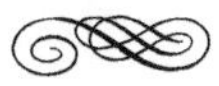

ROSE

I managed to doze off here and there during the ride to the airport. We pull up onto the tarmac and see both Elliot and Leo are there waiting for us.

"Rose, we're here." Mandee informs me, causing me to grunt in sleepy acknowledgement.

My heart aches as I see Leo dressed in black slacks and a tight black button-down shirt boarding the plane. He's upset, I can feel it.

We pile out of the car and grab our stuff before Elliot along with two crew members walk over towards us to greet us and help us with our bags.

"Well hello ladies, these gentlemen will take your bags and if you follow me on board there is a bottle of champagne waiting for us." He explains with a smile.

"Rose looking lovely as always." He smirks taking in my appearance.

"Elliot, I mean this in the nicest way possible, fuck off." I state, my annoyance evident in my tone.

Elliot lets a deep roar of laughter rip through his chest as we continue to walk to the plane. They can't stop asking one another questions, each of them eager to unlock knowledge from the other.

I walk further into the plane taking in the grandness and luxuries that the inside displays. I had flown on beautiful private jets before, but this one was just different.

The last time I had been on a private jet, my hands had been covered in blood. My head begins to pound as I let those memories infiltrate my mind.

As my eyes scan the limited seating options, I notice Leo sitting all the way in the back looking down at his lap, trying to avoid me. I couldn't blame him. I should be doing the same, but I can't help myself, my eyes just gravitate towards him.

I needed to snap myself out of it and sit down. Elliot and Mandee sit at a table together towards the front as they continue their conversation. And I contemplate whether or not to sit with them but decide against it. I begin to walk towards an empty seat not too far from Leo but far enough, so that I can just sit and stew in my emotions by myself. However, as I walk towards my desired seat, he looks at me, those green eyes pulling me in. As I walk closer, I notice the book in his lap, my heart flutters from the sight.

I take a seat on the opposite side of the plane where he is sitting and pull out my phone.

"Nice shirt." He murmurs under his breath. At first, I'm confused but when I look down, I notice it was his shirt that I had grabbed this morning. I must have grabbed it by mistake, when I was rushing. I continue to look through my phone, aimlessly as my heart fights to not explode, from the weight of this grief I'm feeling. Choosing to separate myself from him is so much harder than it should be. It has to be an effect of the soul tie. My body craves his presence. I needed space. I get up and quickly rush to the bathroom. I needed a moment alone. All of a sudden, the plane felt way too small. And although the bathroom was tight, it didn't have the weight of his stare.

I look in the mirror and cringe at the sight of my unruly hair still in the braids from last night. I try to tame it, as a way to distract myself from the anger I know he is feeling. I'm angry too. I'm not choosing to be apart from him, because I want Cain. I'm doing it to protect him. He needs to understand I'm keeping him at arm's length for his protection. That's why I know when the time comes, I will go willingly. Hell doesn't seem so bad compared to Leo dying because of me. As the darkest of all thoughts consume me, I hear a knock on the door.

"Rose. Let me in." He asks, his voice eerily calm. He was pissed, I could practically feel his anger radiating off of him through the door. I close my eyes as I mentally prepare myself to see him. I knew I couldn't hide in here forever. Especially since he would outlive me.

"Rose, open the door, before I break the door down." He commands this time more sternly. I let out a small breath as I try to ignore the flutter of something I refuse to think about between my thighs. Even when angry he was sexy, and that right there was my red flag.

Not having it in me to fight with him, I give in and slowly open the door. The moment I see him up close and feel his body so close to mine, I have to steady myself. His presence was intoxicating, so much more than before. He looks at me for the briefest of moments before he closes the door behind him for more privacy.

"I'm not partaking in this ridiculous separation you have declared." He growls as I feel my back hit the wall in the small space. I close my eyes as I try to center myself. I wanted to give in and jump into his arms, but I knew I couldn't or better yet, shouldn't.

"It's not your decision Leo. It's mine." I state, keeping my voice steady as I dare to look him in the eyes. He remains quiet but lifts his arms to cage me in and leans forward before breathing me in.

"No, my love it is not. You are mine. From the moment I laid my eyes on you and from the moment I tasted you, in every possible way you became mine. And I won't be parted from you."

"Leo please. I can't be responsible for your death. And I can feel it, he will come for you." I whisper, my words breaking as I fight back the tears of frustration threatening to spill. He moves one of his arms so that he can brush away the stray tear with his thumb before he gives me a small grin.

"Rose, he won't hurt me. And he will certainly never hurt you."

He takes my silence as an invitation to lean down and kiss me. It's soft and borderline cautious. However, it was enough to break my restraint and without any hesitation I wrap my arms around his neck and pull him in. He was mine, just as much as I was his. I wanted to relish in what should be our glorious reunion, but I couldn't. He had lied to me. And as much as I wanted to forget all of that, I couldn't. At least not right now. So, using my last bit of strength, I pull away from him, and quickly move out from under him to where the door is on the opposite side of the small space.

"I want to be with you, more than anything and I believe you full heartedly when you say that you'll protect me from Cain. But Leo, you lied to me, continuously. You have a history with Marie, my blood ancestor." I argue, as I look him straight in the eyes, refusing to back down. He couldn't fix this with a kiss no matter how skilled his lips were.

He remains silent for a few moments before walking over to where I stand and places his hand to my heart, then grabs my hand and places it over his own. There's no heartbeat.

"You told me once that you didn't care that I didn't have a heartbeat because yours beat enough for the both of us. That's because my heart is a mirror of your own, and it always has been. Yes, I lied but it is only because I thought I was protecting you.

And when it comes to Marie, it was all a fantasy, a mirage. Nothing was ever real, not like how it is when it comes to you and me. You quite literally make my unbeating heart beat to the melody of your breath. Because you being here with me alive and well, is the only thing keeping me standing." He confesses.

I stay silent, his words hit me like small bullets to the chest.

"I forgive you."

The smile that spreads along his face is enough to assure me in my response. He slowly leans down and places his soft and inviting lips onto my own and kisses me. Claiming me as his.

We stay like this for what feels like a long time until Elliot knocks on the door informing us that we need to take our seats as we would be departing soon. Leo pulls away from me and holds out his hand for me to grab. And as both of our hands intertwine, I can't help but physically feel the stitches that intertwine our souls pull tighter together. Reassuring me that they could never be severed, not even by choice. We would always be bound to one another.

We take our seats in the back of the plane, sitting right next to one another as our plane finally takes off to Paris.

***

The flight went by smoothly. Leo and I spent the majority of it sleeping and holding one another. We needed to make up for the last few days of not being together. I didn't mind. I loved being near him, and to have his body close to mine. During the last hour of our flight, I woke up to Elliot and Mandee, in the middle of a history lesson. Leo sleeps right through their chatter, looking absolutely adorable might I add. He looks innocent and peaceful when he sleeps. His cold and rigid demeanor vacates his body as he relaxes and loosens up under the spell of slumber.

After staring at him for too long, and feeling like an absolute stalker, I look over to where Elliot and Mandee are sitting. They truly have taken a great amount of liking towards one another.

As I stay laying out on my chair, just listening to everything else and not my own thoughts, I overhear Elliot explaining to Mandee the difference between gypsies and witches. He explains how gypsies are the children of seers and angel blood. They are gifted with sight and intuition and sometimes special powers. They are also considered soldiers of Lucifer. They're supposed to protect and keep the peace amongst the children of the dark. Witches on the other hand are part of the supernatural order. They are immortal and born with great power some more than others depending on their lineage. They were the creation of Lucifer and Lilith, along with vampires. It seems that the darkness created through both Lucifer and Lilith was enough to conjure these creatures.

As I lay still, overhearing everything, the pilot jumps on the intercom and explains to us how we are going to be landing soon. I start shifting in my chair and sit up, Leo does the same as we both strap in. He gives me a smile as his beautiful green eyes look into mine. So many promises swirling around within them.

"Did you sleep well, love?" He asks, his voice husky and strained from sleep. I nod my head and smile as I take in everything that has happened along with the sight that is him.

Elliot and Mandee must hear us shuffling around in the back because they both turn their heads towards us.

"You two, slept the whole flight." Elliot points out.

"Well not all of us can talk for eight hours straight Elliot." Leo grumbles.

"Well not all of us decided to take a vow of silence for the last two hundred years." Elliot retorts, causing me to let a small giggle escape my lips. It was true, Leo is a man of very few words. However, when it came to me, he was always able to express himself comfortably. It was one of the things that I loved about being with him.

We land safely and we all pile out of the plane and grab our bags. The ride to Leos and Elliot's Chateau is silent. Elliot and Mandee ride up front while Leo and I sit in the back of the massive SUV that picked us up. The sexual tension between Leo and I is enough to drive me insane, but we sit silent. His hand is on my thigh throughout the entire ride, tormenting me as I focus my attention on undoing my braids from earlier and throwing my hair into a messy bun. I was trying my best to remain distracted. However, the moment the car pulled up to the most beautiful Chateau I had ever seen, like something from a fairytale, the tension had reached its breaking point and so had we.

Chapter 30

ROSE

Elliot and Mandee, get out first and pull down the seat for Leo and I to exit. The boys take it upon themselves to grab the luggage from the back of the car as Mandee and I stand breathless taking in the sight of their home. It was absolutely breathtaking.

The moment all of the luggage is out of the car, we all begin to make our way inside. The entrance and the rest of the house from what I can see is absolutely stunning. The beautiful architecture paired with the beautiful French provincial design was gorgeous. We walk further in and close the door behind us before Elliot turns to us with a small smile across his face.

"I'm going to make myself a drink. Mandee my dear, would you care to join me?" Elliot asks. Mandee nods her head in acceptance and follows him into the next room. Then in a flash I am in the air and thrown over Leo's shoulder. I can't help the squeal that escapes my lips. I was mortified, but I couldn't seem to find it in me to care. As Leo moves quickly towards his desired destination, he lays a playful slap to my ass.

"That my darling Rose is for trying to leave me." He states, as he chuckles from his own action. He then barrels into a room down the next hallway and throws me onto the comfiest bed I have ever laid on. It felt like a literal cloud.

Leo stands before me and watches me, as I take in the room around us. It was absolutely beautiful and ornate. The room was regency inspired and held such a luxurious charm to it. I am in complete awe of the scenery that surrounds me. It truly looked like something built for royalty.

"Well, is it to your liking?" He asks, smiling from my obvious infatuation.

"I love it." I say, as I continue to take in the beautiful scene before me. Noticing all of the intricate details from the paintings that are hung on the wall to the beautifully picked out drapes. Every detail in this room was meticulously chosen to tie the room perfectly together.

"And I love you." He says, as he leans in and kisses me feverishly. It's as though I can feel his want flow through his kiss and seep into my soul.

"I want you." I pant when I pull away from his addictive lips. I swear the more he gave the more I wanted. Then before he could say anything else, I pulled him towards me again and locked my lips with his, hungry for his touch. My fingers run through his hair as I try to pull him in as close as possible.

He deepens the kiss by invading my lips with his tongue. He leans me back and crawls on top of me as he breathes me in. His lips disconnect from mine as he pulls away slightly and rips my shirt open with a desperation that can only be described as frantic. He kisses down my neck to my stomach with sloppy kisses marking me as his as he sucks and bites teasingly. He hurriedly pulls down my sweatpants as I kick off my shoes. He kisses every inch going down my thighs as I play with his hair. I pull him back up towards me, so that I can feel the sensation of his kiss.

Once I am left in my bra and panties, he looks at me with evident desire in his eyes. I manage to roll us over and I begin to unbutton his shirt as he looks at me, anticipation building in the air between us. As soon as the last button comes undone, he leans up and finishes removing his shirt. I push him to lay on his back once more, enjoying the control I have and leave a trail of kisses from his happy trail to his chest. I make sure to kiss every part of the scars that mark his skin. I need him, I want him and more importantly I love him. Finally, once I reach his neck and jaw, he grabs onto me and flips us over to where he is now hovering above me, his vampire face on full display.

He looks away ashamed. I wished more than anything that he could see himself the way that I do- beautiful.

"Leo look at me." I whisper, placing my hands on his face forcing him to look at me. I gently trace the veins that surrounded his eyes and place my finger on his lips looking more intently at his fangs.

"I love you...all of you." I proclaim, reaching up to kiss him. At first, he is cautious but then he lets himself relish in it. I move my hands and unbuckle his pants pulling them down along with his boxers, freeing his very large and very erect shaft.

"Needy, are we?" He asks, pulling away, showcasing his normal face. I nod my head, growing more and more impatient. I want to feel him inside me. I want him to consume me and take away any fear that is currently rattling around in my mind.

"My beautiful Rose, I live to serve you." He smirks. He moves his way down, placing a rough kiss on my inner thigh, pulling my panties down. Then without warning he bites into my inner thigh. I moan in absolute pleasure the pain only making it feel better. Being with Leo has truly blurred the line between pleasure and pain.

"I had no idea I had this much of an effect on you love." He grins, as he moves himself, to my very open and exposed dripping entrance, licking his lips from my blood. I swallow out of embarrassment from his statement. It was embarrassingly evident just how much of an effect he had.

He then bends down and licks me clean, savoring my need for him, my *want* for him. I let a small moan leave my lips, when his fingers start teasing my entrance. His thumb lazily circles my most sensitive spot, before he pumps two fingers inside of me. I moan in pure bliss. He pushes them in and out slowly, as his eyes remain on me, wanting to see my every reaction and hear my every moan. His eyes only grow darker from the sight in front of him.

"Leo please." I beg hoping he would stop teasing me and give me what I truly crave.

"As you wish." He grins, then fastens his pace, as I continue to squirm and pant from feeling my stomach tighten as I try to further open my legs, from the amount of pleasure he was igniting. I was ready to release at any moment.

"I'm going to..." before I can finish, he takes them out then places them in his mouth, tasting me off his fingers. I could have climaxed just from that sight alone. However, I wasn't given the chance because in a flash he thrusted his erect member into me without any mercy. I yelp from the blissful pain of him intruding my tight space. However, when he starts thrusting himself in and out of me a few more times, the pain instantly turns to the most pleasurable feeling I have ever experienced. My eyes practically roll to the back of my head as I moan out in pure ecstasy. I call out his name over and over again, the feeling of our colliding bodies becoming one, edges me on further, shaking me to my very core.

"Leo! Faster." I cry out as I run my fingers down his back, feeling his scars.

He keeps his motions steady and continues his movements as he reaches down and kisses me. I want to taste him.

"Fuck Rose it's like this pussy was made for me." He practically growls after disconnecting from our kiss.

"It's always been yours." I cry out, causing him to thrust into me faster.

"Bite me." I beg wanting to feel my orgasm with that extra added intimacy. He stops then looks at me, unsure.

"Please!" I beg. Then without any hesitation he brings his fangs down and bites my tender flesh. He sinks his fangs into my neck and continues his rough movements. Then as if a wave of absolute ecstasy and euphoria washes over me, I release harder than I ever have before. He still works himself inside me trying to reach his release.

"Let me help you." I plead. I want to make him feel good. He stops and smirks knowing what I was proposing. He takes himself out of me and rolls over onto his back. Still reeling from my orgasm, I get up and move to my knees in front of him. His beautiful shaft is still erect and already covered in cum from my orgasm. Without any hesitation I kitty lick his tip causing him to groan. I take him into my mouth going as far down as I can. I instantly moan from the taste of him causing him to let out a low groan of absolute pleasure. I gag as he hits the back of my throat but absolutely love the feeling of my mouth being filled with him. He watches my every move, as he moans in pleasure. His eyes on me only encourage me further.

I continue to bob my head up and down, when I feel him reach out his hand and touch my neck. He swipes his finger on the blood seeping out of my wound, he brings it back to his mouth to taste it. His face morphing into the one Lucifer gave him. God save my soul, but it is the most erotic sight I have ever seen. Using it to fuel my motions, I continue to bob my head until I feel him twitch. He places his hands in my hair guiding me with the movements he needs until I feel him release into the back of my throat. I swallow everything he gives me with a smile on my face causing Leo to groan from the sight. He lifts my chin up and smirks as I look up at him through my long lashes.

"My naughty little angel." He coos, placing his thumb on my swollen lip and drags it down, his eyes boring into mine.

I nod my head then climb onto his lap and curl myself against him.

"Only for you, my love."

We clean up and make our way back into the living room where Elliot and Mandee are drinking martinis. We both take a seat next to one another on the sofa across from them. The silence is palpable as Elliot looks at us. When his lip turns up into a devious smirk, I have no doubts he knows what just transpired.

However, he doesn't mention it and begins to discuss what he thinks we should do. Apparently, all of us need to figure out how we are going to take down Michael and make sure Marie doesn't get the chance to come back and also what deal we can possibly make with Cain, that would release me. It seems that all the tasks discussed are impossible, especially killing Michael, based on all the complications Leo and Elliot keep throwing out every time Mandee or I make a suggestion. It appears the older the vampire, the harder it would be to kill him, which makes sense.

"My aunt mentioned that I have Hellfire in my veins. Is that something that could help when it comes to destroying Michael and taking down Cain?" Mandee asks, causing Elliot to place his Martini glass down and give his full attention to her.

"Hellfire. You are a rare gypsy indeed. Your skill will most definitely come in handy when it comes to winning this war, Mandee, but we must start training as soon as possible."

"Is there any way I have the same gift? I mean, I know that my abilities are apparently being blocked but is there a way we can figure out how to remove that block?" I ask.

"No, only members of that bloodline carry that fire in their blood, but there are two other gifts you could possess. I don't know the specifics, if I'm being honest, but what I do know is that the gypsies house three main gifts. Hellfire, Darkness, and Chaos. Most gypsies have the power of sight and intuition; however, three very rare and powerful bloodlines carry one of these magics within them." He explains.

I stay silent, for a moment until I remember what Cain tells me every time, he comes to visit me

"I will unleash the darkness in you that resides." I repeat silently. My mind becomes so focused on that, that I don't even realize when they switch the topic to how they are going to outsmart Michael. Leo looks over at me as if curious to know what has me so occupied, but I just give him an assuring smile and join in on the conversation. I decide to think about Cain's words later.

"Halloween is a month away, there is a lot of work that needs to be done. The first thing we need to do is get rid of Michael, then once Cain descends on earth, we will finish him off once and for all. However, the key lies in finding the weapon capable enough to kill him." Elliot states.

"Cain doesn't die the way that vampires or witches do?" Mandee asks.

"No, although he shares both life forces in him, he has angel's blood inside of him. Lucifer changed him using his blood, and when that blood was forged with the magic that Lilith provided to turn him into the ultimate killer, he became fully immortal." Elliot explains, causing a feeling of uneasiness to surge through me.

This wasn't going to end well; I could feel the darkness creep up my spine as if warning me of the darkness to come.

After a couple more hours of back and forth between everyone tossing ideas on how to deal with Michael effectively, we all decide it would be better to regroup after we all go to sleep and adjust to the new time zone. Before Leo can drag me back to his room, I decide to go to the bathroom that is connected to the room he gave me and splash some water on my face. When I look up into the mirror, a blackness takes over and lures me in. Violet eyes watch me through the glass. And then the mark on my shoulder burns.

"Stop! Please!" I scream out.

"Oh, my little doll, this is only the beginning." He purrs, when everything stops.

Chapter 31

ROSE

The mirror goes back to being a mirror rather than a black abyss with eyes and the pain that once was crippling disappeared. However, when I looked closer into the mirror, something seemed different. It rippled. I slowly placed my finger onto the surface and instead of hitting a hard surface my finger went through it, and then all of a sudden, I was pulled into a bright light. Right as I feel like I am falling, I land on what feels like a hard surface- marble. I look around and notice that I'm now in what appears to be a palace where a party is happening. Ball gowns and coat tails is all I can see. The powdered wigs and corsets really magnified the fact that I was no longer in the modern era where women were actually allowed to breathe and embrace their natural beauty.

I walk through the sea of people making my way down a path that I somehow know to take. I open the extravagant doors that lead into a beautiful hall with mirrors plastered everywhere. I now understand where I am. I am in the Palace of Versailles- the hall of mirrors. I keep walking until I see him. I can't miss those green eyes even if I wanted to. I walk closer and there he is, dancing with who I can only assume is Marie. I am relieved to see that we had little resemblance, but she did have some qualities that proved we were related. As I get closer, I see her lean into his ear to whisper some-

thing. Her eyes meet mine. For a brief moment I am absolutely terrified, until I realize she can't see me. I look back and realize who she is looking at...Michael.

I approach her trying to hear their whispers.

"Leo my love I can't wait much longer." She whines pouting her small but plump lips while batting her eyelashes, taking in all of his attention with her big brown eyes- that do hold a resemblance to my own. They hold a small trace of seductiveness to them. My chest aches as I see Leo, his innocent human soul falling for her devilish tricks. He looks so different, yet similar. His hair is longer and pulled back, but his green eyes still hold a brokenness to them. His lips are full and as kissable as ever.

"I know love, but I have to meet with the guests then we can leave, I swear to you." He smiles hoping she'd follow suit. She lets a small grin line her perfectly painted lips.

"I want to spend eternity with you, my love." He whispers, pulling her close then kissing her softly. My heart stings from seeing him with her. Jealousy is starting to work its way into my heart.

"I love you, Leonardo." She whispers, breaking the kiss, then quickly glances back at Michael who is holding a menacing gaze.

Trying to remain focused, I realize the room has become blurry and before I know it, the image shifts. We're no longer in Versailles; instead, we are in a house, a grand house. I walk past the open door and there standing in the room was Leo. He is in a white puffy shirt and trousers, by the window looking out into the stars as I walk over to him and stare out the window alongside him. He looks over in my direction and for a split second I think he can actually see me. However, I am mistaken because when I look behind me, Marie appears in what seems to be their definition of lingerie. Leo's eyes widened in admiration.

He was in love. Not like a normal modern-day love that is filled with materialism and self-masochism, because you're constantly killing yourself to appease them to keep them with you. This love was different. He was in love in the purest form. He was a man who saw a woman who made his heart beat a bit faster than normal, that made his mornings seem worth waking up for. He was completely and utterly consumed by her. "Beautiful, Cheri." He gushes as she walks closer to him. He stays in his stance mesmerized by her walk.

"Leonardo, are you ready?" She asks. He shakes his head, eager to begin this new chapter. Standing from this angle I can see an all too familiar shadowy figure outside the window, it had to be Michael- sneaky bastard.

"I want to be with you forever." He confesses. She smiles at his candor and runs her fingers through his perfect dark brown hair. I want to scream for him to not do it.

He kneels before her and moves his head to the side to expose his neck. She licks her lips as her vampire face exposes itself, before she bites into her skin and makes him drink from her wrist. After a few seconds she moves him off of her. She then kneels in front of him and kisses him. I can't help but look away. I didn't want to see one of his more intimate memories with another woman. Then I hear the groan. I look back and her fangs had descended into him. His eyes roll to the back of his head as she sucks the blood from his human veins as he gives himself to her. She finally pulls away once she had finished draining him.

Then without warning two men dressed in black cloaks burst through the door. Marie quickly pushes herself away from Leo, dropping him onto the floor bleeding and dying.

I quickly run over to him. He looks weak and fragile. It is an unfamiliar sight to see.

Marie tries charging at these men; however, she is halted when one of the men grabs her by her wrist and disappears into thin air. Leo cries out in excruciating pain. My heart shatters all over again. I want to help but it is no use. The man that came in with the other looks at him and does absolutely nothing.

"Welcome, soldier." He laughs cynically, before disappearing as well. I crouch to his side as he lays there vulnerable and in pain. His screams are horrid. The pain in his features from the change and not being able to save her is like nothing I have ever seen.

"Marie!" He screams over and over again.

His veins then begin popping up all over his body, his jerking movements becoming more and more manic. He is transitioning. The process seemed torturous. He clutches at his chest as he cries out. Tears escape as I watch him scream out in pain. His cries echoing in the room. He went through this all by himself.

"Leo!" I scream, over and over again.

I try screaming for the millionth time when I am suddenly transported back to the bathroom. And before I can even begin to try and understand what just happened, I hear the sound of that sinful voice.

"Now you see. He loved her enough to change for her."

"No, he was manipulated. I saw it with my own eyes." I try to reason not letting his words hit their mark.

"Rose, let me love you the way you were meant to be loved. There is no one but you in my heart." The voice taunts, and once again the mirror turns black as those violet eyes watch me.

"I don't want you." I bite, my anger rushing to the surface. Then the scene of Leo in absolute agony hits me once more except this time, I can feel it. The immobilizing pain and absolute agony hits me in waves.

"You might not want me, but tell me this, would his heart break the same as it did for her, when you and I inevitably come together?" He asks. My body shakes from the agony, as my throat loses the fight to hold in my scream. Not knowing what else to do, I punch my fist into the glass. The mirror shatters around me, the shards hitting the floor as my hand bleeds.

He was gone.

However, the pain and sorrow still surged through me. I try to focus on my surroundings, but blood and glass is all I can see until Leo rushes into the bathroom. I fall to my knees, and Leo is right there to catch me. His hands grab mine and he gently inspects my wounds as I try to calm myself down.

"Rose what happened. Tell me love. What's wrong?" He pleads, as he forces me to meet his gaze.

"I saw it, you were in so much pain, and no one was there." I cry, still trying to regain my grip on reality.

"I don't understand." He states, desperately.

"I think Cain pulled me into one of your memories. I saw the night you changed. Oh my God, Leo it was horrible and I'm so sorry. I could feel the pain you had to bear." I cry, as I hold his gaze. He looked shocked from what I had just told him.

"Why was it so painful?" I ask in between sniffles. I can still feel the pain he felt in my bones. It's a haunting feeling; one I never want to feel again.

"It's not, but my transition was a little different. You see when you change everything becomes heightened and more intense. Sadness becomes despair, love becomes obsession, and heartbreak becomes inconsolable. So, when they took her from me, that feeling of absolute heartbreak quite literally amplified to the feeling of having my actual heart ripped out of my chest."

"You loved her, Leo. As much as you try to deny it, you cared for her deeply." I whisper, as I let the full memory hit me. Leo frowns from my candor and gently places one of his hands on my cheek.

"My human self, cared for her; this I won't deny. But that love died the moment my heart stopped beating. All that was left behind was my hurt pride and obsession, over losing her to another. None of it was real. Being with you has shown me that love is more than just the desire of the flesh. It is more than just surface level similarities and weightless words that have no feeling. Love is what lies underneath our exterior. You and me Rose, we are connected but it is more than just the soul tie, our hearts beat as one and our souls are sewn together. The words we speak to one another is a language only our souls can decipher. You and I are one."

I stay silent, letting his words give me the comfort I so desperately needed, but then I remember something from that memory.

"Michael was there when you were turned, why didn't he stop them from taking her?" I ask. Leo thinks it over, trying to make sense of it.

"They probably overpowered him." He reasons.

"Marie was falling in love with you. The idea that she wasn't is false. I saw it, the way she looked at you is the same way I do. You can't fake that. I think Michael didn't fight to save her because he's the one that sent for her to be collected. I mean think about it, they were on the run for hundreds of years continuously evading Cain. Then all of a sudden right as Marie turns you, she gets taken. You were supposed to be nothing more than a pawn in Marie and Michael's sick relationship, Leo. She broke the rules and Michael punished her." I explain, piecing the puzzle together out loud.

"I mean if that's true, then Michael is even more dangerous than we thought, the guilt of sending her away must be eating away at him. Even if he was jealous of me, and angry at Marie, he would never do something he thought would truly hurt her. He probably thought that the soul tie would come up faster than what it did. He didn't bank on those two extra centuries." Leo states, his worry evident on his face.

"He will stop at nothing to get her back." I mumbled, thinking his thoughts out loud.

"What happens now?" I whisper. Leo looks around noticing the broken glass and blood that surrounds us from my still open wounds.

"We fight. And we don't stop until everyone who tries to separate us is dead. You are my forever Rose, and no one will separate us- not even the devil himself."

About the Author

Katelyn Alexandria is currently pursuing her MBA while also writing spicy supernatural stories. She has always loved anything having to do with paranormal lore. When she is not writing, she can be found spending time with her family and friends, along with her two adorable dogs. She enjoys reading, drinking an alarming amount of coffee, and listening to jazz music.

Make sure to keep up with her future releases and any other news by following her on her socials below:

Instagram: @kate__alexandria

TikTok: @xokatexo_